A Tw  of Queens

(A Tudor Tragedy)

by

Anne Stevens

Tudor Crimes: Book 8

TightCircle Publications © 2016

This book is dedicated to Boffin.

Foreword

The rivalries between the great of the court continue to fester. The year will see unfold, the struggle for power between Thomas Cromwell, and his arch rival, Queen Anne.

Having helped to bring down one queen, Cromwell is now compelled to go up against another, much more powerful consort. The King sways, like a rowan tree in the wind, waiting for his secret wishes to be guessed at, and then fulfilled.

Anne Boleyn holds the fate of all of England in her two hands, and struggles to give the king that which he most craves - a son. She is ready to do her duty, if only the king can manage to do his. Men are fickle in love, and kings are the most fickle of all.

Even as Thomas Cromwell's faction, and the supporters of Anne Boleyn prepare for the final conflict, Henry is prepared to throw everything out of kilter, because of one small whim. In a dangerous age, one smile, and the touch of a soft hand, can change a country forever. The smile, from Jane Seymour, may be all it takes to throw England into turmoil.

There are some who await the outcome of the struggle in eager anticipation, for their lives depend on it. A victory for Anne will mean death for all who have ever stood in her way. Margaret Roper is the keenest observer, for her father, Sir Thomas More, is in the most imminent danger.

He has read the oath to the king a thousand times, and has come to the one, and only conclusion a man such as he can reach. He cannot take it. Margaret, his daughter, is acknowledged to be the cleverest woman in England, and can stand up to a hundred lawyers. She is not prepared to give up the struggle.

There is, surely, a small chink of light, and she thinks she has found it. There is a possible way out of her father's situation, but she must enlist the help of a man whom her father roundly detests: Thomas Cromwell.

When you sup with the Devil, it is advisable to take a long spoon, and Margaret Roper must engage with Cromwell at his own time of greatest danger. The blacksmith's boy hopes to save a realm, and the lives of all his people, and he wonders if the sparing of his old friend is beyond even his great capabilities.

1   The Audience

"I have given my word, Master Cromwell." Rafe Sadler does not know where he has found the courage to approach his old master, but he is here, in the lion's den, tweaking the, less than benign, beast's tale. "I have promised her," he adds, lamely.

"Then bloody well un-promise the girl," Thomas Cromwell shouts back at his most favoured young lieutenant. "You have no right trying to arrange such a meeting for me. Why, you are not even in my service, since the king stole you away. What are you thinking of, man?"

Rafe Sadler is not one to beg favours from Thomas Cromwell, and is now demanding something that might bring grave danger to the door of Austin Friars. He wishes Thomas Cromwell, the king's most respected councillor, to meet with Rafe's childhood friend, Margaret Roper. The woman, who Rafe admired when he was a young boy, is the daughter of Sir Thomas More.

"She seeks only to save her father, sir."

"If I am seen to be favouring More's cause, just now, I lay myself open to attack from the Boleyn faction," Cromwell explains to Sadler. "You know the queen wants poor old More's head, and will have it, the moment he refuses to take the oath. If I interfere with her plan, she will whisper to Henry, and say that I am against the monarchy."

"The meeting need not be in public," Rafe explains. "What if it is kept secret, and you, and she, are the only two present?"

"Then that leaves only one to tell these hypothetical secrets to the world," Cromwell snaps. "One word from her, about anything I may, or may not, say about her father, and the fat is, well and truly, in the fire. Queen Anne will see us as a bevy of ravens, turning on her."

"An unkindness," Rafe Sadler mutters.

"I do not mean it to be." Cromwell does not wish to fall out with his right hand man, and looks for consoling words.

"No, I mean that it is an 'unkindness of ravens', master … as you would say a herd of cattle, a gaggle of geese, or a …"

"Bastard of Boleyns?" Thomas Cromwell says, and they both smile at the dangerous jest. "I cannot see how I can meet with young Margaret, without anyone knowing. The Boleyns watch my every move."

"They do, but they do not watch the comings and goings of my wife."

"And what has my poor, sweet Ellen Barré got to do with all of this?" Thomas Cromwell smells trouble, and wonders if it is too late to avoid unpleasantness, or worse.

"She comes and goes all day long," Rafe explains. "If, just once, she were to change dresses with Margaret Roper, and have her come back here to Austin Friars instead, who would notice? Why, they even look alike. Same hair, same features, and same…"

"I do see what you mean, Rafe," Cromwell replies, "but I doubt it would work."

"It did."

"What?" Cromwell is stunned by the audacity of the man. Rafe Sadler is the steadiest of all his young men, and would never enact a plan without involving Cromwell, and first seeking his permission. "It worked?"

"Like a charm, master."

"When?"

"Just now," Rafe says. "Did you not see Ellen passing the door to your study, with a bale of washing on her shoulder?"

"Dear Christ in Heaven, you have done all of this without asking me?" Cromwell is horrified at the prospect of the Roper girl being under his roof, and wonders if, even as they speak, Boleyn agents are watching.

"I did, sir. It is just that Margaret has put it into practice, a little earlier than I said. Will you see her?"

"I doubt I can do anything about it," Thomas Cromwell pleads. "Must I be forced to tell her, to her face, that her father is already a dead man?"

"If need be, sir," Rafe says. "After all, two ravens must make an unkindness."

"This is no time to jest," says Thomas Cromwell. "Have your washer woman come to me, here, but do not let the servants see her. I will listen to her pleading, take a deep breath, and break her heart. Sir Thomas More was my friend, once. I …oh, never mind. Bring the girl down, Rafe, and damn you for your idiotic kindness to her."

He positions himself, back to the fireplace, and facing the solid oak door. The damage is done, he thinks, but he still smiles at the simple ruse. His assumption that it was Ellen Barré passing his door, reminds him that keeping things simple is often the best way. Had he wished it, Rafe Sadler could just as easily have smuggled in King François of France, dressed up as a plump, rather ugly, kitchen maid.

He hears muted voices on the landing, then the sound of daintier feet than Rafe's descending to the hall. There is a gentle tap at the door, even though it is a little ajar.

"Come!" He tries to make his gruff voice sound gentler, and a little more inviting. Cromwell is becoming a very gentle lion, to those he loves, or admires. In this case, he feels both emotions, and recognises that he is on very dangerous ground.

"Master Cromwell, I thank you for this kindness," Margaret Roper says, as she enters, and curtseys, prettily, to him. She is wearing the Spanish style of hat, which frames her triangular features, perfectly. High cheekbones, a thin nose, and cupid lips, are but adornments to her eyes. The eyes are large, and have an intelligent, knowing look, that penetrates your soul. The king once remarked that were she a man, he would have her on his Privy Council, rather than waste her to marriage. She is a very beautiful young woman, and he can see how easily she can sway men to do her bidding.

"It is an unkindness, or so Rafe tells me," Thomas Cromwell replies. "Queen Anne is set on bringing your father down, my dear girl, not I." He offers her a chair near the fire. "I knew your father when he was a student, at university. I was a ragged little boy, and would run errands for him, and the other gentlemen, for a penny a time. Once, he threw me a shilling, instead. I held it out, and waited for him to see his mistake, but he just smiled at me, and asked my name. Then he said to me, 'Take it, Tom, and may it help to keep you honest."

"Ever the optimist, my father," Margaret replies, tartly. "Perhaps he should have slipped you a golden angel or two, instead?"

"You come to insult me, Margaret?" Cromwell says, smiling at the clever, unexpected, riposte. "I used to dangle you on my knee, when your father and I were dear friends. What do you want of me now?"

"I want to try and save my father."

"A noble sentiment," Thomas Cromwell responds. "Then that is simple, my dear. It is just a matter of his uttering a few words, with his fingers crossed behind his back, if need be. Tell him to do as lesser men do, and take the damned oath."

"He will not." Margaret states this, as if it is an obvious, and unalterable fact of life.

"You mean he cannot, because of his religious faith?" Thomas Cromwell says.

"No."

"Then what?"

"I cannot say."

"You talk in riddles, Meg!" Cromwell cannot help but admire the girl's obvious courage, and wonders what game she is about. "Will he take the king's great oath?"

"No."

"Then he is condemned to death, as a traitor."

"How so?" Margaret asks. "For he has not given any reason why he refuses the oath."

"By God, who thought this little idea up?" Thomas Cromwell says.

"It is my idea, sir." Margaret does not flinch from his studious gaze, and he is forced to pull his eyes away from hers, first.

"Of course. I always knew you were a clever one," Cromwell tells her. "I see where you are going with this, my dear girl. The king will not condemn your father or, indeed, any man, without some proof. If a man refuses the oath, yet gives no reason, it can be supposed that a part of it offends him."

"Just so," Margaret says. "But which part, pray tell?"

"No sir, I will not answer to you," Cromwell replies, playing his part in the little mummery. "It is simply that I will not take the oath. I will not answer any further."

"Then what do you object to?" Margaret asks, smiling.

"I stand on what I say," Cromwell tells her. "I will not take the oath, and I will not say why. The clever simplicity of it frightens me, girl."

"Will it work?" Margaret asks.

"No. They will find a way around it, if they think hard enough." Thomas Cromwell watches the flash of despair cross her face. "Though it will surely give his earliest inquisitors some pause for thought."

"Who will they use?" Margaret asks.

"In the first instance, they will send Archbishop Cranmer, who is a dear old friend, along. He will speak with your father at Utopia, in a casual way, and try to get him to either take the royal oath, or condemn it. Though he will be as fair to your father as he can, it is in his best interest to appease both Henry, and his vengeful queen. Poor old Cranmer must be considered an enemy … though a benign one, who will not twist your father's words."

"Archbishop Cranmer has visited Utopia, and eaten at our table many times," Margaret says.

"He will not hold that against your father," Cromwell jests, and recalls how poor the fare is at Utopia, even in times of great bounty. "He is but the opening gambit, and Sir Thomas must not be drawn out of position. He must deflect any questions about the oath, and if pressed on the matter, shrug, and say it is not something he has yet thought of. You have to understand that the oath is yet to be made public knowledge. Have your father deny having even read it, officially."

"Yes, how can you possibly comment on something which you have not yet officially read?" Margaret Roper asks. "So, the old archbishop is gently rebuffed by us. He will go back and explain the situation. What next, Master Thomas?"

"Anne will be furious, of course. The queen will push for the text to be made available to all, and have a copy hand delivered to Utopia," Cromwell says. "That will take about a month. Then, he will be approached again. It could be by any of the clever young fellows we are surrounded by. They might send Richard Rich, who is a devious toad, Thomas Dacre, a man of no morals, or even our own Rafe Sadler. Whomsoever is chosen, he will be told to demand an answer to the king's great question: Will your father take the oath?"

"Then he will refuse." Margaret wonders if she can get her father to remain silent over his reasons. "He will turn them aside, even if they come at him by the dozen."

"He must. They will try to trick him into some reply which, as lawyers do, can be twisted into a weapon against him. He must simply refuse the oath, without giving a single reason. That will eat away another couple of weeks ... more if they send Rafe Sadler, who can be devilishly slow, in matters of law." Thomas Cromwell explains. "Queen Anne will become more and more irate, and urge the king to much firmer action. He will, eventually, seek me out, as his best advisor, and ask for my advice."

"What will that be?"

"Why, the same as what it was over Cardinal Wolsey, and what it was over his divorce," the Privy Councillor says. "I shall preach caution, pointing out that the rest of Europe are waiting for him to become a bloody tyrant. Henry hates not being adored, and will listen to me, for a little while, at least. Queen Anne, however, will make his life more and more unbearable, until he demands action against all those who still refuse to take the oath."

"Is that when they shall come for him?" Margaret asks him.

"The king will demand that I 'do something', and there will be nowhere to hide," says Cromwell, with a twinkle in his eye. "I will inform His Majesty that your father should be arrested, on suspicion of treason. It is then that Sir Thomas might consider a deal."

"A deal?" Margaret is immediately suspicious. "What kind of a deal, Master Cromwell?"

"You used to call me Uncle Thomas, as a small child, Meg," Cromwell says to her.

"I am wiser now, sir," she replies. "What deal?"

"First, they will ask him to swear the oath, but only in writing."

"Ha! Do they think him a fool?" Margaret asks. "Why, if he either swore, or refuted the oath in writing, he is lost. One way, he writes his own death warrant, and the other has him refute his faith, and put Henry above God the Almighty, the Son, and the Holy Spirit. He will not write a single word!"

"Of course not." Thomas Cromwell is calculating each stage in his head, and thinks that, by now, ten or twelve weeks have passed. "Once he refuses to speak his mind, they will take him from Chelsea, down river to the Tower of London. Then they will row him inside, through the Traitor's Gate, and place him in a small, quite uncomfortable cell, with a high window, and a slatted wooden bed. On the way, they will let him pass the torture room, as if by chance, where the rack, and hot braziers are to be seen. Men have been known to break down and cry at this point."

"A wasted ploy," Margaret Roper mutters.

"Quite so, my dear. They will not be able to torture him," Thomas Cromwell explains to her. "Henry cannot let the King of France, or the Holy Roman Emperor, think that so illustrious a man as your father is being broken on the rack. No, they will take away all of his books, yet leave him with as many writing materials as he wishes."

"Are you sure?"

"Yes. I will order it to be so, in the hope that Sir Thomas commit's the folly of writing about his position, and his inability to take the oath. I am, after all, the king's councillor, and Henry will expect me to do as much. Warn him of my duplicity, and tell him to write nothing contentious."

"Then my father languishes in a damp, cold cell?" Margaret Roper wonders how her frail, ageing father can stand up to such harsh treatment.

"Not so damp, and not so very cold," Thomas Cromwell replies. "Colonel Will Draper is a close friend to many who work in the Tower, and shall see to whatever creature comforts your father may ask for. By now, we will have gained, at least, three precious months."

"Gained?" Margaret is beginning to perceive a distant light of hope, and it is a torch, held aloft by Thomas Cromwell, and his Austin Friars young men. "You keep my father alive for three more months?"

"Oh, no." Thomas Cromwell pours a glass of wine, and offers Margaret some. She shakes her head. Her husband, William Roper is a staunch Roman Catholic... this week, at least ... and he frowns on strong drink, outside of the Communion. "We have just started. The king will wish to appoint someone to destroy Sir

Thomas, without any international fuss. He will try to give the task to me, and I will, regretfully, refuse him. As a man of the law, I must point out that the only man for the job ... investigating the previous Lord Chancellor ... is the current encumberant."

"Sir Thomas Audley?" Margaret Roper shakes her head in bewilderment. "The man does not have the wit, or the courage, to conduct such an important interrogation. Does this really suit our purpose, Master Thomas?"

"Yes, dear Tom Audley," says Cromwell. "I suggested him for the post, of course, and we are now the greatest of friends. He will see that the inquisition of your father is carried out in as gentle a manner as can be, and goes on for as long as possible. He will restrict the questioning to one hour a day, at my request, and ask questions I suggest to him. They will be designed to be deflected easily by your father."

"Then we have saved him, for a few weeks longer."

"Precious, golden weeks, my dear Margaret," Thomas Cromwell says. "In twelve, or fifteen weeks, almost anything can happen. Imagine if Queen Anne fell from grace, or that the king found his mislaid scruples, or regained his long lost courage? Under those circumstances, there might well be reprieves, or even pardons handed around. Putting heads on spikes is not the way to go about running a country."

"Then you know of something, do you not, Master Cromwell?" Margaret is hopeful, for the first time in months.

"Only that those weeks give us all hope," Thomas Cromwell replies, evasively. "Do not press me. Go to your father now, and urge him to keep silent on the matter of the king's oath."

"He will not listen to me," Margaret says. "That is the main reason I come to you as I do."

"Ah, I see." Thomas Cromwell smiles, and shakes his head at his own gullibility. "You want more than a short audience, my dear. You want me to convince your father for you. I cannot. I will be watched, every step of the way."

"Perhaps, but no one watches your nephew, Richard, or your cook, or your…"

"Enough!" Cromwell is beaten by the cleverness of a woman, and his love for an old friend. Rafe, and Margaret, will have him disguised as a servant, and smuggled into Utopia in the blink of an eye. "I refuse to impersonate Richard… for he is much bigger than I, and my cook has no reason to go to Utopia."

"Master Oakley visits us once a fortnight, with a gift of food, authorised by yourself, sir," Margaret says. "You need only pull down a cap, and swathe yourself in his clothes. A basket of pies and bread, and a jug of ale, will complete the mummery!"

"God's teeth," Thomas Cromwell mutters. "Even then, should I escape my watchers, and arrive, safely, at Utopia, your father will refuse to see me. Since I drew up the laws to help the king re-marry, we have not exchanged a single civil word."

"No, but you have fed us, out of your own pocket," Margaret Roper reminds him. "Rafe explained about the deliveries of firewood in the winter months, the odd cask of ale, and the loaves of bread. I also know that Miriam Draper, who is a Jewess, is most Christian of all. She sends pies, and fresh caught fish, twice a week. Her fellow says that they are surplus, and would be thrown away, as Miriam only sells the freshest products."

"She, like you, has an answer for everything," Cromwell says. "Miriam can afford such gifts, as can I."

"Then it is time my father stopped being so arrogant," the young woman says. "He never asks where our generous bounty comes from, but surely he suspects. It is only fair that he grants you an audience."

"Your father might see it otherwise, and have me thrown out," the Privy Councillor replies. "He can be so … stiff necked."

"I am relying on his curiosity," Margaret says. "He will wish to know why you aid us… and mere charity is not an answer for it. You must give him a reason for your generosity. Then you can broach the subject of the oath. That is when he might throw you out."

"Perhaps I should send Mistress Miriam to plead my case," Cromwell jests. "She might fare better than I fear I will."

"I thought of that," Margaret says, "but she is travelling."

"Yes, she is abroad," Cromwell replies. He does not like the idea of Miriam, who is only several months from giving birth again, trying to deal with wily French merchants. "She has been offered a deal that seems far too good to miss."

"Then let us hope my father thinks what you have to say is also 'too good to miss', sir!"

2 Comings and Goings

The sturdy cog is under full sail, almost as soon as she clears Dover's deep harbour. Miriam has been on board since arriving with a cargo of wool from Sudbury. Once the captain secures his precious load, they navigate their way up the coast, before turning out into the gently heaving Channel. It is a fine day, and the crew expect a smooth, uneventful crossing.

"Your first trip to Calais, Mistress Draper?" Jake Timmins, the ship's master asks. He still finds it difficult to understand how a mere girl can own a fleet of cogs, and run a successful trading business, but he likes her, and enjoys being one of her ships masters.

"My first trip abroad," Miriam replies. This is not strictly true, as her father and mother brought her to England from Spain, almost twenty years before. Her parents, long deceased, were of the Jewish Mordecai family, but it does not do to boast of such a connection in London. Jews are hated in England, and they are banned from living in Henry's realm, on pain of death. So, she and her brother Moshe, known by all within Austin Friars as Mush, pretend to be English born. It is a fiction supported by legal documents 'uncovered' by Thomas Cromwell, and certified as real.

"Calais is a filthy hole," the captain tells her. "Will you have someone to protect you, once we land?"

"Master Cromwell has kindly asked for his agent in Calais to meet me," Miriam informs him. "Once you land me, I have arranged for some passengers to join you, for the return journey. A Spanish doctor and his family. See they are as comfortable as you can manage, and do not let the crew meddle with them."

"I run a tight cog, mistress," Jake Timmins tells her. "My crew know what I will do to any who disobey. This is the best run boat in your fleet, madam."

Miriam smiles. That she has enough cogs to warrant them being called a 'fleet' pleases her. Twelve cobs, and two sea going ships is not something to be sneezed at. If this new business deal works out, she will become an agent for a powerful group of wine growing families in Portugal, and Northern Spain, and the Draper fortune will swell to marvellous proportions.

" I have no complaints, Master Jake," she replies. "You have the lowest spillage of all my captains, and I trust your excellent mariner's skills. I will be three days over my business, and will be ready to re-cross the Channel on this coming Saturday."

"Tides willing, mistress," Jake says. "How is your stomach?"

"Full, and ready to bring forth more fruit," she says. "Or do you mean something else, sir?"

"Oh, I have seen many a sturdy fellow throwing up his dinner, mistress," the captain replies. "I wonder only if your delicate condition causes you to feel any sicker than is usual for such a voyage?"

"Not at all, captain," Miriam tells him, as she takes in a great breath of fresh, salty sea air. "My stomach is as sound as can be. I must have good sea legs."

"Then will you share our food?" Jake Timmins asks. "You are welcome to a slice off our roast."

"Thank you, but no," Miriam replies. "I will wait until we are in

Calais, and Cromwell's agent comes for me."

*

"Any reports?" Will Draper asks, as he comes into the bare stone room he has requisitioned from the Keeper of the Tower. It is little more than ten feet by twelve, and contains a desk, two old chairs flanking the fireplace, and a chest for papers. Captain John Beckshaw looks up from the paperwork in front of him, and jumps to attention. Draper waves him back into his seat, and wonders when the young Yorkshireman will cease being so deferential towards him.

"Nothing of note, sir," the young man replies. "I have made arrangements for the Spanish doctor and his family to be sent on to Exeter. I also have documents, sent from Austin Friars, which show them to be from Toledo. It is a strange business sir. Why should we be confirming these people are …"

"Yes, captain?"

"Nothing, sir." John Beckshaw is slow to realise, but sees now that it is another Jewish family who are being resettled by Miriam Draper. He has no evil in his heart for Jews, and actually admires Will Draper's wife. "Forget I spoke."

"Very well. Then we have no other business?"

"Nothing from the king, sir," Beckshaw replies, "but I have a rather strange letter from someone claiming to be the Sheriff of Hertfordshire."

"Oh, does the fellow have a name?"

"Sir Walter Beasley. He claims to be a long standing friend of yours, sir." John Beckshaw holds out the letter.

"That is putting it strongly," Will replies. "Sir Walter used to be an Under Sheriff of St. Albans. Our paths crossed a couple of times, and I was able to secure him a promotion. Sheriff of Hertfordshire now, is he... I wonder what he wants?"

"Help. It seems he did you a favour, and hopes you will remember him with kindness."

"I owe him nothing," Will protests. "The fellow presumes too much."

"He is beset by a monster," John Beckshaw says. "Though he does not specify what kind."

"Oh, there are many different kinds then?" Will smiles at the credulity of his young recruit, who he has made a King's Examiner, and raised to the rank of Captain of Horse.

"Why yes," Beckshaw replies, solemnly. "There are great wolves in the far northern reaches, bears, both black and white kinds, huge snakes, and tusked pigs. Then there are the kind who infest the seas. There are behemoths of the deep, and fish with daggers for noses, and things with many tentacles, I am told. Finally, there are the beasts that are conjured up from the bottom of a wine bottle. Sir Walter appears to be suffering from the latter."

Will Draper peruses the letter, and frowns. Sir Walter, a gruff, no nonsense sort of a man, in his late fifties, lacks anything like an imagination, yet he writes about 'creatures with burning coals for eyes', that slither through the forest, and devour anything that crosses their paths. The closing lines speak of a local man, ripped apart, as if by a huge beast.

"Whatever the cause, Sir Walter mentions a man who has been killed, in a most hideous way." Will considers his options. The Sheriff of Hertfordshire has no influence in the royal court, and there is no possibility of profit from such a case, but letting young John Beckshaw investigate will be good practice. "Stories about monsters unsettle people, and can disturb the king's peace."

"Then we will investigate?" John's face lights up at the prospect of action.

"I think we must," Will says. He has nothing to keep him home, with Miriam away, and such a diversion might prove entertaining. "The king leaves these things to my discretion. Have two horses made ready, and draw enough supplies for five days. We will set off at once."

"Shall I reply to Sir Walter?"

"There is no point," Will says. "Even if we use a royal messenger, he will only forewarn the Sheriff by a few hours. No, let our involvement be a surprise for all concerned. It is strange how news of our coming often makes people become tight lipped."

"What about arms, sir?" John asks. Will sees that the young man is perfectly serious.

"Well, I do hear of seamen, hunting great whales, with barbed spears," he says, suppressing the need to grin. "Or we might prevail on the Keeper of the Tower to loan us a pair of cannon from the ramparts."

"We would need at least a dozen horses to pull ... ah, you jest, sir." John blushes. He is yet to grow used to his commander's quirk-some humour, and often finds himself the butt of gentle jokes by the Austin Friars young men. "My slow Yorkshire wit fails me again, I fear."

"It does well enough for me, John," Will replies, trying to make light of the young fellow's dour nature. "I am coming with you, purely so that I might watch how you proceed. This investigation is yours."

"Really?" John Beckshaw says, more than a little surprised. "Then I shall have the shire horses made ready, and arrange for the cannon to be delivered."

"No, I meant..." Will tumbles into the trap, and shakes his head at his own stupidity. "Well played, John. I walked into that, did I not?"

"My humour seems to grow apace with my rank," John says, smirking at his commander. "Perhaps swords, and a couple of pistols will suffice, after all?"

*

Mary Boleyn is tired of life in the depths of Sussex, and yearns to have news from the royal court. It is months since her sister has banished her, and she spends her days running the small house, and few acres of farmland given her by a reluctant, and parsimonious king.

"Jem Potter, have you fed the pigs?"

"Nah, mistress."

"Why not?"

"Du nah, mistress." the dolt replies. The servants are the laziest people she has ever come across, and they know that, with no master on the land, they can get away with whatever they please. "It don't seem long since last yah asked me."

"And did you do it then?"

"Nah, mistress." The fellow ambles off, intent on catching the milk maid in the barn. Lady Mary Boleyn might be important in London, but that is a world away, and if she was held in such good stead, why has she now been banished to a tiny village on the high Sussex weald?

Mary stands, trembling with impotent rage, and wonders how she is ever to get through the next few months. The land is left untended, and the livestock are seldom looked after as they should be. She lives in a state of chaos, and does not know how to cope from one day to the next. She can feel the tears welling up in her eyes, when a horseman comes into view. He is still a half mile distant, when she recognises the familiar shape, and almost cries out in joy.

Mush Draper has been riding most of the morning, and, after several wrong turns, he has found his destination. He slows the horse to a canter, and waves at the small figure in the distance. She begins to jump up and down, and wave her arms at him. He reigns in his mount, and slips from the saddle. Mary is in his arms before he can draw breath.

"Mush!" She crushes into him, and pushes her lips against his, with frantic longing. "You have come, at last. What took you so long to seek me out?"

"They would not tell me where you were sent," Mush replies, truthfully. "Then I overheard the Duke of Norfolk talking to that wastrel of a son of his. The boy was complaining that you were on his land. That narrowed it down a little, to Surrey, and half of Sussex. I got the lad into a drinking bout, and he told all, before passing out. So, here I am."

"Yes, so you are."

"Who be this?" Jem Potter, the steward, appears from the direction of the milking shed. "There ain't enough food to feed another mouth."

Mush smiles at Mary, and perceives, at once, that she is the butt of a bully, who thinks himself the cock of his own small dung heap. He bows to her, as if in court.

"With your permission, My Lady," he says. "The king, and his queen, your sister, sends their warmest regards, and ask that I assure myself of your wellbeing. You, fellow… what are you here?"

"Steward."

"Sir … or master." Will steps close up to the big, brute of a man, and stares up into his pig-like eyes.

"What?"

"What … sir!" Mush hardly moves. A slight inclination of the head, and the man staggers back, holding the bridge of his nose.

"Ugh!" he grunts. "You bastard!"

"Oh, dear," Mush says to the man. "Manners, I fear, must be taught." He gives Jem Potter a sharp, back handed slap with his leather gloved hand. "When your better is present, you say 'sir', 'mistress', or 'master'. Clear?"

"Why, you dirty…" The steward reels back from two more slaps. "I'll have the Sheriff on you!" Mush hits the man, hard, in the stomach, and he doubles up in agony.

"One more word, and I will gut you like a fish, Master Dog," Mush snaps. "Now, you have my permission to get off this land. The Earl of Surrey deeded it to me after a game of cards, last evening, and I am the master here."

The big oaf cannot believe what he hears, but is too scared to refute what the olive skinned young man is saying. He bows, and begs the master's pardon.

"I bin' at the cider too much, sir," he grovels. "Dunno wha' cum over me."

"A bucket of slop, if you are not off my land, at once. Or would you rather argue?"

The big man backs off, then turns and starts running. He makes for the ramshackle barn, and grabs up a long handled pitchfork. He returns, waving it at Mush, who simply draws his sword, and prepares to meet an attack.

"You can't throw me off of here," Potter growls. "I got my rights."

"You have raised your hand against the lawful master of this land," Mush says, coldly. "The choice is clear. Either fight, or hang."

"Hang?" Jem Potter falters. It is beginning to dawn on him that he has overstepped the bounds, once to often. "You didn't say nothing about no hangin' … master. I jus' wanted my rights."

"You have the right to live… if you drop the fork, and run, now." Mush steps forward, and points the sword at the cowering bully. "Come back, and I will have the Sheriff hang you from the nearest tree."

The man drops the pitchfork, and runs. This time, he heads across the cow pasture, towards the nearest village, where he will spend what few copper pennies he has getting roaring drunk. In the morning, he will understand what he has lost, and move on, in the hope of finding another position.

"Thank you, kind sir," Mary says, curtseying to him.

"I will find you a decent, new steward, tomorrow," Mush tells her. "Are the other servants capable?"

"The milk maid is a slut, and the two field hands feared Potter too much to say anything against him."

"Then they may stay," Mush says. "I have Surrey's paper, and will sign the land over to you, as soon as I can find a sober enough magistrate. I will arrange for you to have a reasonable pension, until the place is making enough money."

"And in return?" Lady Mary Boleyn asks. Mush is ten years her junior, yet is treating her as a father would his daughter.

"A bed for the night?"

"There is but one in the main house, sir."

"That is inconvenient," Mush replies. "Though I am sure we can come to some, mutually beneficial accommodation."

"You are a wag, sir," Mary says, smiling. She has not been happy for months, and Mush's arrival seems to bode well for her immediate future. "Perhaps, if we squeeze in, closely…?"

*

"Ahoy, aboard!" The tall young man hails from the dockside, and starts up the narrow gangplank. "I come for Mistress Draper."

"What is that?" the captain asks. "Who are you, fellow?"

"Peter Yale," comes the reply. "I am Master Cromwell's agent in Calais."

"The devil you say!" the seaman curses. "Mistress Miriam left here a half hour since… with Master Cromwell's agent."

"I assure you, sir, that I fulfil that role."

"Are there two of you then?"

"Sir, what are you saying?" Peter Yale demands. "I am sole agent in Calais, for Thomas Cromwell. Where is my charge?"

"Gone, sir," The captain is ashen faced now, and does not know what to say for the best. "A young fellow came, claiming to be Cromwell's man. Mistress Miriam went off with him!"

"Sweet Christ, man!" Yale cannot believe his ears. "Then the lady has been taken by an impostor. How did they leave?"

"On foot," the captain replies. "Though the rogue claimed to have a coach waiting a street or two away, where the road widens, and is better cobbled. He even took her valise up onto his own back!"

"I must report to the Governor, at once," Yale snaps. "He must raise the soldiery, and close the city gates at once."

"Too late, I fear," Miriam's captain says, with dread in his voice. "I am returning toLondon on the next tide, and will send messages to Master Cromwell, and to Colonel Draper too. By God, sir, but they will have our heads for this days work, and no mistake!"

"I do not understand," Peter Yale asks the cog's horrified captain.

"Why would anyone wish to kidnap Will Draper's wife?"

*

The clothes are authentically worn, and smell of every ingredient in a kitchen. Cromwell is as alike to his cook as possible, and he has even adopted the fellow's shambling gait. He lumbers from the boat, as it lands at the jetty, and sets off up the lawn, to Utopia's once grand entrance. Margaret is waiting for him, and opens the door, at once.

"Ah, Master Oakley, I see you have our victuals," she says, and ushers Cromwell into the great hall, which lacks a good fire, and is bitterly cold.

"What is it?" Sir Thomas More says, starting up from a doze. The book on his knee slides to the floor with a soft thud.

"Christ's Thunder, but it is cold in here, Tom," Cromwell growls. "Surely, you have enough chopped wood, do you not?"

"Thomas Cromwell, is that you?" More says, rubbing at his sleep hooded eyes. "Has Anne Boleyn sent you to murder me now, to save the expense of a long trial?"

"Hush, man," Thomas Cromwell replies. "Where will my lawyers fees come from if there is no grand show trial? A man of my worth is paid by the hour, these days. We must make your court proceedings last as long as we can."

"Margaret, how could you let…"

"Leave the girl alone. Her only crime is to love you too much, you miserable old fool." Cromwell sits, unbidden. "I come to discuss our defence."

"Our defence?"

"If the Boleyn woman brings you down, how long will it be before she wants my head?" Thomas Cromwell asks. "Your star is allied to mine, sir, and we stand or fall together, I fear. They will send Archbishop Fisher against you first. You must refuse to discuss the oath with him, Tom."

"Ah, do I perceive a strategy then, Cromwell?"

"You do, if you let me stay a while."

"I have nothing to offer you."

"I have brought it with me, old man," Thomas Cromwell tells him. "Fresh bread, a pie, and some ale. Let Meg serve it up to us, whilst we speak… please. For friendship sake."

"For old friendship's sake." More is pedantic, and does not wish Cromwell to think he still loves him as a friend. "A few minutes will not hurt, I suppose."

"After Cranmer has failed, they will send some clever young fellow, who will try to lie you into submission. They will say that you need only write down your acceptance, or pen the reasons for your refusal. Do not give them any."

"Then I am to stand on my refusal, and not offer any reasons?"

"Yes." Cromwell sees the light of reason flicker across his friend's eyes, then die.

"It will not work," More tells him. "They will simply legislate around the difficulty."

"I know, but it will give us valuable time."

"For what?" Despite his reservations, Sir Thomas More is interested in what Cromwell has to propose. As a student, he used to throw the young Cromwell a coin, now and then, and marvel at his clever repartee.

"To work on the king, and against the queen," Thomas Cromwell tells his old friend. "After all else is tried, they will take you to the Tower of London, and try to terrify you into taking the oath."

"I think I can stand a little pain before I die," More says. "Besides, they will not want to look bad in the eyes of Europe. Henry is a thin skinned soul, and hates to be criticised."

"They will lock you up, and demand that you either sign, or give your reasons for refusal. You must refuse to say what it is you object to. Simply refuse."

"It might give us a few months, I suppose," More says, "but the fact remains, I will not take the oath. You, and all of your lawyers have done far too good a job of things. I have dissected every word, a thousand times over, and there is not even a chink of light to give me hope."

"I know, but if Queen Anne were to … fall from grace … the king might forget to press the oath on you, and those of a like mind." Cromwell hopes this chance will enervate his old friend, and give him the strength to carry on the fight.

"It is a slim chance." More does not seem convinced.

"Take it, for Meg's sake," Cromwell tells him.

"At the last, I am willing to die for my beliefs, Thomas Cromwell."

"And I am willing to live for mine, dear friend." Cromwell can say no more. It is now down to Sir Thomas More's cleverness of wit, and the vagaries of time. He adopts his shuffling gait again, and starts to leave.

"Thomas."

"Yes?" Cromwell says, from the door.

"I knew it was you, at once." More sighs. "Take care, my friend, for you hold your own life dearer than I do mine."

"If I fall," Cromwell replies, "then, like it or not, everyone will go with me. I pray to God that day never dawns!"

*

Captain Jake Timmins goes straight to the castle, the moment he lands back at Dover, and reports to the

Warden of the Castle, who sends a fast galloper to London. The man delivers his news to Austin Friars first, then goes on to see who else will drop him a coin for what he knows.

By chance, he is relaying the news to the Duke of Norfolk, when Charles Brandon, who is back in favour at court once more, overhears. Despite being under a cloud with Cromwell and his faction, he considers Will Draper to be an honourable man, who has helped him in the past, and he resolves to have him told of Miriam's disappearance as soon as he can. He seeks out one who knows most things in court, and approaches him, with some trepidation.

"Doctor Theophrasus… a word, if you please," the Duke of Suffolk whispers to the big, olive skinned man, dressed in the soft, black gown of the medical profession. The venerable old man pauses, on his way to the throne room, and casts Brandon an interrogative glance.

"Do you ail, My Lord?" Adolphus Theophrasus asks, with a slight smile playing about his lips. Lord Suffolk can cure himself in a moment, by stopping all of his drinking, and staying up all night gambling, and whoring about the city.

"Not I, sir," Brandon replies, rather stiffly. "It is just that I seek Colonel Will Draper, and know you are close to him."

"I am quite close to the whole Draper family," the doctor says, carefully. Adolphus Theophrasus is part Greek on his Athenian father's side, and part Hebron Jewish, through his mother. This manifests itself by giving him an olive skinned, and exotic appearance; ideal for his chosen profession, where patients choose a doctor for his ostentation, and mystical looks, rather than any innate medical skill he might possess.

He is a man of some wealth, these days, ever since he and Will Draper were able to save the old queen from poisoning. He now has a medical practice, situated in a small, but lavishly furnished house close to Whitehall. The doctor is much sought after by those rich idlers who enjoy following the latest trends in medicine. Some, but only behind his back, call him a quack, whilst others claim he is the greatest anatomist since Leonardo

Da Vinci, who learned his trade on the bloody battle fields of Italy.

The Lord Chancellor's office are mindful of his heritage, and would like to expel him from England, on the grounds that he has Jewish blood in his veins, but find they cannot.

Apart from now being a physician to the royal household, it seems that, on further enquiry, the good doctor's closest blood relatives are from a small town in the depths of rural Cornwall; a fact attested to, and confirmed by documents uncovered by some of Thomas Cromwell's people.

They are clever forgeries, of course, but of such a fine quality that they surpass the originals in many ways.

"I have news of Miriam."

"Does she need a doctor, so soon?"

"She has been stolen away, sir," Brandon says. "Will needs to know, but he is shunning me, at the moment."

"Do you wonder?" Theophrasus growls. "The girl is kidnaped?"

"In Calais."

"Then we must act," the old doctor says, firmly. "You must put aside your petty differences, and find Mush.

Have him round up some able fellows, and take a cog across the Channel at once. In this way, we will have men on site. I will attend to the king, and then send out to find Colonel Draper. Are you up to that, sir?"

"You ask if I am sober enough," Brandon tells him, and drops his head in shame. "I shall do as you ask, and will not touch another drop, until Mistress Miriam is brought safely home again."

"I find myself to be irrefutably English, thanks to Master Cromwell," the doctor tells Suffolk. "A Cornishman, in fact. This means I can hold my wealth in London. So, tell me, young man, are they going to ask for a ransom?"

"God alone knows," Suffolk replies. "The Drapers are worth many thousands, I hear, but why take her captive abroad?"

"To elude Master Cromwell's long reach?" The doctor shrugs. "Now, be off about your business, My Lord Suffolk, and I will tend to that which is my portion."

3   Amongst the Beasts

Hertford is a pleasant enough little town, with a commanding, stone built, Norman castle, and a twelfth century priory, which is still fighting, forlornly, to remain within the Roman Catholic faith. It is overseen by a council of twelve burgesses, who employ a bailiff, and rely on the local County Sheriff to administer justice.

Sir Walter Beasley has come to his higher office late in life, and finds anything other than petty thievery, and drunken brawling, to be beyond his abilities. It is this fear of his own inability which drives him to call on an old acquaintance for help.

"You sent no word of your coming, Colonel Draper!" The garrulous older man bustles forward, and holds out a welcoming hand to the younger man. "Are you alone?"

"I am, Sir Walter." Will's companion, John Beckshaw is entering the town by another road, and is going to spend a few shillings in Hertford's various inns and taverns. This unofficial approach often loosens tongues, and provides otherwise concealed facts, and snippets of gossip.

"Might you tell me all that you know, so far?"

"A beast is abroad," Sir Walter states.

"Facts, sir?" Will asks.

"A month ago, a sheep was found on the heath, with its throat ripped open, and its body dismembered, as if some great animal had torn away the flesh," Sir Walter reports. "I was sent for, and saw the terrible sight with my own two eyes. I set a patrol on the heath, for the next week, but the beast never returned."

"Then came a second attack?" Will guesses.

"Horrible. An animal from the same flock as before. Gabriel Haddow owns many of the flocks about here. He called me in, and I can honestly say that I have never seen such a brutal slaying. The head was severed, and huge portions of the carcass ripped off, as if by sharp teeth."

"You investigated, of course," Will says. "What did you find?"

"A couple of paw prints in a patch of muddier ground. Each one as big as a man's fist." Sir Walter shudders at the thought. "I had called off my men, but the night before, and kick myself for my impatience. Had they stayed abroad, the beast would have been seen… even hunted and killed."

"I doubt it," Will tells the Sheriff. "I have hunted wolves in Ireland, and they are a shy breed. They can be seen, only when there are none to see them."

"True." Sir Walter frowns, and thinks what he might suggest next, but Colonel Will Draper is ahead of him.

"We must post more men at night," he says. "During the day, we can organise a hunt. The local burgesses, and the nobility will love a chance to scour the heath, from end to end."

"You have the king's authority, Will," Sir Walter replies, happy that someone else is ready to take the blame. "Tell me what to do, and it shall be done."

"Master Sheriff!" A boy, about eleven years of age is in the open door, and hopping from foot to foot.

"A moment, child."

"But, sir!" The boy cannot be denied. "The beast has come again, in the night."

"But there were two men patrolling the whole heath," Beasley says. "Tad Blake, and Gabriel Haddow. Did they see nothing?"

"Tad was off abed with a whore," the boy explains, "and it was left to Master Haddow to face the beast!"

"Gabriel Haddow faced the beast?" Sir Walter feels a flood of relief. "Thank God, for he is a goodly huntsman."

"It ate him, sir." The boy relishes the effect of the news on the two gentlemen. "Tore him apart. We found the head in one place, and an arm in another. Master Haddow is half devoured, and his horse has claw marks ripped down one flank."

"Where about, lad?"

"The northern end of the heath, sir," the boy replies, pointing vaguely to his left. "Half of the local men are guarding the body, with scythes and daggers, but Bill Abbot, the farrier, says the creature will have magical strength, and might even be able to fly through the sky ... or disappear."

"I once came upon a vicious, hungry wolf," Will Draper says, then pauses for dramatic effect. "Its pelt made me a fine saddle lining, and stopped my arse from aching. Whatever it is, my sword, or my pistol will stop it. Now, take us to the place where this murder has taken place."

"Murder?" Sir Walter is puzzled at Will's remark. "How so?"

"If a beast causes the death of a man, it must be killed," Will explains. "In Halifax, some years ago, a pig was tried, and hanged, after trampling its old master to death in the sty."

"Then must we have a jury of twelve cows, or a panel of clever sheep?"

"We need not go so far," Will tells the Sheriff. "Let us first establish the facts of this case, shall we?"

*

"I have a mind to spend the rest of my days here," Mush says. Lady Mary Boleyn is naked, and lies in the crook of his arm. "Is that to your liking?" Mary kisses him, and simpers into his olive skinned chest.

"Forever… or until I grow too old for you," she says.

"I do not notice the years," Mush tells her.

"No? I am far too old for you, my love." She kisses him again. "One day, you will ride away, and never look back."

"Until then, I am yours," the young man tells her. "The new steward starts today, and I have warned everyone within riding distance, that you are under the protection of Thomas Cromwell, and that I am his agent. Upset you, and I will visit swift retribution on them."

"Listen, I can hear a rider," Mary says, trying to rise. Will pulls her back down, and runs his hands over her firm, naked body.

"It is just a rider," he says. "keep warm, and I will see the fellow on his way. Mush crosses, quite naked, to the window, and throws it open.

"A sight for sore eyes!" The lone rider calls up from the back of his horse. "This will make a pretty tale, around the breakfast table, at Austin Friars!"

"Barnaby Fowler, how come you to be here?" Mush reaches for some clothes.

"The court gossips," Barnaby replies. "The tale of you fleecing the Duke of Surrey, and demanding this particular estate is all about. It is a wonder queen Anne is not already signing your death warrant!"

"Very funny," Mush says. "Now, what is so important that you…"

"It is Miriam, my friend," Barnaby says.

"She is in Calais."

"She is taken, Mush," Barnaby Fowler tells his friend. "Some trickster lured her away from the boat, and she is taken. Lord Suffolk fears a ransom demand will come. Some of us are crossing the Channel later today, and I come to see if you will join us."

"How many are we?" Mush is almost dressed, and is busy concealing his throwing knives about his person.

"Me, Richard Cromwell, Suffolk, you, and Tom Wyatt." Barnaby Fowler confirms. "Doctor Theophrasus thinks they might be foreigners, and wish to negotiate on their own territory. Which is why Tom Wyatt demands to be invited. He speaks French, the Flemish dialects, Italian, and Latin."

"Saddle my horse," Mush cries. "I will be down in a moment." He crosses to the bed, where Mary has turned her back to him, lest he sees her tears. "I must go, my dearest one," he says to her bare back. She does not answer, and he runs from the room.

Ever since being told she was the king's plaything, men have taken their pleasure, and then left her. Her life has slid, remorselessly down into ruin, until Mush. He is like a hero from the tales of King Arthur, but he is as flawed as they. Within each man is a beast, and a woman can only pray it remains hidden from her.

It is only when she hears the sound of a second horse, and the gabble of men making plans that she climbs from the bed. She watches from the window, as the two comrades gallop away, towards the Dover road. She watches until they quite disappear from view, and she wipes a hand across her eyes.

"See what I mean, Mush? She mutters through the rolling tears. "You never look back!"

*

Miriam is blindfolded and gagged, and someone, a strong man, drags her across a wooden floor, to a chair. He pushes her down, until she sits, then removes the cloth from her eyes, only to tie it across her mouth instead. She blinks in the dim, candle light, and tries to identify her captor. He is as big as Richard Cromwell, has a shaved head, and the expression of someone who is little more than a simpleton.

"You may look," a voice says, from the gloom, but I will not tolerate your petty mewling. Nod if you promise to remain silent, unless you have something important to say."

"Why am I here?" Miriam asks the question, as soon as the big fellow removes the gag. There is nothing but silence. "When they realise I have been taken, you will be hunted down, and punished. Let me go now, and spare yourself the gibbet, or the headsman's axe!"

"Let them hunt," the voice replies.

"I am with child," Miriam says.

"That is more of a factor in my favour," the hidden voice tells her. "It will add a little salt to the meat. How much does your husband love you, Mistress Miriam Draper? A thousand Ducats, or ten thousand?"

"We are not rich."

"You lie. You own a dozen boats, a warehouse, and enough market stalls and shops, to sell all your trade goods." The voice sounds as if he is reading from a prepared document. "I am told that a ransom of fifty thousand golden Ducats is not a problem."

"My husband will pay," Miriam says. "Though it will take a little while."

"He has a week, then I shall have Hugo here snap off a finger of yours, and sent it to him," the voice explains. "Each delay will result in a further mutilation. After a month, there will be no more fingers, and we will start with your toes."

"He will pay, without delay," Miriam bargains, "but it is I who am in charge of the finances."

"Poor Colonel Will." The man steps out into the light, and Miriam is disappointed that she does not recognise him. He is tall, and has the air of a soldier about him. "How comes he to be a man of such high rank? Did he buy it, with his woman's money, or did he spin enough lies to make himself into a hero?"

"He is the King of England's Examiner, and the rank goes with the gravity of the position," Miriam replies. She refuses to be baited by her captors, and will defend her husband's honour to her last breath. "Soon, he will be investigating you, sire, and coming to some conclusions."

"His wife leaves a cog in Calais harbour, and vanishes from sight," the man says. "My agent is not known in the town, and is already safe in Flanders. He can search Calais from top to bottom, and shall find no sign of his lovely wife. Let him ask, or set a reward, if he will, but he will find no trail to follow … save the one I set for him."

"Why not name your price, and be damned with it," Miriam spits. "He will pay good gold for my safe return."

"Gold?" Her captor laughs out loud. "Is that how your people see the world … Mistress ben Mordecai? Do you sit around, counting your money, and thinking that you own men's souls?"

"You dislike Jews?" Miriam asks. It might be that she is taken for another reason … rather than for ransom. "Do you wish me harm?"

"No, and yes," the man replies. "No, I do not dislike Christ Killers, I loathe them, and yes, I most certainly do wish you harm. I want to see you crawling on the floor, begging the pain to stop, with your husband on his knees, with my knife at his throat."

"Thirty thousand golden Ducats."

"The money means nothing."

"Sixty thousand." Miriam says, softly. Hugo, the giant guard makes a funny sucking noise with his teeth, and glances across at his master.

"Sixty thousand Ducats, Master Baglioni," the man says. "It will pay for a new…"

"Shut up, Hugo," the man snarls. "We will have every piece of gold Draper possesses, and we will have even better than that. We will have him, his gold, and his wife."

"But the gold…"

"Enough!" Baglioni touches a hand to the hilt of his sword, and starts pacing the room. "Did you leave the message, as I instructed?"

"Yes, master," Hugo replies. "It shall be delivered to the Warden of the Fortress, by one who does not know what he does."

"Like you, Hugo," Baglioni says. "Each fragile link will lure your husband closer to me. First, he must leave the safety of England, then he must forsake the high walls of Calais. Once he is outside your king's realm, we are on equal terms."

"You mean to kill him, and me," Miriam says. "The name Baglioni, means something to me. My husband often tells the tale of how he destroyed the power of the condottiero, and saved Venice from being sacked. You are a Baglioni, are you not?"

"I am," the swarthy looking man admits. "I am Angelo Baglioni, a cousin of the greatest condottiero in Italy. In time, I was to become one of his most trusted *tenentes*, and form my own condottiere. We would have conquered the whole of Italy, and made it into a mighty empire."

"My husband called Malatesta Baglioni 'a clever bandit', and often boasts of how easily he was brought down."

"Murdered."

"What?"

"Murdered, by your husband's mistress, a young, very beautiful courtesan, called Pippa Micheletto," Angelo Baglioni tells her. "Did he not mention that part of the heroic tale to you then, Mistress Miriam? He took her as his whore, and she killed my brother to please him."

"You are a liar!" Miriam's conviction comes from the strength of her love for Will, and the assurance, from her brother, that her husband was the only man in Venice who resisted the charms of the attractive Italian courtesans.

"Then why do you not know her name?" Baglioni asks, sensing another way to hurt the family he is sworn to destroy. She wonders at the girl's omission from the story, when it would be a simple matter to name her, and jest about how all the lads fancied her. "Is someone keeping secrets from you, poor Miriam?"

"My husband is faithful," Miriam states. "He is a man of his word, and when he finds out about this, he will swear to kill you. It is a simple fact, Angelo Baglioni. Will Draper will come for me, and kill any man who stands in his path!"

*

"I hate boats," Charles Brandon, Duke of Suffolk explains, between bouts of retching over the side of the little cog. "Why cannot they build a bridge across this troublesome sea, so that we might ride in comfort?"

"The wind is too strong, and there is not enough stone and timber in England," Tom Wyatt replies, nonchalantly. "That is why they are going to build a tunnel underground."

"What?" says Suffolk. "A tunnel, between England and France? I have heard nothing about such a grand scheme."

"Of course not," Barnaby Fowler puts in. It is a wonderful jest, and he can see great merriment in so ridiculous an idea. "The lawyers are still trying to buy up the coast in Suffolk, and France, before the price of land goes too high."

"Suffolk is mine!" Brandon says.

"Exactly," Tom Wyatt tells his friend. "Your sandy coast is worth but a pound an acre, but the moment they wish to build a tunnel from France, they need a place to come up. Good coastal land will be fetching a thousand pounds an acre!"

"Dear Christ!" Suffolk realises that he shall soon be a rich man. "They must buy my land then."

"No, friend," Richard Cromwell says, picking up on the jest at last. "Set up a toll at the tunnel mouth, and charge every wagon five shillings, and every man, woman and child a florin, to use the gateway to England. You might even charge the Frogs a little more. Why, inside a year, you would be as rich as Uncle Thomas."

"Who is running this venture?" Suffolk asks. "Be it us, or the French?"

"Neither," Tom Wyatt explains. "For the part in the middle belongs to King Neptune, and he has his own ideas!" The small company can restrain themselves no longer, and burst into laughter.

"Blast your poet's eyes, Tom Wyatt," Charles Brandon curses. "How can you jest about such an important thing? Why, someone should dig a tunnel… for it would save me getting sick every time!"

"Damn, but I wish Will was with us," Mush curses. "How could he go off, and not leave word of his whereabouts?"

"Doctor Theophrasus will track him down," Richard Cromwell tells them. "He has the use of all our agents, and will have Will in Calais, the moment he is found."

*

"What manner of beast is it that can rip a man's head off so cleanly?" John Beckshaw asks, as he studies the dismembered remains of the Burgess, Gabriel Haddow. Will Draper shrugs his shoulders. The colonel is standing back from the rough wooden table that has been set up in the castle, where Sir Walter has his office. "See the body, where the claw marks are evenly spaced here, and more ragged here. It is not the work of a wolf, or even a bear, master."

"My name is Will. You must begin to call me by my given name, John. It will make for a better working relationship. I agree that it is not a wolf, and we have not seen bears in this part of these islands for two, or three hundred years."

"Then what?"

"You are in charge, John," Will Draper reminds the younger man.

"Think back to Skipton, when the mad Irish priest was fomenting rebellion against the crown. You thought matters through, and came to a well reasoned decision. This is no different. Take all that you know, and separate it into two: that which you actually know, and that which you think you know."

"You confuse me, sir... I mean, Will." John Beckshaw is a decently educated country fellow, who just needs his mind sharpening in the ways of investigation, and the art of smelling out lies.

"When you wake up in the morning, you know it is day, but you do not know it is a good day, until you open the window and establish the facts." Will tries to make it as simple as he can for his new recruit. "It is not enough to think the sun is shining, John, you must look up, and see it hanging in the sky."

"Then I must take nothing on trust?" the Yorkshireman asks.

"Unless you have no other choice," Will says, smiling. "If the king says it is raining frogs outside ... we have no option, but to accept his word. Otherwise, doubt everything, until it can be proven, or discarded."

"What of gossip?" John asks. He has been in the town, and about the taverns incognito, and has heard enough tittle tattle to fill a bible.

"The same applies," Will replies. "Listen, and sift out the useful parts. Sometimes, two casually uttered phrases, from different sources, will corroborate that which you suspect. Enough drips of gossip can turn into a lake of truth. The important thing is… think!"

"What about any talk of unnatural things?" John asks his comrade. "I know you sneer at monsters, and evil spirits, but what of witches?"

"Hush, John, that is a dangerous word." Will Draper has had dealings with Irish witches, banshees, and talk of spirits before, and knows how frightened the locals can become. Many an innocent woman has burnt for her odd way of looking. "Witchcraft is apt to cause panic amongst those less educated than we."

"Not here," John explains. "Prudence Wells lives in the town, and she is well thought of, as a healer, and a foreteller of things not yet happened. I spoke to her."

"Did you now?" The King's Examiner can tell from John's slight blush that she is not the usual wizened old hag of folklore. "Is she old … or young?"

"In her twenties, I would guess," says John. "She came to me, and said that I would find that which I seek. No one knew I was with you, and I was shaken. Then she said a funny thing."

"What?"

"She said 'an angel has gone before a prophet', and sat by my side."

"Lucky boy," Will Draper says. "Anything else?"

"Yes, she spoke of you. She said, 'there is another man with you … and he must know that what was here is now there, and shall not come back here, until Hell freezes over.' It scared me, and no mistake."

"Cleverly phrased words," Will says. "They can be interpreted in a dozen ways, to suit her needs afterwards. Unless she can give you some hard facts, have nothing more to do with the woman, John ... No matter how pretty she is!"

At that moment Sir Walter Beasley erupts into their presence, leading Timothy Stay, a tired looking Austin Friars messenger by the elbow. The Sheriff is red faced, as if he has run all the way from London himself. He pushes the bedraggled fellow towards Will Draper, like a sacrificial offering.

"Tell the colonel, you damned fool!" Sir Walter demands. "The oaf has been riding all about the town, asking after you, Will, instead of coming to the proper authorities. I found him just now, about to ride on to St. Albans!"

"You have a message for me, lad?" Will asks. The young man nods, and takes a deep breath. It is memorised, and he has been warned to deliver it, word for word.

"From the Greek doctor, Master Will," he says. "He bids me say: Come at once. Mistress Miriam is further abroad than we wish, and your attendance is urgently needed."

"This does not bode well," Will says, glancing at Sir Walter, who has no idea what the message may mean. "I must return to London at once, John. You shall remain here, and conclude the investigation."

"Who would dare?" John asks. He understands the cryptic spoken message to mean Miriam is held abroad, and cannot understand how anyone could benefit from such an act. "Is it for money?"

"That is for me to find out," Will Draper says. The message tells him what he needs to know, and the details are for him to uncover later. For the time being, he must reach London, speak with Thomas Cromwell and Adolphus Theophrasus, and make his plans.

"But Will," John Beckshaw says, white faced. "Is not that what Mistress Prudence foretold to me? Miriam was here, and is now there … and may not return, until Hell freezes over!"

"Ah, you have met Pru Wells?" Sir Walter Beasley says, oblivious of the sudden shift in the chain of events. "She foretells happenings with the most amazing success, and is a damned pretty wench, what?"

4 The Searchers

"Every single, stinking hovel in Calais has been searched," Richard Cromwell says, as he throws himself down onto a long bench. "Bring me ale, girl."

"Then we must widen our range, and seek my sister in the outer Calaisis area," Mush replies. "There must be many hiding holes in the Calais hinterland. Will may arrive on the very next tide, and I cannot tell him we have found nothing out."

"We cannot invent anything," Suffolk says. "Colonel Draper must know nothing else can be done, until we receive a ransom demand."

"Three days, and two nights have passed, without a word," says Barnaby Fowler, dourly. He is a practical, hard headed lawyer, and speaks as he thinks. "Any ransom demand would, surely, have been delivered by now. The Warden of the Fortress is holding enough of Master Cromwell's gold to buy Calais, twice over, but no-one yet asks for it. I am beginning to get a bad feeling about this whole business."

"My sister is alive," Mush snaps.

"I suggest nothing otherwise, Mush," Barnaby replies. "My thinking is that the abductors have Miriam for other reasons. Do not jump to the wrong conclusion, my friend, I merely say that they do not want our English gold."

"Then what, in Hell's name, are they after?" Charles Brandon, the Duke of Suffolk asks. He is in constant, chronic debt, and cannot think of anything more important than gold.

"What if they have taken the wrong woman?" Richard Cromwell says, from behind a huge mug of strong ale.

"The wrong Miriam Draper?" Mush asks. "How many rich women named Miriam, married to men called Draper do you think there are in Calais?"

"Not many, granted," Richard admits. "I only meant that they mistook her for another woman altogether."

"Then why not release her… or cut her throat, and dump the body?" Barnaby Fowler asks. He sees Mush's discomfort at the thought, and reassures him, again, that Miriam is alive. "The abductor asked for your sister by name, my friend. There is no mistaken identity here. Whomsoever has taken her wants something from one of us. Either they seek to force Master Cromwell into a certain course of action, or they want Will to pay the price."

"They must know how strong we are," Mush offers. "Why, we can put a hundred men on their trail. We have agents across France, Flanders, and all of the Holy Roman territories. There is nowhere for them to hide, for any length of time."

"Peace, friend," Suffolk advises. "We must do as Will Draper does. Think it through. Though I am not as good at it as he, I must confess. If they do not want money…"

"Then they want something else," Tom Wyatt says, as he strolls into the low tavern. "They want attention. They wish the might of Austin Friars to be directed here. They want Master Cromwell worried, and Will Draper frightened for the life of his sweet wife. They want everything they hate to be in one place, so that they might destroy it. There, is that clear enough reasoning, my friends?"

"Then it is not an enemy of Will's, but of us all?" Suffolk asks. "I do not understand. What have I to do with these mysterious foes, Wyatt?"

"Nothing," the poet replies. "You chose to involve yourself, if only to recompense Thomas Cromwell for your previous poor behaviour, and so, you have become one with us. All that remains is to puzzle out who wants us hurt, or even destroyed."

"Pope Clement?" Richard Cromwell asks, and the others all laugh aloud. The Roman Catholic church's supreme head on Earth is a dissolute old scoundrel, who has the most complete lack of morals anyone could imagine. He is interested in wealth and debauchery, not revenge. Besides, how has Thomas Cromwell ever really hurt him, other than in some ephemeral, political, way?

"Clement is a worthless arse," Tom Wyatt says, "but he would never stoop to kidnap. His cardinals might, I suppose, but which one of them could be bothered, and for what possible reason?"

"What about an ally of Sir Thomas More?" Mush voices what is but a mild suspicion in his mind.

"Too honest," Charles Brandon replies. The Duke of Suffolk speaks with the conviction of a dissolute waster, who understands other men's morals, even if he cannot abide by them. He shakes his head. "Why, he would have to pray for a year if he ever thought of such a wicked thing. besides, he does love Cromwell, almost like a brother, despite everything. Nor would the fellow strike in Calais. His power, or what remains, lies in London, and the Low Countries."

"Then we are looking for a foreign hand?" Barnaby Fowler says, then realises that they are going over the same old ground, yet again. "Some powerful rogue, who does not yet know to fear our power... and ... but, of course, why did I not think of the damned fellow sooner ... Anton Fugger!"

"What?" Suffolk has never had any dealings with foreign bankers, and has not heard of the rich Germanic financier.

"Anton Fugger," Barnaby repeats. "He is very rich, and the master humiliated him once. We stole a wagon load of treasure from him, when he sought to forge English money, and ruin our economy."

"The banker most certainly has the man power," Richard Cromwell agrees. "He sent mercenaries against us in East Anglia, and has the wealth of a hundred Spanish gold mines in the New World to draw against."

"Is he the sort of man who would seek such a winding path to revenge?" Tom Wyatt asks. "Surely, he is more the sort of fellow who will pay a gang to set upon his foe, and hack him down."

"True, but he must remain a consideration," Barnaby insists. "Men will behave in odd ways, if they feel their honour has been slighted, or they have been made to look foolish, and Fugger was the laughing stock of the Holy Roman Empire, after we finished our dealings with him."

"Is he an old man?" Suffolk asks. In his mind, all bankers are miserly and old. They huddle over counters, and stack neat piles of silver coins all day long.

"Not at all," Barnaby Fowler responds. "Why, I doubt he is much above forty. He loaned money to Emperor Charles, against the prospects of gold in the Americas, and struck lucky. The wealth of Peru, and the Caribbean Islands flows into his coffers. It is said that he will choose the next pope, and has enough influence over the emperor to dictate his foreign policy."

"He sounds like our own, dear, Cromwell." Suffolk sees his remark is not well taken, and decides to keep his mouth closed for the time being. He understands that he is not a member of their exclusive band, and that he is there only on sufferance.

"Uncle Thomas has the measure of Fugger," Richard tells them. "He knows how easily we can get at him, should the need arise."

"Ah, then the dagger story is true?" Tom Wyatt asks. He is a collector of gossip, and is not adverse to weaving what he hears into his more risqué poetry. "I thought it a silly tale, put about to frighten little children."

"Not children," Mush replies. "The story goes that Fugger went to bed, in one of his many castles, surrounded by a small army of bodyguards, sworn to keep him safe. He awoke, to find a dagger driven into the top of a nearby table. 'See,' said the message, 'we can reach you, no matter where you may be', and the shock almost killed Fugger. Or so they say."

"Then the man would be a fool to kidnap one of our people," Barnaby Fowler says. "Perhaps we are trying to be too clever. What if it is just some rogue, who saw a chance to grab off a pretty girl."

"How did he know to present himself as Cromwell's agent?" says Mush. "No, this smacks of a well planned business. They took Miriam to get at … whom? Apart from Cromwell, and Will Draper, who else would care?"

"You," Tom Wyatt offers. "Could it be you, Mush, who he seeks to punish? What if you have hurt someone on your travels, and they have decided to revenge themselves on you now?"

"Am I that important?" Mush is aghast at the thought. His only recent visit to the continent was his disastrous decision to journey to the Holy Land. He was no more than half way across France, when his beloved wife, Gwen was stricken with some sudden illness. Within days, his wife was dead, and Mush was on his way back, broken hearted. "I met no one on my trip across France. Nor, to my certain knowledge, did I offer offence to any person going. I was in no fit state, coming back, to hurt any living soul."

"We all still grieve for her," Richard says, sincerely. "My father was Welsh, as you well know, Mush, and Gwen and I would gossip for hours, in our mother tongue."

"It is not I they want," Mush insists. "I spent my early childhood in Spain, and then England, these last few years. Apart from that I ... sweet God ... I went to Venice. How could I overlook such a thing?"

"We had a good time there," Richard replies, with a rueful smile. "Tom Wyatt spent his time with the Pope's pretty whores, whilst we had to fight off half of Italy."

"I stood with you at the final battle," Wyatt complains. "I still do not understand how we overcame such odds. Their condottiero was too rash. Had he hung back, and outflanked us, he would have won the day."

"Instead, he ended up as our prisoner," Mush says.

"He would make a strong suspect," Barnaby Fowler tells them, "had he not died in such a horrible way.

Will Draper was actually talking to him, when a courtesan gave him poison to drink."

"Not so," Mush replies, as he recalls the aftermath of the fight, near Perugia. "Her name was Pippa Micheletto, and she was not some expensive whore. Her father was a spy for the Doge of Venice. Her family were murdered, right before her eyes, by Malatesta Baglioni."

"A pretty young thing," Richard murmurs. "Baglioni saved her, for his own amusement, but she escaped, and came to warn us."

"Yes, with that strange priest," Mush says. "He held a cross in one hand, and a double edged axe in the other. The men followed him into battle, as if he were a saint."

"Father Geraldo," Tom Wyatt confirms. "Though he was not as he seemed. He was a soldier, once, and was intent on raising an army of faithful priests, to take Christianity to the New World. His real name was Ignatius… something or other."

"Father Ignatius Loyola, my son." The poet swings about on his stool, and peers into the darkness of the next booth. A tough looking set of eyes gleam back at him. Then the man who has spoken leans forward, into the light of the single candle on his table.

"You!" Wyatt stands, and almost crosses himself. "Where, in Hell's name did you spring from?"

"May I join you?" Ignatius Loyola stands, and comes around, into their private booth. Barnaby Fowler notes the gleam of a lethal looking dagger at the priest's rope belt. He is dressed in a black smock, and has leather sandals on his feet.

"Gentlemen," the poet says, gesturing to the middle aged priest. "Father Ignatius Loyola, late of Italy. You know Richard Cromwell, and Mush Draper, I recall, and this is Master Fowler, our lawyer, and Charles Brandon, our very own Earl of Suffolk. Now, I repeat... what are you doing here?"

"Trying to right a terrible wrong," Loyola says. His voice is sonorous, and seems to reach right into a man's soul. "It has been a long journey, and I have come close to stopping all of this twice, but Baglioni is a wily devil, and has evaded me, each time. Now, he is on his guard, and his men seek me out. I have become the hunted, my friends, just as all of you, and Will Draper, have."

"How came you to know we are here?" Mush asks. He is suspicious of this new development, and does not hold the same reverence for priests that seems to be affecting the rest. "You speak of Baglioni, as if he still lives. Will Draper watched him die an agonising death, and we buried him, and those of his men who fell in battle, in the red Umbrian earth. Is he then a vengeful spirit?"

"God, but I *really* hate vengeful spirits," Richard mutters.

"I was drawn here," the priest replies. "You must have many questions, and I will try to answer them all, but for the moment, you must trust me."

"Why?" Barnaby asks.

"Because there are four armed men sitting by the door, watching us, and another two outside. This foul place has a privy, at the back, but they will have men watching there too. You are not the hunters, gentlemen, but the hunted."

"He speaks the truth," Mush mutters. "The two by the far window also seem overly interested in us. That makes them about ten or twelve to our five."

"Six," Ignatius Loyola says, as he fingers the hilt of the broad bladed knife at his hip. "They will not try anything inside, but once we make to go out…"

"They might think to take us, as we leave," Tom Wyatt guesses. "A sudden mêlée, and a few strangers are dead, killed by men who melt away into the night."

"Does anyone have a good idea?" Barnaby Fowler asks. It is true that he stood alongside his friends in the great Welsh fight, and received a stab in the leg for his trouble, but he is a lawyer, rather than a fighting man. He also knows that Suffolk, though handy at jousting, has never been in a murderous street brawl before. As for the strange priest, who has come out of thin air, well, he might run at the first hint of trouble. "Only three of us know how to fight, hand to hand. I fear the worst, my friends."

"God will protect us," the priest says. "For he is the burning light that …" Ignatius Loyola closes his eyes, and nods, as if in answer to an unheard voice. "Yes, Lord… I see… the light is the way!" He opens his eyes, and mutters for them all to be ready.

Once out of the confines of the low tavern, they must fight their way to either the fortress, where troops are stationed, or back to their inn, which can be easily guarded against attack. Tom Wyatt sees that they must act in concert, or die, piecemeal.

"Once outside, we form up into a tight wedge, with blades at the ready. We turn to the left, and make our way to the fortress's main gate. The guards will see, and come to us. Once inside, we are safe, for a while."

"I helped bury Baglioni," Richard grumbles. "Must we now kill the bastard all over again?"

*

John Beckshaw, Lieutenant of the King's Horse, and presiding King's Examiner, is feeling cold, and stiff. It is well past midnight and, against his better judgement, he has agreed to stand watch on the broad heath. Sir Walter Beasley, and a dozen others are positioned in key areas, so that they can confront, and kill, the ravenous Beast of Hertford.

"It is a cold night, Master Beckshaw." The young man almost leaps out of his skin. The woman is suddenly beside him, and he has not heard her approach. Prudence Wells is a slight, very pretty young woman, and Beckshaw is able to quiet his nerves quickly.

"You should not be abroad, Mistress Prudence," he says. "If there is a beast abroad, you would make a most satisfying meal."

"Do you seek to devour me then, John?" she replies, kneeling down beside him. "I can read men's eyes."

"I could never hurt you, mistress," Beckshaw replies, truthfully. He has spoken to the girl but once, and finds that he has a strange affinity to her. "You hold a strange attraction for me."

"There, that was not so hard to say, was it?" Prudence says, softly. "I have been waiting for you, these twelve months gone, and had almost given up hope."

"Waiting for me?" the young man is confused, but can tell she is speaking in earnest. "How can that be?"

"I 'saw' it. I saw a young man coming from the north, and I knew that he would save me. I saw it, as clear as day, and I saw hints of the beast."

"You have seen this beast?"

"Not with my eyes," she replies, seriously. "In my head. It is a darkness, that moves about, feeding on fear. It wants something, and I am not sure what."

"Can you describe it to me, Prudence?"

"Please, call me Pru… as we are to be married."

"What nonsense is this?" John demands. "You and I are to be married?"

"Yes, if you stop the beast," Pru says. "That is all I can see, in my mind. It is up to you, John… stop it, or lose me."

"You speak in riddles."

"What did Master Draper think?" she says. "He has lost that which he most loves, and will not see her again, until Hell freezes over. I do not understand what comes over me, but I am seldom wrong, John. We will wed, after the beast is …" She breaks off, as a gunshot echoes from the darkness.

In a moment, men are running from cover, and making for the sound of the pistol shot. John Beckshaw and Pru are first there, and find Sir Walter standing, and pointing into some nearby hawthorn bushes.

"It was there!" he cries. "Blood red eyes, coming closer, and closer. The beast was almost upon me, sir. It is huge, and… dear God, I think I might have hit the creature."

John Beckshaw waves for the rest to stay back, draws his own pistol, cocks it, and moves into the bushes. Almost at once, he stumbles on a hunched form, and kneels to examine the corpse. After a moment, he stands, and returns to Sir Walter and the others.

"A fine shot, sir," he reports. "Right between the creature's 'burning' eyes. You seem to have bagged a sheep!"

"Then we are no better off," Sir Walter growls. "Damned sheep should be in a pen. Right, you fellows, that is it for the night. I doubt any beast would stay within a mile of us now. Master Grey, see the men are fed and … Master Grey, damn it, where are you?

There is a quick head count, and all are accounted for, except Sir Walter's steward. On the way back to the town, they find, hanging from a low tree branch, a freshly severed arm.

"The beast has outwitted us," John Beckshaw says, as he examines the gruesome discovery. He has them split into pairs, and search the immediate locality. After a half hour, they find enough hacked about body parts to know that Master Grey has, unlike them that night, met the terrible Beast of Hertford.

"Have the men bring what we have of poor Master Grey back to town," John Beckshaw commands. "Then tell them all to get some rest. We are at a disadvantage in the dark, Sir Walter, and must restrict our searches to the daylight hours."

"The beast roams at night."

"Yes, but must lay low, during the day. If we put a line of men with sticks across the heath, and beat out anything hiding there, our quarry might take flight. Whatever this thing is, it cannot turn invisible, can it?"

"You saw what happened," one of the men calls. "We were all armed, and stationed to block every path through the heath. If the beast was on all fours, it would have had to go through the undergrowth … like Sir Walter's sheep."

"True enough," another adds. "Grey must have seen the thing, and should have either shot at it, or screamed for help."

"A bad business," says a third man, and they disperse, grumbling, to their various houses.

"The men will not want to go out again," Sir Walter tells the young King's Examiner. "This beast has us all frightened. Why, if it can move, without making a sound, what will stop it coming into the town, and feeding on us, as we sleep?"

"You must stop all that talk," Pru says, sharply. "John Beckshaw will save us. I have seen it, Sir Walter."

"Will not your father wonder where you are, Mistress Wells," the Sheriff of Hertfordshire asks. "It is late, and he will be missing you."

"He is asleep, by the fire," Pru replies. "In a moment, a hot ember will fall, and land on his bare foot. I must dash!"

"Strange girl," Sir Walter says, as Pru vanishes down a narrow alley. "She has the sight, of course, but that does not make her a witch. Her father should get her married off, rather than refusing perfectly good suitors."

"Then she is betrothed?" John Beckshaw is curiously disappointed. For a while, back on the heath, he almost believed her wild claims, and he still finds her to be a most attractive girl.

"No, not as such. There are, or rather were, two who press her, and each is comfortably off, but she refuses them both. She claims some fellow is going to sweep her onto his saddle, and ride away to a land of wonderment. We all think she is just a little mad, of course ... but there is not a better looking wench in all of Hertfordshire!"

"You may be right, Sir Walter," John Beckshaw replies. The girl is like no other he has ever known, and he almost wishes that what she 'sees' in her mind, is true, for a pretty wife is an asset to any man. It is only when he is back in his own room, and drifting off to sleep, that a half formed thought comes to him. It emerges from the darkness of his own mind, and skips about, like some untamed satyr in the woods. At one point, he almost grasps it, but it eludes him, until the light of dawn comes in through the window, once more.

He sits up in his narrow bed, and smiles. The solution has come to him in the night, and he can see the whole, sordid thing, laid out before him. He is in no hurry to dress, and he takes his time over a sumptuous, and leisurely breakfast, whilst the town of Hertford awakens, and starts another day. There is no mad rush to find Sir Walter Beasley, for John Beckshaw is certain of one thing, and one thing alone. The 'Beast of Hertford' will not go out hunting again, until darkness has fallen.

"Ready, Master Beckshaw?" Sir Walter asks, when he finally decides to call on the King's Examiner. He finds him, washing down the last of his repast with a half flagon of watered down beer. "I thought you were going to stay abed all the long day."

"Not I, sir," John Beckshaw replies. He is almost unable to suppress his pleasure at the resolving of his first investigation. "For I have a terrible beast to catch, today!"

"In daylight?"

"Why not?" the young Examiner says, with an enigmatic

smile. "For the monster must have a lair, and we have but to track him down."

"Him, sir?"

"Oh, yes, Sir Walter," Beckshaw concludes. "It is a 'he' we seek, and no mistake!"

5 Revelations

"I swear," Richard Cromwell says through a swig of cooling water, "that I have never seen the like of it before. Our priest is a man after my own heart, only cleverer!"

The rest are within the confines of the fortress's gate house, and slapping one another on the back, more in relief than joy. Even Mush Draper, who has seen enough fighting for a lifetime, can still not quite believe what has happened. They have bested at least a dozen armed men, without a single scratch to themselves.

"Everyone is cleverer than you, old friend," Tom Wyatt says, as he tries to catch his breath. "Though, I must confess, to not realising what the fellow was about. When he ordered up those flagons of lamp oil, I thought him mad."

Father Ignatius Loyola is a man of God now, and tries to avoid taking life, wherever he can. The simple expedient of throwing the oil over their adversaries, and advancing on them with a burning rag, wrapped about a stout stick has the desired effect, and they fall back, terrified of the immediate risk of immolation. The six comrades are out into the street, and making for the fortress in a moment. Their assailants dare not come too close, lest they be burned alive by Father Ignatius Loyola.

"The Lord moves in mysterious ways," Suffolk tells them, as he sheaths his dagger. He is pleased not to have had to fight without the comfort of armour, and a broad sword, in his two hands. "Now we know who our enemy is, though I cannot understand how he has managed to dig himself out of an Umbrian grave, and come all the way to Calais."

"It is not he," Loyola says. "The dead will not rise again, until the day of resurrection. Malatesta Baglioni murdered his own uncle, and an older brother to become the Lord of Perugia. Once having assumed his position, he used his influence, and his military power, to gain favours for the rest of his people. He had an illegitimate brother, of a similar age, whom he loved more than the rest of his family."

"I wager he treated his horse better than his blood kin," Mush mutters. "The man was evil, through and through."

"He was," the priest explains, "but he loved his half brother, who is called Angelo. The young man is, by a curious twist of fate, both half brother, and cousin, to the Condottiere. He was placed in the bosom of Mother Church, and became, first, a priest, then later on, a cardinal."

"What... so young?" Tom Wyatt asks. "I doubt he can be little more than forty, now."

"Pope Clement owed favours to Malatesta Baglioni, and sought to pay his dues by advancing the bastard brother to an exalted position within the church. Once made into a cardinal, Angelo received grants of church land, and was able to accrue vast wealth. He was a poor sort of a priest, and he has become an even poorer cardinal."

"Then this Cardinal Baglioni comes for revenge?" Suffolk asks. "Why does he act against us all?"

"Because he can," Ignatius Loyola tells the duke. "In Italy, if someone kills your brother, you swear a vendetta against him. Once sworn, it cannot be rescinded, and you must kill the killer of your brother. You might even go further, and kill the killer's brother. His family then revenge themselves on you, unless you get them first, and so it goes on. They are a strange race… creating great art with one hand, and killing with the other. I put it down to the weather."

"Spain is hot," Richard says, recalling his brief stay in the country, on his way to Venice. "Are you not Spanish, Father Ignatius?"

"We spend our extra energy worshipping God," Loyola replies, with a slight smile. "You protestants cannot possibly understand."

"How came you to be involved?" Mush asks. He is eager to save his sister, and wishes to hear out the priest's tale.

"I was in Rome, hoping for an audience with His Holiness, when I came across Cardinal Baglioni. He was spending a fortune, trying to find out all about his brother's death. I knew that he would, eventually, uncover my part in the business, and send men after me."

"So, you ran away from him?" Mush asks.

"Of course I did," the priest replies. "I slipped out of the Holy City, and made my way to Venice, where I knew Pippa Micheletto was living, after her marriage."

"Pippa whom?" Suffolk asks.

"No matter," Mush snaps. "Go on, priest!"

"I arrived, only to find she and her new husband, Bartolommeo Rinaldi, had left for Genoa. It was their intention to board a ship for Spain, and travel on to England."

"Bartolommeo was a good friend to me, in Venice," says Richard Cromwell. "He is a nephew to the Doge, and fought well alongside us, against Malatesta Baglioni. He and Pippa said they wanted to visit England."

"Quite," the priest says, softly. "So, I sought a word with the Venetian Doge, and told him of my fears for any who helped bring down the condottiero. He sent out his agents, and they came back with the most awful news imaginable."

"Dear God, what has happened?" Tom Wyatt asks.

"You remember Giovanni Ipolatto?"

"Yes, he rode with us, and died in the last battle," the poet replies. "I had sworn to see his wife and family were taken care of, and delivered his share of the spoils to his widow. It was enough to keep them, until mourning was past, and she could re-marry. I doubt she was more than twenty two, or three."

"Some men came, from Perugia," Ignatius Loyola continues, though he does not want to tell the story. "They found where Ipolatto's family lived, and murdered them all. The wife, her children, her mother, her father, and two younger brothers. Vendetta, you see. Cardinal Baglioni has sworn to avenge his half brother, and kills, wherever he finds anyone who can be implicated."

"Seven innocent people," Mush says. "How were they guilty, Father Loyola?"

"They were guilty, by association." The priest sighs, and wonders how much bad news these young men can listen to in one sitting. "As was Antonio Puzzi's brother, his widowed mother, and a twelve year old sister."

"Bastards!" Richard cannot believe such barbarity.

"The murders were spread across Venice, and Verona," Father

Loyola explains. "Puzzi's sister was a virgin, and it is bad luck to kill such a one, so the men who came, raped her first, then cut her throat. I almost lost my faith, when I was told."

"Then Cardinal Baglioni is reaping a harvest of blood," Mush says, coldly. "Such a man can only be stopped in one fashion, and he will kill until we halt his rampage. Miriam is in his hands, and I fear greatly for her life."

"He will keep her safe, until all his enemies are drawn into the open," Loyola tells them. "He has only to kill Will Draper, and his allies, and the task is almost done."

"Almost done?" Richard asks. "What of Pippa, and Bartolommeo? They are still free, are they not?"

"Angelo Baglioni's men caught up with them in Gerona. The Doge's agents in Spain arrived just too late. Giovanni fought well, and killed three of them, before he fell, and Pippa…"

"Tell us, priest," Mush says.

"She swallowed poison."

"The same way she assassinated Malatesta Baglioni," Tom Wyatt says, and nods his head. It seems fitting that the young girl was able to choose her own death, and so cheat the condottiero's bastard brother of his revenge. "A remarkable girl. One day, I will sit down, and pen her story. I will make her live forever."

"That is small recompense," Mush snaps. "We must bring this animal out of his lair, and slay him. Once Will arrives, we shall gather our strength, and prepare for the final confrontation."

"He is rich, and has many well trained men in his service," the priest tells them. "I have spent months, running from him. The Doge begged me to stay in Venice, where I could be protected, but I could not. Baglioni blood is evil, and must be expunged from the land. Like cat and mouse, I move from hide hole, to hide hole, and seek to find a weakness."

"Have you?" Mush asks. "Is there a way to defeat him?"

"Had he stayed in Rome, or even Italy, he remains untouchable. You cannot kill a cardinal, without the most awful repercussions." The priest smiles then. "Last week, he crossed out of the Lombard provinces, into Savoy. He intends to be present, when the final moves are made."

"Then he is here, in Calais?" Richard needs to see his foe, and cannot do with all this mystery.

"I doubt it," Loyola replies. "He is not that stupid, my dear old friend. He will stay in France, or perhaps he will position his forces in the Holy Roman Empire's lands. That would make him closer to his main ally."

"He has support from Emperor Charles?" Barnaby Fowler asks. He has remained quiet throughout, but knows something of the emperor, and his ways. "I doubt Charles will furnish him with troops. He hates Henry, for casting off Queen Katherine, but this affair is not grand enough for him. We are all pawns, in his mind, and not worth the taking."

"I do not mean Charles," Father Ignatius Loyola tells them all. "There is one, who pours gold into the Roman coffers, who calls himself…"

"Anton Fugger," Tom Wyatt says. "Then he is in this too?"

"Fugger seeks to buy his place in heaven," the priest explains. "He finances His Eminence, and 'donates' vast sums to the various cardinals. In return, Pope Clement has granted a dispensation to Anton Fugger, allowing him to bypass purgatory, and go straight to heaven."

"There is no purgatory," Richard says. "The Tyndale bible tells us so. We are all God's lambs, and he will treat us all with equal grace, when the time comes. Hell, however, is very real, and awaits all those who do not find favour in God's eyes."

"You have a very odd way of believing, my son," Ignatius Loyola tells the big man. "You claim that God deems us either 'good', and worthy of heaven, or 'bad', and fit only for the eternal fires of Hell. What of those who are mostly good, but with a little bad in them, or those who are bad, but do the odd good thing?"

"Can we leave this for another day?" Mush asks. "We have evaded our enemy, for now, and should rest. Come the morrow, and our leader will be here."

Richard Cromwell has never heard Will Draper referred to as their leader before, but he understands the sense of it. In battle, or when outwitting an enemy, he is a true leader of men, and can be trusted above any other man. Though Thomas Cromwell is the cleverest man in England, his way of leading is different. He seeks to influence situations, until his will be done, and often gets his own way, without those he uses even knowing.

"Then let us hope he comes with reinforcements," Barnaby Fowler concludes, "for we six cannot win this war on our own."

"God will provide," Father Ignatius Loyola says. On his journeys, he has been collecting together priestly soldiers, for his great crusade into the New World, where he has been told, by God, to spread the light of Christianity. Though they do not yet number a host, Loyola knows them to be amongst the toughest men in Christendom. "Even now, the army of Our Lord, Jesus Christ, is girding its loins, and making ready for its first, great battle, against the forces of Satan."

"Amen," Tom Wyatt mutters. "I hope they have a few cannon!"

*

The small band of Englishmen, and a lone, Spanish priest, retire for the night, safe in the knowledge that the fortress of Calais is impregnable. They will sleep, or try to, and wait for the morning, and what it may bring.

It is that same morning, in England, when John Beckshaw, the King's Examiner, awakens, full of hope. He is refreshed from the few hours of broken sleep, and finds that he has, as if in a dream, come to a startling solution.

"A fine morning, Sir Walter."

"After a bad night," the Sheriff curses. "Another brutal death, and the loss of one of Abraham Polly's best sheep. He is talking of having me up before the magistrate!"

"Pay the man what it is worth," Beckshaw tells him. "But first, answer me this, sir. Mistress Wells is a fine looking girl, and of the age to wed, yet you say her father refuses two very good suitors?"

"He does not," Sir Walter replies. "It is all her own doing, my friend. She turns them away, saying a better man is coming."

"I suspect her father was angry at her." John Beckshaw knows that for a girl to go against a father is a cardinal sin, and one not to be tolerated lightly. "Did he beat her?"

"He dare not," the Sheriff explains. "For she has the sight, and strange things can happen, if she is upset."

"Then he did nothing?"

"He made her swear an oath."

"I see. In my experience, swearing oaths leads to nothing but heart ache and trouble. What did she have to swear to?"

"Why, to choose between her suitors, if no better comes along in seven weeks."

"Seven weeks?" the Examiner is taken aback by such an unusual choice of time. "Why, pray tell, did he set it at seven weeks?"

"He did not. It was Prudence who stipulated the period of time," Sir Walter tells him. "She said that a man would come for her, in exactly seven weeks. If not, she would marry one or the other of her suitors."

"When was this?"

"Let me think … ah, yes. About seven weeks ago. I say, that is an odd to do. I wonder where this fabled man is coming from?"

"So, she must decide who to wed?"

"Not any more, I suppose." The

Sheriff does not yet wonder why the Examiner is so curious about Pru Wells and her love life. "I suppose the choice is made for her."

"How so?" John asks, but thinks he already has the answer.

"Why, my steward, Master Grey, killed by the beast last evening, was a suitor," Sir Walter replies. "I would guess that she must marry the living one."

"What of Gabriel Haddow?" John asks.

"The burgess?" Sir Walter shrugs. "I doubt his wife would have let him court Mistress Wells."

"Then we must make haste, sir, and arrest our murderer."

"Murder, you say?" Sir Walter frowns. This fellow is as odd as Will Draper, and seems to have some knowledge he does not yet possess. In the event of failure, he will be easy to blame. "Give me a name, and I will have the fellow in chains, before you can blink again."

"I do not know his name, sir, but you do."

"What, another riddle?" Sir Walter is becoming annoyed at this little game. "Very well, must I guess?"

"No, for the list is short. Who else wished to marry Pru Wells?" John Beckshaw asks.

"Ezekiel Longbutt, of course," the Sheriff says. "He is a butcher, by trade, and one of the richest men in Hertford. Poor Zeke is quite mad with love for the girl. I do not see what this has to do with our beast though."

"There is no beast," John Beckshaw explains. "There has never been a beast. It has never been seen."

"It ripped apart the sheep, and two men."

"It did not. There is no beast. Think, man." John Beckshaw wonders at the man's slowness of wit. "If a beast did not do it, then these crimes have been committed by a man."

"Ezekiel Longbutt?" Sir Walter Beasley shakes his head in disbelief. "Why would he kill so randomly? A sheep, then a lone man. No, it is mad."

"Is there anything more maddening than love?" John asks. "If you know that she must choose between you, or one other, the solution is clear. Kill your rival."

"Grey?"

"Yes. The trouble with that though, is that everyone in the town knows he is your love rival," John continues. "How then do you get rid of him? Why not commit a series of random murderous acts, and get the populace up in arms. There is a terrible beast amongst us, they think. The bodies are hacked apart... not torn with claws, or teeth, but hacked with a sharp knife, or a keen meat cleaver. Then, once we all believe the beast is killing at will, you murder your rival."

"Dear God!" Sir Walter is catching up, fast. "Of course. He is a butcher by trade, and knows how to make a carcass look as if some creature has been at it. You are right. Once the beast is to blame, he can kill with impunity. What do we do now?"

"We must have proof." John Beckshaw thinks for a moment, then smiles. "Unless, the fellow admits his guilt."

"How do we get him to do that?"

"Let him know that Pru Wells was right. A man has come, who will take her onto his horse, and ride away. Give out that the hunt for the beast is to go on, even though the King's Examiner is leaving, with his newly betrothed lady."

"Sir, you are either clever, or mad." Sir Walter suppresses the urge to think it is the latter. "He will become enraged, if what you surmise is true. He is besotted with the girl."

"She loves me, sir," John confesses. "She has foretold these events, and we must allow things to run to their conclusion."

*

"Will you always love me?" Pru Wells asks, as they ride across the heath.

"I thought you could see such things," John replies. "You said I would come, and I came. You said we would wed, and we shall wed. Can you see no further, my love?"

"No, there is a dark veil." She settles into his arms, and sighs. "It is as if my life will go one of two ways, and the divided path is hidden behind the veil."

"Then you do not know what will happen in the next…"

"Sir!" A great brute of a man is barring their path. In one hand, he carries a huge cleaver, and in the other, a butcher's knife. "Climb down from your horse, for I will have words with you."

"Ezekiel?" Pru Wells tenses. "What is it?"

"This is Hertford's great beast, my love." John reaches, stealthily, for the pistol hanging on his saddle. "Am I right, Master Longbutt?"

"Climb down, Pru, you are staying here, with me," the man growls. "This … creature is not the one for you."

"What are you saying?" Pru shivers with distaste for the wild eyed butcher. "I was never going to marry you, Zeke Longbutt."

"I've earned the right," Zeke snaps. "You must marry me, after all that I have done for you… all the… blood."

"You killed Gabriel Haddow," John says. "Then you killed poor Master Grey. You really think we would believe some sorry tale about ravening beasts?"

"Get down, you dog!" Zeke Longbutt steps forward, and brandishes his cleaver. "I have already killed for you, woman. Now, come to me, or I will not baulk at killing again!"

"Is that proof enough, Sheriff?"

"Enough to hang the fellow, Master Examiner," Sir Walter says, emerging from a clump of shrubbery. Other men break cover, and point their weapons at the beast, Zeke Longbutt. "Will you come quietly, or must we carry you back on a pole, like the monster you pretend to be?"

"I love you," the man says, and something in his voice makes John Beckshaw react. He draws his pistol, and cocks it, even as the big butcher lunges at them. Both he, and Sir Walter fire together, and the beast screams, and twists away. He is wounded, and is now at his most dangerous. The townsmen come at him, screaming in rage. The men circle him, wary of the arms he still wields, and he rushes onto their short pikes and knives. They thrust, in concert, and he finally goes down, in a tumble of arms and legs. In one, last, defiant act, he throws back his head, and howls. The blood curdling death cry has his tormentors cross themselves in superstitious horror, and several fall to their knees, and offer up a prayer.

John Beckshaw holsters his pistol, and slips a free arm about the shivering girl. There is to be no trial, or execution, and he can set off, back to

London, without further delay. The girl half closes her eyes, and smiles in relief.

"The veil is lifted," Pru Wells says. "Now, I can see the way ahead."

"Does your future involve me?" John asks.

"You know it does," Pru replies, happily. "We will go to London, and I shall live in a big, empty house. I see a child, but no mother, and I see you travelling, without me."

"We will live at Draper's House, at first," John Beckshaw agrees. "There is a young child … little Gwyllam … and an absent mother."

"You must travel, to help make things well," Pru says. Then she frowns, and closes her eyes. Dark thoughts begin to crowd, unbidden, into her head. "Oh, God save us, John, my love. You will leave me, and I shall not see you again … until Hell freezes over."

"It will take more than the pit of Hell to keep me from your side," Beckshaw says. He is a modern man, and does not believe in such things, he tells himself. "Besides, from what you say, Will Draper must be by my side, and I trust him with my very life."

"Your path will lead you into the valley of the shadow of death," Pru Wells mutters, "and you must fear no evil."

6   Meetings

Will Draper throws his bundle over one shoulder, and slips over the side of the cog which has brought him, swiftly, from England. The cobbles of the Calais dockside are firm underfoot, and he is pleased to be on dry land once again. Since leaving Adolphus Theophrasus in London, he has had no further news of his wife, and he is almost sick with worry.

It is a short walk from the dockside to the huge gate of Calais' fortress, and he is challenged, almost at once by alert guards, who expect an attack from any quarter. The sergeant at arms, a big, broad-chested fellow, bars his way, and demands that he declare himself at once.

"Colonel Draper, the King's Examiner," he replies. "I have papers to prove my…"

"No need, sir. The Duke of Suffolk has warned us of your coming, and you are expected, sir," the man says, as he gestures for his men to throw open the gate. "My Lord Suffolk is within, and has left orders for him to be awoken, whenever you arrive."

"Is there any news of my wife, sergeant?"

"Your wife, sir?" The man shrugs his broad shoulders. "I am not privy to what is afoot, sir, but Lord Suffolk and his men were in a running fight earlier. We had to rush out, drive off a gang of ruffians, and bring them all to safety. There is no woman amongst them… though they have found a strange priest."

"A priest?" Will Draper is puzzled. "Then you must take me to Lord Suffolk, at once, so that I may find out what is going on."

"At your command, sir." The big sergeant leads him inside the huge keep. He enters a narrow, stone-walled corridor, then pauses, and turns to Will, diffidently. "Begging your pardon, Colonel Draper, sir, but I was wondering if you might have need of a few good men. If so, myself and some of the others are looking for something more than this shit-hole garrison duty."

"Yes, I might need some reliable men. Fellows who can handle weapons." Will sees that the big soldier is hard muscled, and has the appearance of a tough, no nonsense fellow. The man is a well trained professional, and is quite wasted by being posted to a garrison town. "Name yourself, sergeant."

"Edward Wesley, sir," the sergeant replies. "Though folk do call me Big Ned, on account of Corporal Ned Foskett being a small sort of a chap. Folk calls him Little Ned, because of it, but he is the dirtiest fighter I ever did come across. We would suit you very well, Colonel Draper."

"Have any of you ever been to war?"

"Little Ned did a year in Ireland, and me and the other lads spent the summer before last, killing Scots raiders. Lord, but they took some beating. The duke almost gave up."

"Northumberland?"

"Cumberland, sir." Big Ned smiles. "Harry Cumberland is a fighter, sir, whilst Lord Percy, beggin' your pardon, is a drunken arse wipe. No offence meant."

"None taken," Will replies, and suppresses the wish to laugh out aloud. "Keep yourselves ready Ned, and I will send for you, when I am ready." Big Ned raps his knuckles on a low linteled door, and throws it back. Several men are slumped in chairs, asleep, or half asleep. One of them stands upon Will's entrance, and holds out a welcoming hand.

"God be with you, my son."

"What in Christ's sweet name are you doing here, Father Ignatius?" Will asks. "What news of my wife?"

"It is a long, depressing story, my friend," Ignatius Loyola replies. "Though I must tell you, at once, that we have no bad news of Miriam."

"Will?" Mush is awake now, and rousing the rest from their various slumbers. "Get up, you laggards. Will has need of us!"

"Thank God you are here," Tom Wyatt says, yawning. "For we are in sore need of a guiding hand."

"Then tell me everything you know of events," Will Draper demands, "so that I might find a way forward. Has there been a ransom demand yet?"

"Calm yourself, Will Draper," the Spanish priest says. "It is a half brother of Malatesta Baglioni behind all of this, and his motive is vengeance."

"I thought that accursed family died out with the death of the condottiero," says Will.

"No, Malatesta has a bastard brother," Richard Cromwell replies. "Calls himself a bloody cardinal, he does … and murders women and children."

"Then we know our enemy," Will mutters. "That is half the battle won, my friends. Tell me it all, no matter how trivial it may seem, and we shall see what is to be done. For come what may, this foul creature must be brought low."

*

"This is a most pleasant surprise, old friend," Sir Thomas More says, as he gestures for the archbishop to take a hard seat by the fire.

"I was passing," Archbishop Cranmer replies, and he sees how lame an opening he has made. "I was on my way to Westminster, and thought I might just … drop in."

"After eight months?" More gives out a small, cackling little laugh, and closes the book on his knee. "You walk slowly, Archbishop. Can not the diocese afford you a horse, or a palanquin to ride in?"

"Still mocking me, old friend," Cranmer responds. "Can I not visit an old mentor anymore?"

"And ask after his health'?" More shakes his head. "The king frowns on me. You would not dare come here, without his express permission."

"Henry asks after your health."

"I fear I will not die of natural causes," Thomas More says.

"Cromwell tells the king that your heart is weak, and that you might not last out the winter. Is this true, old friend?" Cranmer asks because, were it true, Henry need take no further action against the ex Lord Chancellor of England. The king can leave him to die in peace, and avoid offending the intelligentsia, and nobility, of Europe.

"My poor heart is truly sick, Cranmer," More says, slyly. "Though I hear yours is even sicker. Is it true what I hear? Must you avoid embarrassing confrontations with other high churchmen, lest they refute your rather unexpected appointment?" Cranmer has to swallow this from More, because it is the truth. He has had to avoid men like the bishops Stokesley and Longland, who are conservative, and resent his sudden elevation.

"I was in Rome when the call came," Cranmer replies. He is suddenly the one being questioned, and does not know how to return to the topic in hand. "It was a surprise to me, also. Before being made archbishop, I have held only minor posts in the church."

"Do you wonder then that some of the bishops might seek to make an embarrassing personal challenge to your authority?" the wily More continues. "Why, even dear old Stephen Gardiner does not support you. He sits on the fence, and waits for Henry to tire of your failures."

"I shall not fail the king. Or is that what you wish... that Henry does not get his way?" Cranmer hopes More will forget himself, and utter some slander against Henry, but the old Lord Chancellor is no fool. He smiles, and shakes his head, as if instructing some recalcitrant schoolboy.

"What if, by doing the king's bidding, you fail Anne Boleyn?" More says. "Can a dog have two masters, old friend? What if one does not like the way you bark?"

"You seek to anger me," Cranmer says. "I came, but to ask after your health."

"And I have told you. My heart is sick, Cranmer. Are you not sick of the way your fellow high ranking prelates object to the power and title you have been given, or of how they argue that the Act of Supremacy does not define your role?"

"They accept me, now," Archbishop Cranmer states. "I am now acknowledged as the supreme churchman within the realm."

"They accept you, because Tom Cromwell has taken on the office of the vicegerent. That makes him the deputy supreme head of ecclesiastical affairs, second only to His Majesty."

"Cromwell is a lawyer," Cranmer says, evasively. It is true that only Cromwell is strong enough to bring the other bishops to heel, and that he is creating another set of institutions that will give a clear structure to the royal supremacy. "I bear no resentment to Vicegerent Cromwell."

"That is fortunate, for though you are an exceptional scholar, you do lack any political ability. It is a poor statesman who cannot even outface a few clerical opponents. You do well to leave those tasks to Tom Cromwell."

"The man is a useful servant," Cranmer says, coldly.

"Thomas Cromwell is an eternal optimist," More tells his visitor. "He sees an opportunity under every stone. I think he might have made rather a good Archbishop of Canterbury."

"Again, you mock me." Cranmer says. "I am not here to listen to your political and religious observations. The king charges me to put certain questions to you."

"Then get on with it," More snaps. "What do you wish to ask of me… old comrade?"

"The king wishes to know if you will take the oath?" There, it is said, and Tom Cranmer can breath again. He does, in truth, lack the courage to face up to things, and finds it hard to displease anyone, without support. It is up to Sir Thomas More now, to give either a yea, or a nay to it.

"What oath?"

"The oath!" Cranmer's throat constricts, and he can hardly spit out the words. He feels as if he has been drawn into a trap, but cannot yet see what it is. "The Oath of Obedience to His Majesty, King Henry, of course."

"Ah, that oath." Sir Thomas More smiles, benignly at the increasingly confused prelate. "We are in the backwoods, here in Utopia, Your Excellency, and did not realise ... this oath you speak of has been passed into law then?"

"Of course. Two days ago."

"Then how could I express an opinion?" More says. "Why, I doubt the printers have yet run off enough copies for one to reach old Tom More, here in Chelsea."

"You have not yet read the oath?" Cranmer begins to see how he is to be tricked, and is annoyed at his own stupidity.

"I have not yet received an official copy of the new oath," More tells him, springing the trap. "How can I pass comment? What if this oath is badly written? What if there is something in it that goes against the king, and it has not been noticed by all the other lawyers?"

"I shall have a copy sent to you, at once, my dear Sir Thomas," Archbishop Cranmer says, with a slight smile playing about his lips. "After all, how can I expect a man to swear to an oath, when he has not yet read an *official* copy?"

"Will you stay, and pass on what gossip you have?" More asks. "How is the king keeping? What news of the queen?"

"Which one?" Cranmer asks.

"Ah, I see you still wish to gain something from our conversation, my friend." More nods his head, and considers his answer. "Why, is this not what all this is about, Cranmer? Then let me say this, without embellishment … there is but one queen."

"Ambiguity," Cranmer replies. "Forget I even asked. Instead, let me make a general observation that Queen Anne is well, but that the Dowager Princess of Wales is not."

"Then I am glad for one, and sorry the other," Sir Thomas tells the churchman. "And what of King Henry?"

"He loves you, above all men," Cranmer says. "He charges me, in secret, to say this to you. If you can see your way clear to taking the oath, privately, he will not mention it again. All shall be as it was before."

"Oh, dear," More says. "If it is kept secret, men will think I have not sworn. They will whisper against the king, and abuse his good name. I cannot allow that."

"For the love of God, Thomas... take the damned thing!"

"Goodbye, old friend." More opens his book, and resumes reading from where he left off.

*

John Beckshaw is impatient to be off, and does not want to hang about the front door of Austin Friars, waiting for an audience with Thomas Cromwell. He is the king's man, and not one of the Privy Councillor's lackeys, he thinks. At that moment, a great, barrel bellied, oriental looking man appears, and holds out a welcoming hand.

"I am Doctor Theophrasus, physician to the king, and a friend of Master Cromwell, young man."

"John Beckshaw, at your service, sir," the young man says. "I wish to speak with Cromwell, at once."

"He is not at home. I hear the good folk of Hertford can sleep easily in their beds again, Lieutenant Beckshaw," Adolphus Theophrasus asks. "It seems their fabled beast was but a man."

"I do not believe in terrible monsters, sir … unless they are men," John Beckshaw replies. "I am here to join the expedition to Calais, which is leaving soon."

"How can you know that?" The doctor's left eyebrow goes up in involuntary surprise. "It is being arranged in the strictest secrecy. Why, even I do not know…"

"Three cogs, each filled with supplies, soldiers, and Master Cromwell's most trusted young men," John replies. "I need only know the departure point."

"If the secret is out…"

"Only I, and my betrothed know," the young King's Examiner says. He does not wish to explain the truth, because he does not really believe it himself. "She… sees things."

"Oh, a diviner, is she?" the doctor takes the news with a pinch of salt. "They are few, and far between, in this backward country, but in the far off East, almost every province has such a one. Is she very pretty?"

"Yes, I think so."

"Then that is why they have not burned her yet," Adolphus tells him with a wry smile. "You must have her keep her power secret, if she is to live into old age, my friend. Now, I will have my servant take you to the assembly point."

"Thank you, sir."

"Your woman… did she foresee the outcome of this business, at all? The doctor has had many experiences with seers, and knows that their insights can vary from the odd clever guess, right up to detailed information, but it is seldom clear, until afterwards.

"Only that I must go, and there will be bloodshed. She also says that neither I, nor Will Draper shall come home, until Hell is frozen over."

"That is unfortunate," Adolphus replies. "We do not know yet who the enemy is, nor do we know his numbers. It rather sounds to me as if there is going to be some great conflict. Perhaps an Armageddon?"

"Come the next tide, Colonel Draper shall have over a hundred men at his back," John Beckshaw says, staunchly. "One way, or another, he will find a way to bring his Miriam home."

"Then let me summon my servant, and speed you on your way," the doctor tells him. "For the tide will soon be in our favour!"

*

"I am bored, Charnley," Henry declares, stomping across the throne room floor. Sir Paul, a relatively new hanger on, and a friend of George Boleyn's, tries to think of something to lighten the king's mood. He sees Thomas Cromwell, hovering by the door, as if eager to escape, and whispers to the king.

"Cards, sire, but with a difference," he says.

"How so?" The king is intrigued.

"Let us draw in some old stick, who does not usually play, and frighten him with huge wagers."

"Splendid. Who shall we…"

"Cromwell is over there."

"Not Cromwell," Henry says. "He is not likely to…"

"He would not refuse, Your Majesty, would he?" Charnley knows how much Anne Boleyn hates

Cromwell, and sees a chance to score against the king's favourite councillor.

"No, but…"

"Master Cromwell, come and join the king, and I, in a friendly game of cards." Sir Paul Charnley produces a hand painted deck of cards, and gestures to the table, set up in the light of the window. "He would see how brave you are in a game of chance, sir."

"Then I must surrender to His Majesty's wishes," Cromwell says. "Though I must warn you, in advance, Sir Paul, that I cannot possibly lose."

"Then I would be foolish to play you, Thomas," Henry says, warily. He has an unswerving belief in the innate cleverness of his blacksmith's boy, and senses that he is telling the truth. "I shall sit out the early hands, and admire how you two play."

"As you wish, sire," Sir Paul says. The Earl of Wiltshire, and his son, George Boleyn are listening, and draw near, hoping to see Cromwell shown up. "What shall we play, Master Cromwell?"

"As I know no games, might we not simply draw cards, and the highest wins?"

"If you wish."

"Check his sleeves, Paul," George Boleyn sneers. "The scoundrel might have a …"

"Leave the room!" Henry is close to having enough of Thomas Boleyn's idiot son, and cannot let his insult to Cromwell pass unchallenged. "You actually dare to offend Master Cromwell … and in my presence!"

"Pray, let him stay, sire," Cromwell says. He pushes back both sleeves, and displays his exposed forearms for all to see. "For, as I have said, I cannot lose. Here, I have a purse, sir. Will you count the contents?"

"I am a gentleman," Charnley says. "I do not need to display my worth, for my word is quite enough. Leave that purse in sight, fellow, and we shall soon lighten it."

"And the stakes, Sir Paul?" Cromwell asks.

"A pound a turn?" The young man usually plays for the customary shilling a turn, but wishes to frighten his opponent with a stiff wager.

"Ten." Cromwell states the amount with cold deliberation.

"Twenty, if you like." The words are out before Sir Paul can stop his foolish mouth, and he must abide by them.

"Or fifty?" Henry puts in, as he begins to enjoy the jest. He loves a game of chance, yet does not understand the subtleties of gambling. There is not a man alive who would wager so much money on the turn of a single card.

"Why not make it a round hundred?" Thomas Cromwell says, his face as calm, and unmoved as if he were discussing the weather, or the price of wool. Sir Paul Charnley's heart misses a beat. A hundred pounds can keep a gentleman for twelve months. To wager such a huge amount on the turn of a single card is unheard of, but he has a certain dexterity with the deck, and trusts to his own cleverness at dealing.

"A hundred it shall be," he says, nodding to George Boleyn, who returns the action. It is a tacit agreement to back him, should things not go well, which George is happy to make. His friend can slide a card from the bottom of the deck with practiced ease, and they have won many a wager by the trick.

"Excellent," Thomas Cromwell says. "Now, we must have a fair umpire. Who better than the king? Sire, will you turn the cards for us?"

"At your service," Henry says. He takes the deck, from a dumbstruck Sir Paul, and gives them a rough shuffle. "King shall be high card. Let each man know that the highest card wins. I shall deal to Sir Paul first, then to Master Cromwell. Is that understood?"

"And His Majesty's word is final?" Cromwell knows that none might contradict him. "Then, for a hundred pounds... sire?"

Henry flips over one of the painted pieces of card, and drops it in front of Sir Paul. "Eight." Henry mutters. He turns a five over for Cromwell, and there is a polite ripple of applause from the small crowd of watchers. Charley has won a hundred pounds, and Henry is perturbed. Cromwell is infallible, and boasts that he cannot possibly lose. George Boleyn slaps his friend on the back.

"That has shown the upstart!" he announces.

"Again?" Cromwell asks, and the small crowd of courtiers gasp, in unison.

"If you wish." Charnley is no fool. He is already a hundred up, and can only lose the same back. The king grins, and turns over a four for Sir Paul, who curses, then smiles, as Thomas Cromwell is given a three.

"Ah, I see I am improving," Cromwell says. "Next, we shall tie, and then I shall start winning."

"As you say," Charnley replies. "Again then?"

"Again."

"Thomas…" Henry frowns. "Enough, my friend."

"Oh, if Sir Paul wishes to run away… then I shall let him."

"How dare you!" the man almost stands, but is conscious that any violence in Henry's presence is forbidden. "Turn again, sire!"

"Queen," Henry says, as he flips the next card. Cromwell closes his eyes, and smiles, as a nine is placed in front of him.

"Thomas, I think…" Henry's eyes implore his councillor to stop. Some men draw bad luck to them, and this now seems to be the case with Cromwell.

"Sire, I cannot lose," Cromwell says, stubbornly. "Let us make it two hundred on the next turn."

The cards land, and Cromwell's seven is beaten by Charnley's painted king. The man is five hundred up, and smiling at his great fortune. The watchers think that the king's favourite councillor is mad, and many of them smile at his obvious undoing by a better card player.

"Let us say five hundred pounds, on the next turn," Cromwell says. His eyes are slightly glazed, and his top lip seems to tremble, ever so slightly. Charnley glances to George Boleyn, who returns his gaze with a blank, noncommittal look. Poor George, his friend thinks, have you so little courage? Sir Paul nods his acceptance of the wager.

"Ten of Hearts," Henry says. He pauses, as if unwilling to turn again. He sweeps the next card from the deck, and throws it down, face up.

"Five!" Charnley cries, unable to believe his fortune. "That is a thousand pounds you are down, Cromwell. Enough?"

"Again, Your Highness." The room falls silent. "There is a purse of one thousand pounds on the table, sir. Match it, and we shall carry on."

"Why should I?"

"It is a matter of honour, sir," Cromwell says. "When King Henry couched his lance, and charged twenty thousand Frenchmen, who was first to break?"

"By God, yes!" Henry's blood is roused at the false memory of his brave charge. He forgets that he was hemmed in by five thousand of the best troops in England, and facing an ill trained rabble, ready to run at the first sign of battle. "I went at them, and never flinched. It is a matter of honour, Sir Paul. Honour!"

"I shall not back down, sire," he replies, unable to get out of it. "Pray, turn the cards."

"Queen," Henry says, glumly, then flips over Thomas Cromwell's painted card. "Great Christ above ... a king!" he cries.

"Ah, then we are even again, Cromwell says. "Another thousand wager, Sir Paul?"

"What?"

"Remember how our own, dear King Hal swept the field clear of Frenchmen?" Thomas Cromwell mutters.

"Damn you, Cromwell... you doubt my nerve?"

"No, sir, only your good judgement."

"Turn!" Charnley demands, forgetting his manners, and to whom he is speaking. Henry looks from one to the other of the players, and licks his lips. His fingers are damp, and the cards slip across his fingers. He turns the top card over, and there is a sigh of relief, as a king appears. The king sighs, and turns the next card over for Cromwell. It is another king. The hand is void.

"Turn again, if you please, sire" Cromwell mutters to the king. Henry nods, and deals Charnley a ten of spades. The next card is flipped over, and smiles up at Cromwell.

"Why, sire, it is your own dear queen, for she is festooned with hearts!"

"Oh, Christ!" Sir Paul Charnley is horrified. He has, in the space of a quarter hour, lost a thousand pounds.

"Again?" Thomas Cromwell asks, then smiles, shaking his head. "I cannot be so cruel, sir. Pray, go and lick your wounds."

"After you have paid Master Cromwell his thousand," Henry says. "It is my rule, gentlemen. I never allow gambling debts to remain unpaid, lest it causes greater ill feeling."

"I have no ill feeling for Sir Paul," Cromwell says. "After all, he was kind enough to let me play on credit."

"But you placed a purse on the table," Henry says.

"Your Majesty instructed me to make a treasury loan to Sir Paul, after George Boleyn petitioned you to help him. I was here to hand over the sum to him, and obtain his signature on the loan. You must have heard me tell him I had a purse, but he bade me leave it on the table."

"Then that money is mine!" Charnley curses.

"It was, sir," Cromwell says. "You gambled it away. Surely, you must know that I would never have let you stop, until one card favoured me? The worst that could happen was for me to break even with you, and the best … that I won the last hand."

"But you might have lost," Henry says.

"In which case, I would have kept playing, until I won." Cromwell explains. "Once it became a matter of his honour, I could not lose. He was lucky that I won so early on. Had we gone on another five hands, he would owe me … sixty four thousand pounds."

"Then you sat down without any stake money?" Henry asks, his face creasing into a smile.

"Am I not a gentleman, sire?" Cromwell replies, with a rye smile on his lips "Is not my word good enough?"

"Then that coxcomb still owes me a thousand pounds," the king realises. "What a jest on the Boleyns. They make me lend, then it is lost … to my finest minister."

"Who owes you your commission, sire," Thomas Cromwell says. "Shall we say a hundred, for your excellent umpiring skills, Your Majesty, or shall we turn a card?"

"What, and let you steal my kingdom?" Henry roars out laughing, but he sees that his minister has taught him a valuable lesson, about when to gamble, and when to stop. "Have we any news? I am still bored."

"The Portuguese envoy is in London. They wish to sign a full treaty with us, at once. I believe it will be on very favourable terms to us, sire."

"How so?" Henry is confused. "I thought the French had their trotters in that particular trough?"

"It seems not, sire," Cromwell says. "It seems that the French launched an unprovoked attack on the Portuguese port, at Tangiers. They bombarded the city walls, then sailed away."

"Damn it, I thought that admiral Travis was supposed to be keeping the French locked up in their own harbours."

"He is, sire," Cromwell explains. "One third of the fleet is in safe harbour, being refitted, and one third is cruising the Channel, daring the French to show their noses."

"And the last third?"

"With Admiral Travis, sire. On their way back from an overseas mission."

"Oh, where?" The king is intrigued, and wonders which far flung spice island has been raided, and whether he is any the richer for it.

"Why, did I not mention it earlier, sire?" Thomas Cromwell says, in a melodramatic stage whisper. "Tangiers."

"You clever dog, Thomas," Henry mutters. "You use my navy like a diplomatic tool, rather than a weapon. What about the Spanish? Did not their fleet wish to contest Admiral Travis' safe passage to the Barbary coast?"

"Apparently not," Cromwell says, with a wink. "They received a secret letter from their ambassador, stating that you had authorised a fleet to sail to the Americas, and ravage it, from end to end."

"What, little Chapuys told them that?" Henry asks. "What on earth for?"

"It seems he saw a certain document, on my desk... and misconstrued it. Poor fellow."

"By God, Thomas, we must put the sainted fool on a nice pension," Henry says. "For he is worth a dozen men o'war!"

7 The Mouser

"You do not need my permission, lad." Will Draper is cleaning the barrels and firing pans of his pistols, for the tenth time since he arrived in Calais. His sword, taken in battle, from an Irish High Chieftain, is in the fortress' forge, being re-edged for him. "It is for you to decide if you are ready for marriage."

"Pru is the most beautiful girl I have ever seen," John Beckshaw gushes. "I knew, the moment I…" He stops boasting about his new love, as he realises how much Will must be hurting.

"Then good luck to you, John." Will says. "I cannot give you a raise in pay, but you must stay at Draper's House, for as long as you need."

"We will both return, with our ladies, sir… when Hell freezes over. I cannot help but wonder at the prophesy." John turns, and gestures out of the low arrow slit window. "Three cogs are in harbour, full of munitions, and food rations. We have brought a company of Lord Suffolk's own soldiery, armed with pikes, and thirty of Master Cromwell's rogues. They have the best muskets he could buy. With the volunteers from the fortress guards, and those friends you have here, we number a hundred and twenty."

"No horses?"

"The doctor says he has agents scouring the Calaisis area, buying up anything with four legs. They will be here by morning."

"Another day gone," Will mutters.

"Haste is the enemy of success, my father used to say," John smiles and slaps his commander on the shoulder. "We do not yet know where the enemy lies, but when the time comes, we must have enough force to win the day."

"It is like San Gemini, all over again," Will muses. We fooled Malatesta Baglioni into thinking a huge Venetian army was about to attack him in Perugia, and drew him out of the city."

"And you met him at San Gemini?"

"Yes. A small, hilltop commune, ringed with walls of Umbrian stone." Will Draper recalls the smell of gunpowder, and the screams of dying men. They had held the walls against the odds, until a relief force arrived, then joined in the final battle. "We won the day, and captured the greatest condottiero of all ... Malatesta Baglioni. I thought that would be the end of it."

"Did you not think to ransom him?" the level headed Yorkshire man asks. "The pope would have paid good money for his warlord back."

"That might have been the best solution, but a girl, Pippa Micheletto had sworn vendetta against him. She poisoned the man, right in front of me, and I did not realise, until it was too late. Father Ignatius gave him the last rites."

"And now, he is here, claiming to be the sworn enemy of this new Baglioni."

"Cardinal Angelo Baglioni is no condottiero, but if he is half the man his brother was, we are in for a bad time of it," Will concludes. "How are you with a sword?"

"I used to use a scythe, as a lad," John replies. "I have drawn the sword you loaned me twice, but I do not know how to use it effectively."

"Then we must get you on the tilting ground," Will Draper decides. "For once you have fired off your pistols, a sword may mean the difference between life and death. A few hours training with Tom Wyatt, and Mush, will sharpen you up."

"You seek to make a soldier out of me, in a few hours," John says. "I shall do my best, sir."

"I have soldiers," Will replies. "They will line up, and advance, with pikes held out, and with a line of muskets behind them. What I need, is for you to become a killer of men. I know you can do it, because you killed the men who came to burn my house down, but I want you to do it without a thought."

"I will not let you down."

"Tom will show you how to parry a thrust, and cleave another man's blade from his hand, but Mush will show you how to kill." Will Draper paces the room again, for the hundredth time. He is impatient to be about the business at hand, and wishes that the cardinal would make a move.

"We will have our day, master," John Beckshaw says. "Your friend, Thomas Cromwell bids me tell you that Stephen Vaughan is on the scent, and that he is the best mouser he has."

"Master Thomas jests. Having Stephen Vaughan sniff out an enemy is like setting a cat after a mouse. He is a good diplomat, and an even better spy. He speaks the language like a native, and will go where others fear to tread." Will is reassured. His friends are doing all they can for Miriam, and she will be found, no matter what.

*

"Goat's piss!" Stephen Vaughan spits out the wine, and bangs the cup down on the inn table. "What has a man to do to get a decent drink in this stinking town?"

"Your French is good," a broad, bearded man says, sitting down opposite him.

"I'm Flemish," Vaughan lies to the Frenchman. In Antwerp, he excuses himself as being French, and thus, his slight accent is accepted by all. "Can you not tell from the fine cut of my doublet and sleeves, fellow? You French … you are so unfashionable."

"And our wine tastes of piss," the man scoffs. "You Flemings are always so much better dressed, or have better wine, or prettier women."

"Not so," Stephen Vaughan replies. "French girls are quite delightful. It is the men who are damned ugly."

"You sound as though you are spoiling for a fight, sir." The big man shifts his weight, and rests a hand, casually, on the handle of his dagger.

"I am," Vaughan replies, "but not for nothing, Frenchman. I am a trained man, and never draw a blade, unless there is a purse on offer."

"You are a mercenary?" The Frenchman asks, suddenly interested in this man with a funny French accent.

"I am. I have fought for the Pope against the Venetians, for the Venetians against the Lombards, and for the Lombards against the Spanish. The only buggers I have not fought against, are the French. I have lately been to Savoy, but the threatened war with you lot has turned into so much hot air. I hate these bloody do-gooder fellows, who piously preach about peace, and let honest soldiers like myself starve to death in the gutters of the towns."

"What brings you to Amiens then?" the man asks, scratching at his matted beard. "There are no wars here abouts."

"I thought I might return to Antwerp, or chance my arm in Bruges. The emperor always has need of good men."

"I hear he pays badly," the Frenchman sneers. "He owns a whole new world, full of gold, and spends it all on the church."

"Then I should become a priest," Vaughan replies, crossing himself. "I drink, fight, and chase whores, so should make a fine man of Holy Mother Church."

"Speak softly, friend," the big man councils. "Amiens is a priest ridden city, and your jests can bring the inquisition down on us both. My name is Pierre, friend. What do you call yourself?"

"My name is Marius De Groote," the Englishman tells his new acquaintance. "How do you make your living, Pierre?"

"This and that."

"I thought so. You wear a dagger at your waist, and another tucked into your boot," Vaughan observes, dropping his voice to little more than a whisper. " You are a killer of men, my friend, and it is written in your eyes. Soldier or assassin, I have known your sort before. Now, why do you choose to sit with me?"

"Curiosity." Pierre grins at his companion. "I have a need to know certain things."

"Which I have now fully satisfied … so, bugger off."

"Why so prickly, Marius?" Pierre says. "It is just that you have the look of a man who can handle himself."

"Push it, and you will find out."

"I am not your enemy," the Frenchman replies. "I might even be able to offer you some work."

"What kind of work?"

"Fighting, and killing work, my friend."

"Yet you claim there is no war here abouts."

"It is coming, Marius… it is coming."

"Whom do I have to kill, and how much does it pay?" Stephen Vaughan is relieved, for he has visited a dozen taverns in the last couple of days, hoping to attract the attention of Cardinal Baglioni. Ever since he first heard about him raising men, he has been trying to make contact.

"Some Englishmen." Pierre Rombard shrugs, as if to say 'who cares'. He earns his bread by killing, and one nationality is much the same as the next. "Fighting work, not murder."

"Where?" Vaughan asks. He cannot seem too willing, and no real mercenary would ever entertain landing in England, since Thomas Cromwell's stern lesson. "I hear King Henry's man hangs my kind from oak trees, by the dozen. I fear I must steer clear of English shores."

"They are coming to us," Pierre answers, with a winning smile. "My master pays well, with golden Italian Ducati, and he can protect us from both King François, and Emperor Charles. The French, and Spanish will turn a blind eye to us, and let us get on with our task."

"What about numbers?" Vaughan asks, allowing himself to be gently persuaded. "I do not like fighting alongside peasants with pitchforks, or farm boys who cannot use a pike. English soldiers are the best in the world, and would soon dispense with some rag tag band of half trained yokels."

"The cardinal has hired mercenaries from Rome, France, and the Holy Roman empire. I mean real soldiers, my friend. We have a company of Swiss pike men, and a host of soldiers of fortune, adept with pistols, swords, and crossbows."

"And King François allows this army to march through his lands?" Stephen Vaughan shakes his head in disbelief. "A foreign army marching where it will, and the French leaving it alone... how can this be?"

"My master is a man of great influence in Rome. Cardinal Angelo Baglioni, has a Papal dispensation, allowing him free passage, with his entourage. The king cannot oppose the Pope, or he will risk excommunication, like that bastard *Henri*, in England. That is why he, and the emperor, will turn a blind eye."

"Then I am contracted to fight for a cardinal," Stephen Vaughan says, and smiles at the big Frenchman. "When do we get to it, my friend?"

"Soon. The English are gathering their forces, and will try to raid, once they know where we are."

"And where are we?"

"Why, here, of course," Pierre smirks. "Our men are billeted within Amiens. The English cannot attack a walled French city, so we are safe, until we choose the moment to sally forth. The cardinal says he wants the English general to be sick with worry, before we ride out, and destroy them."

"Why would he be sick with worry?" Vaughan asks the boastful Frenchman. He has two tasks: firstly he must find the enemy, and secondly, he must try to find Miriam Draper. The Frenchman is full of self importance, and wants to display his wealth of knowledge, and how much he is trusted by the rich Paduan cardinal.

"We have the man's wife," Pierre says. "She is a damned pretty girl, though swelling with child. The Englishman, a man called Draper, will make mistakes because of it. A real soldier would shrug, and find another jade to hump. She must be a special kind of woman."

"A woman is just a woman, my friend," the Englishman tells the bearded Frenchman. He asks, as casually as he can; "Is she in Amiens too?"

"Of course. Cardinal Baglioni wants her close by. He has rooms within the great cathedral's cloisters, and he keeps her locked up there. Now, let us find you a room for the night, Marius De Groote, and tomorrow, we will test your metal."

"Action, at last," Stephen Vaughan says. He wonders how soon he can slip away, and confirm where Miriam Draper is being kept. Tom Cromwell's mouser has sniffed out his prey, and needs only let the men waiting in Calais know what is afoot. "Am I to billet in Amiens too?"

"You can share my rooms. I am on duty tonight, and must attend the cardinal whilst he dines. Then it is my turn to stand guard duty. I have to keep an eye on the sentinels, who doze asleep, if I am not there to kick their arses for them."

"Then we are well met, Pierre," Stephen Vaughan says. "Let us stroll around the walls, and you can point out your men. I can leave kick a rump as well as the next man."

"Well said, friend," Pierre replies. He is pleased to have found so willing a recruit, and looks forward to putting his new acquaintance to work.

With luck, he might have the eager Marius take some of his own duties on, and have more time to carouse in the taverns of Amiens. "Let us see if we can surprise them, shall we?"

They climb up to the ramparts of the high wall which surrounds the cathedral, and Pierre approaches each guard in turn. The men acknowledge him, and salute Stephen Vaughan as another man to obey. They obviously fear the big mercenary, who slaps them heartily on the back, and tries to sound friendly. They do not fall for it, and remember how he beat the last man who disobeyed him half to death.

"Good men," Stephen Vaughan remarks. "Have you anyone in the far tower?"

"No, but I take your point. It has a commanding view across the city." Pierre is annoyed that the newcomer has picked out a weakness. "I will see a man is posted there."

"Can I take a look?" the Englishman asks. Pierre Rombard shrugs, and leads the way. The door to the tower is unlocked, and a narrow flight of stone steps leads up to the upper chamber. The single window looks out across the city, and the river runs at its base. "Some view, my friend. Why look, I can see into the convent!"

"Where?" Pierre pushes Vaughan aside, and looks out, hoping to see some nuns. It is a thing he often thinks about, and he wonders if the priests enjoy visiting. "I cannot see..."

"Peace, brother," Stephen Vaughan says. He steps close up behind, and drives his dagger up, through the left side, and into the Frenchman's heart. The man shudders, and slumps down. The Englishman sighs at what he has done, and heaves the dead weight up, and out of the window. It is a risk, and a guard might hear a splash, but Pierre Rombard must vanish, if Vaughan's plan is to work.

*

"You must eat." Angelo Baglioni is annoyed at the stubbornness of his enemy's woman, and wonders if she will ever show a sign of weakness. Since the first day of her capture, she has fought him at every turn. "I cannot taunt your husband, if he sees you have staved yourself to death."

"Then he is coming." Miriam smiles, and picks up a piece of bread, which she softens in the vinegary wine. "I knew he would. In a few days, he will kill you all."

"What can he do against the walls of Amiens?" the cardinal sneers. "Even if he finds where you are, he can do nothing, except wait for me to pick my time. Each day, more men flock to my banner, draw by either gold, or love of God. This morning, my captains could muster almost five hundred men. Hard men."

"They will need to be," Miriam replies, softly. "For Will Draper does not fight like any other man. Even your brother could not defeat him."

"Treachery brought Malatesta down, not force of arms," the cardinal snaps. "He was tricked out of his castle, and ambushed by your husband, and his Venetian scum. Had he managed to unite his forces, Malatesta would have swept them aside, and marched on Venice."

"Your brother was a better soldier than you."

"Eat, woman, or I will forget my carefully laid plan, and hand you over to my soldiers. You will not be so stiff necked, after a dozen of them have used you."

"If you should happen to come face to face with my husband, he will kill you," Miriam says, coldly. "If he thinks you have done me harm, he will not let you die easily."

"I shall choose the time, and the place," Angelo Baglioni tells her. "My men will engulf the few Englishmen who are foolish enough to follow your husband, and the last thing he shall see, is you... crucified before his very eyes."

"You are a true Christian," Miriam replies.

"Guard, take her back to her cell," Baglioni commands. "Make sure she is locked in, and the door is guarded."

"Yes, Your Eminence." The waiting soldier bows, and moves forward, out of the shadows. "I shall see to it, personally."

"Where is Captain Rombard tonight?" the cardinal asked. "Pierre is meant to be standing guard duty."

"Pierre cannot take his drink," the new man replies. His French is good, but is delivered with a thick, Flemish accent. "Though he claims that it was the two dozen oysters he ate at midday. They smelled pretty bad to me, even doused in vinegar, Your Eminence."

"The fool," Baglioni curses. "I will have his rank for such dereliction… Captain…?"

"De Groote, Your Eminence." The young soldier bows again to the cardinal. "I am fresh from the war in Savoy, where my French masters lost their courage."

"Then you are ready for some real fighting," Angelo Baglioni replies. "You shall have Rombard's troop of horse, if he does not recover in time."

"I fear his malaise will keep him out of things," Stephen Vaughan explains, straight faced. The bearded Frenchman, having told the Englishman all he knew, has succumbed to the point of a knife, and is, even now, floating down the River Somme, on his way to the storm tossed Channel. The Englishman turns to Miriam, and reaches for her elbow. "Come, wench. Do not give me any trouble, for I have no time for Jews!"

Miriam, who until now has been studiously ignoring the soldier, glances up, and sees a face she knows. Stephen Vaughan has been a dinner guest twice at Draper's House, and his close shaved head, and twinkling eyes are a welcome, if unexpected, sight. She stands, and lets the Flemish mercenary lead her off.

Stephen Vaughan understands the military mind, and knows that he must look as though he is obeying orders, as he marches Miriam Draper past several sets of guards, and out into the cold night air. They are several streets away from the cathedral, before the simple subterfuge is discovered, and they are able to disappear into the warren of the city, before a serious chase can be commenced.

*

"It is late, for visitors, sir." Margaret Roper will not open the front door of Utopia after dark, and speaks from the first floor window, that is her bedroom.

"I am on the king's business, madam." The man steps back from his hammering on the door, into the pool of light coming from his servant's burning torch. She sees that it is Richard Rich, a clever, though disreputable, lawyer, who often carries out Henry's dirtier tasks, these days. "I must demand entry, at once."

"Demand all you like, sir," Margaret replies, sharply, "but Utopia's door remains closed, unless you have a warrant, signed by a council member, and with the king's seal upon it."

"I have just such a thing," Richard Rich announces, pompously. "See, here it is!" He holds up a piece of parchment. Margaret shrugs her shoulders, and starts to close the window.

"That could be anything at all," she tells the confounded lawyer. "I cannot see it from here."

"Then come down, and open the damned door, madam!"

"I will not open the door, unless I see a warrant."

"It is here."

"I cannot see it from here."

"Then open the …" Richard Rich turns on his heel, at the sound of laughter, coming from the jetty behind him. "Who dares jest at the king's expense?"

"At your own expense, Master Rich," Thomas Cromwell says, as he steps from his own boat. The oarsman follows, and takes the torch from Rich's servant. He holds it up, so that Margaret Roper can see everything, clearly. "Why do you come calling on Sir Thomas More, at night, like some skulking thief?"

"Master Cromwell, you wrong me. I am merely following instructions," Rich blusters, but he is afraid of the older man, and does not want to cause too much offence. "The king bids me question Sir Thomas."

"At night?" Cromwell looks up at Margaret's concerned face, and gives her a cheery wave. "There is nothing to fear, Mistress Roper. Master Rich is merely an over zealous messenger. It might be best to allow him entry, even at this late hour."

"As you wish, Master Thomas," Margaret says. "Roper will come down, and unlock the door. Will you come in, and join us?"

"Why not?" Cromwell replies. He lowers his voice to Richard Rich. "Speak plainly, Rich. Was it the queen who bade you come at night?" Rich contemplates a lie, but decides it is safer to keep to the truth, where he must. Besides, Cromwell's arrival is no accident. Rich realises that he must have been watched by his agents for just such a moment.

"It was, sir."

"And did she tell you to be cruel, and press Sir Thomas for certain answers?" Cromwell knows how these things are done, and is perturbed that Queen Anne is pushing matters along so quickly.

"Yes." Richard Rich cannot hide anything from Cromwell, and in a contest between the Privy Councillor, and Anne Boleyn, he thinks the former will still win out, and he wishes to be on the winning side. "She hinted that I might embellish his words somewhat."

"You mean lie?" Cromwell smiles. "Really, Richard. You would commit perjury for the woman?"

"She can be most persuasive, sir."

"Ah, did she offer money, power, or something of herself?"

"She mentioned only that Audley cannot live forever," Rich confesses. "The position of Lord Chancellor would then be free, and available to a loyal supporter."

"Then you did not know her?" Cromwell is not sure why he asks such an outrageous question, but it makes Richard Rich's face contort in horror.

"Dear Christ above, Master Cromwell!" He steps back a pace, as if the man has slapped his face. "Do not draw me into that matter. If you wish to go down that route, you must speak to other men than I."

"Such as?" Thomas Cromwell is becoming desperate to find a weapon to use against the queen, before she destroys him, and all of his people.

"There was talk of Northumberland, a few years ago."

"That is old news," Cromwell snaps. "What of now?"

"Tread carefully," Rich replies, as the door opens. "For you might be using poetic licence."

There it is again, Cromwell thinks. Northumberland, who has sworn an oath that he has not tupped Anne, and Tom Wyatt, who writes poems about her milk white breasts, and moons after her, like a cast off lover. Neither prospect appeals to him, and he wonders where else to cast his net, before the queen is pregnant again.

"Come in," Roper growls. "It is a sad day, Master Cromwell, when a lawyer's clerk can beard a great man, and in his own home."

"Master Rich will be brief," Cromwell says. "It is fortunate that I was passing, and saw the light outside Utopia. Is Sir Thomas still awake?"

"In the library."

"I have a copy of the oath for him." Richard Rich produces a rolled document. "He is to read it, whilst I am here, and answer but one question."

"Then come this way, and ask," Roper says, sullenly. He leads them down the passage, and into a book lined room. Sir Thomas More looks up from the heavy tome on his lap, and smiles at his guests.

"Why, Master Richard Rich, is it not?" he asks. "I have not seen you since … since you scurried away from my employ, and sought crumbs from the king's table."

"I must find work where I can, sir," Rich replies. "The king bids me give you this. It is a copy of the oath."

"Put it on the desk," More says, vaguely waving his hand to the corner of the room. "I really must finish this first. Have you read Agricola's *De Inventione Dialectica libri tres*, yet, Thomas?"

"Ah, I knew a copy had been brought from Antwerp, but did not know whom it was for," Cromwell replies. "Might I borrow it, after you have finished with it?"

"Of course, my friend. Has Meg offered you some refreshment, Master Rich?"

"Sir, I must insist that you read the oath."

"Of course." Sir Thomas More smiles. "I trust you have brought the other relevant documentation?"

"What is this?" Richard Rich stares at the frail old man, and senses a lawyers trap about to snap on him.

"Rafe Sadler, Tom Cromwell, old Audley, Archbishop Cranmer, and a dozen other fine minds have drawn up this oath, have they not?"

"We have," Thomas Cromwell mutters, subduing the urge to laugh at Rich's plight. More is a wily old dog, and has not yet lost his vicious bite. "Each of us submitted our reasoning, and observations to a parliamentary committee, for scrutiny."

"Then I wish to read their findings, before I read the actual oath," More says. "For these deliberations might convince me that the oath is, after all, sound."

"You say it is not?" Rich says, and almost bites his tongue.

"I can say nothing, until I have read the supporting evidence, Master Rich." Sir Thomas smiles at Cromwell. "Perhaps you can have copies drawn up by your people, and sent to me, Tom?"

"Of course," Cromwell replies, and executes a small, deferential bow to the cleverest man in Europe. "Though it might well take a week, or even two to collect them all."

"No hurry," Sir Thomas More says, with a soft sigh. "I am not going anywhere. You know, Tom, I think it a stroke of great happen chance that you came along when you did."

"How so, Sir Thomas?" Cromwell says, playing up to the grand master of obfuscation.

"Well, had but one of you come, he might have reported back that which his master wants to hear, rather than the actual truth of the matter."

"You insult me, sir," says Richard Rich.

"Do I?" More shakes his head. "It is interesting that of the two of you, it is you who thinks himself slighted.

Why could I not think that poor old Cromwell would perjure himself, for some small, royal, favour? After all, he has always been such a rascal ... even as a small boy."

"Then you will not read the oath?" Rich demands, and Thomas Cromwell grips his shoulder, tightly.

"You really must listen, Richard," he says. "Sir Thomas is eager, not only to read the oath, but to agree to it, if he can. To establish whether he can read the oath, he needs to see the supporting documentation. No lawyer goes into court without knowing the evidence, lad. Tell Queen Anne that the matter is progressing at a goodly pace, and tell the king that the letter of the law is being followed. Do you understand, Richard?"

"Yes... sir." Rich pulls himself free, bows, and turns to leave. Cromwell nods to More, and follows the younger man outside, where the servants wait. He beckons for his man to come over, and the fellow stands between Rich, and the path he must take.

"Richard, this is Master Joe Douglas. Those who know him call him Black Dog, because of his temper."

Thomas Cromwell steps close, and whispers in the young lawyer's ear. "See how he marks your features, like a hound sniffing at his meat? If you stray from the truth, and say Sir Thomas spoke treasonably, he will come for you. I do not use Black Dog to chastise, but to punish. He can make the very pains of Hell seem like a stroll in the countryside."

"You threaten a servant of the king, sir." Rich tries to sound unaffected, but his heart is now racing in fear. Cromwell is not one to make idle threats.

"You are too fond of the queen, Master Rich," Thomas Cromwell says. "Stand too close to the fire, and you will be scorched for sure."

"I will report, truthfully, what Sir Thomas has said, and have the documents he wants sent along." Rich places his right hand over his heart, and bows. It is his pledge to keep the faith, and binds him as tightly as any legal writ. Cromwell terrifies the young lawyer, and he knows that to go back on his word will invite a painful retribution.

"Good man. Though you need not hurry about the business," Thomas

Cromwell concludes. "It is in our favour, if you are a little tardy. By the time Sir Thomas is ready to give his views on the great oath, they may be quite superfluous. The king has a provincial sort of a conscience, and it will not take much for him to reconsider the situation. He will see how it will make him look, and he will waver from his course."

"You think so?" Richard Rich feels as though he must say something in retaliation. "The queen is wearing Henry out in the bed chamber, and is sure to be with child again, soon. She will only have to bear a son, and your conscientious Henry will give her More's head on a spike, and yours too, if she but asks."

"In that event, Richard, feel free to throw your lot in with the Boleyns," Cromwell advises the young lawyer. "Though you must time your actions well. To switch your sworn allegiance, too soon, might well be the death of you. Good night, and sleep well, Master Rich."

8   The Last Vendetta

Stephen Vaughan's sudden appearance at the gates of Calais, with a young woman, in an advanced state of pregnancy, causes some surprise, and when his companion's name is known, the surprise turns to wild rejoicing throughout the town. The young roving ambassador has infiltrated Amiens, the French stronghold of Cardinal Angelo Baglioni, and emerged with the greatest prize imaginable.

It is left to Mush to find Will Draper, and tell him the unexpected news. He is poring over maps of the locality, and hardly looks up. Mush joins him at the table, and sees that two tears, one at the corner of each eye, which betray his suppressed emotions.

"Go to her at once, Will," the swarthy young Jew says to his brother-in-law. "I will search these maps, from corner to corner, and find what you seek."

"It must be higher land, and with a river, or stream, to the fore." Will straightens up, and smiles, as he wipes the teardrops away. "We also need …"

"Enough," mush says,

soothingly. "I know how to pick our battle ground, almost as well as you, brother-in-law. Go to my sister, and show her how relieved you are. Let me stay here, and see to our plotting and planning."

*

"Are we all clear upon our parts?" Will Draper asks the question, but already knows the answer. He has been through much with these men, and trusts each one, for varying reasons.

"You worry like an old maid," Richard Cromwell says. "You know each of us will either do, or die."

"I am glad that Miriam is safe amongst us, again," Rafe Sadler says, "and wonder why we still seek a battle that could have an uncertain outcome. We risk defeat, when we could just slip back to England."

"Stephen Vaughan has earned my everlasting gratitude," Will Draper replies, "but the Baglioni vendetta is still in force. This Cardinal Angelo has murdered people whom I have called friends, and still seeks my blood. He must be stopped."

"Why here?" Tom Wyatt asks. "I mean to say, we are less than a hundred and fifty, against two or three times that number. Might it not be better to lure him to England?"

"He will not do that," Father Ignatius Loyola puts in. "If we flee to England, he will send assassins after us. Clever men, and women, who know how to kill, silently, or poison secretly. We will know no rest, until Baglioni is in Hell. I have a dozen brothers, in Calais, who will fight for us."

"Brothers?" Mush says, with a sceptical smile.

"Converts, from our last meeting, my friend," Father Loyola replies. "They were once men of the Venetian Doge's own Swiss Guard, but they now do their soldiering for God."

"Swiss pike men?" Richard Cromwell remembers the tenacity with which the big mountain men fight, and nods his head in approval. "One could not die with better men," he says.

"Nor live with better," the priest replies with a gentle reproof. "To squire death is a vanity, my son. God will make those sort of decisions, not mortal men."

"Well said, Father Ignatius," Will says. "I, for one, have no intention of dying. Not with Miriam safe, and my second child almost here. I must have her safely back in England soon, lest my child is born on French soil. Now, my friends, are we ready for the task ahead?"

"Of course we are," Tom Wyatt confirms. "It is only that we are going into the unknown … and on such an inauspicious day."

"How so?" Richard Cromwell is superstitious, and frowns on taking chances on a day of ill omen. "Are the stars against us, Master Poet?"

"It is March the Fifteenth today," Mush explains. "The Ides of March… Julius Caesar."

"Who?"

"The Roman emperor, who was stabbed to death on this very day," Tom Wyatt explains. "Though that must mean the day is well starred for us … for Baglioni is of the same race, is he not?"

"Then let him fall too," Will Draper pronounces. "I ride to Amiens within the hour. You must remain behind, Tom, as discussed, and you also, Father Ignatius. I will take Mush,

Richard, and twenty well mounted horsemen."

"What of I, sir?" John Beckshaw asks. "My place is by your side, is it not?"

"Your place is back here," Will tells his assistant. "You are to obey Tom Wyatt, in all things. If we are destined to lose, you must escort my wife back to Calais, and get her on a boat to England."

"As you wish." The young Yorkshire man can see the sense of it, but still wants to be in the thick of things, for as long as he can. "I'll find a good trumpeter, from amongst the men."

"A trumpeter?" Richard asks.

"Of course," Beckshaw replies. "How else will the citizens of Amiens know that the English army are at their gate?"

*

"Your Eminence, the Englishman is here." Angelo Baglioni glances up from his meal, and frowns.

"Here?"

"At the gate of the city, sir," the soldier replies. "He has about twenty men with him. He has a trumpeter, riding back and forth, and demands your presence."

"The dog!" Baglioni has expected something, since losing his hostage, but hardly this. "What does he want?"

"To meet you, in single combat."

"The fool. With twenty men at his back, he knows he cannot fight us. Send out a company of horse. He will turn tail, and withdraw. Have the men follow, and try to stop him getting back to Calais. I will follow with the main army."

"As you wish, sir, but..." the captain is about to ask why they are letting themselves be drawn out of the city, so easily, when he sees the look on his master's face. His hatred for the Englishman is so palpable, that it is pointless offering advice. The mercenary is content in the knowledge that the English colonel has only a hundred and fifty men under him, at most. Even if they are all trained soldiers, they are outnumbered four or five fold, and will not have any heavy cavalry.

The moment Cardinal Baglioni's cavalry emerge from the main gate, Will Draper and his small band turn tail, and gallop off towards the nearest crossing of the River Somme. They keep to a steady trot, and draw the cardinal's men relentlessly on.

"There are only a hundred, or so," Richard says. "We could turn on them, and cut half of them down, before they realise what is happening."

"And Cardinal Baglioni remains, safely inside Amiens," Mush replies. "With the rest of his force. No, we must retreat, slowly."

The snail like chase continues into the morning, and, just before midday, they come to the place found by Mush, and chosen by Will, to be the final battleground. The main English force are drawn up in a straggled line, between two enormous haystacks. To the fore are an assortment of Swiss pike men, Big Ned Wesley, and thirty two foot soldiers from the Calais garrison. Behind are a motley assembly of mounted men, armed with pistols, swords, crossbows, and lances.

Will and his small force splash across the ford of the stream, gallop up the slight incline, and join the main body of men. Father Loyola's men step aside, and allow them to ride to the rear. The King's Examiner knows that the following cavalry force will not attack. Instead, they will wait for the rest of Baglioni's army to materialise. They will have numbers heavily in their favour, and might expect an easy victory.

"Tell the men to eat, quickly," Will commands. "Baglioni will only be an hour behind."

"Are you sure they will fight?" Tom Wyatt asks.

"Would not you?" Will replies. "We are a sorry looking bunch, and he has three, or even four times our numbers. He will send his heavy knights against us, to smash through our pikes, then pour in with his light horse. Once our line breaks, it is simply a matter of encircling us, and ending it."

"You fill me with confidence, Will," Wyatt mutters.

"We will stand, Tom," Richard says. "Just make sure you do your part!"

"I shall lift more enemy purses than you do this day, you marrow head," Wyatt tells his friend.

"Marrow head?" Mush sniggers. "Why, you really are a poet, Tom Wyatt, after all!"

*

"Captain Paulio, heavy horse to the fore!" Cardinal Baglioni commands. The huge war horses are twice the size of the usual cavalry mounts, and are specially bred in the wilds of Romania. Their riders are encased in heavy armour, as are the horses, and they can smash through even a double bank of levelled pikes. The mercenary force is a hundred strong, and have never been bested in the field of battle.

"As you command, Your Eminence." Paulio approves. He can see the lines of pikes, but they are not nearly dense enough to deter a single charge. "Then might I suggest a flanking movement, to either side of the haystacks? We can…"

"No!" Baglioni knows such a manoeuvre can allow time for a few to escape, before the cordon is tightened. "Allow the heavy horses a fifty pace start, then follow with the light cavalry. I shall lead the second wave, and we will ride straight for them. Tell the men to ride through them, then swing about, and come back. I do not want any of the English to live. Is that clear?"

"What about Draper?"

"Take him alive, if possible," Baglioni says. "Also, search to see if his slut is with him. If so, she shall suffer first, before I kill my brother's murderer."

"The land they stand on is inside the Calais jurisdiction," Captain Paulio tells his master. "The English will complain to King François about our actions, and demand he do something."

"François has a dispensation, waiting to be signed by me, on behalf of Pope Clement," Cardinal Baglioni replies. He smiles, knowing that the French king will express shock at such an outrage, and swear to detain the cardinal. Then, regrettably, the man, and his army will cross into the lands of the Holy Roman Empire. Another complaint, to Charles V will result in a similar response, by which time, Baglioni will be back in Lombardy, and on his way to Rome.

"Then God is with us?"

"Can you doubt it?" Angelo Baglioni slaps his favoured captain on the shoulder. "In two hours, the English will all be dead, and my army will be rich men. I have enough Ducati, waiting in Rome, to make every man comfortable for the rest of his natural days... unless..."

"Unless, sir?"

"Once in Rome, we will have enough force to ensure the next papal election. Clement is an ailing old man, and will not last much longer. With so much gold, and an army behind me, I might well become the next Pope. Then you, my friend, would be the first general of the Papal Army, and all of Italy would tremble before us."

"Your brother sought to conquer Venice," Paulio replies. "It is only fitting that you complete his great work."

"Well said, my friend," Cardinal Baglioni tells him, "but first, we must exterminate these English vermin." Captain Paulio nods, and spurs his mount to the front line. The solid, terrifying, line of gigantic warhorses, each with a completely armoured man on its back, stands like a living fortress.

Once it begins to move, no man, on foot, or mounted, can withstand it.

From a steady walk, the heavy cavalry will break into a strong gallop, and hit home with devastating effect. The order is given, and the unwavering line sets off to cover the scant three hundred yards that separates them from the feeble line of English pike men, and gentlemen with swords. The horses are trained to snap, and rip flesh with their teeth, and stamp on fallen men. The only, faint, chance of survival, is to turn, and run.

*

"Great Christ!" Barnaby Fowler mutters. "Those beasts look more like armoured elephants than horses."

"Calm yourself, friend," Tom Wyatt replies. "Just be ready, on my command, and hope that Master Beckshaw is also prepared."

"I hope so," the lawyer says. "For I am still aching from dragging these bastards all this way!"

"Stand fast, lads," Will Draper says. He is leading his horse up and down the thin line of men, encouraging them to hold their ground. "Another hundred paces, and they are ours. Now, Father Loyola, you must leave some of these evil bastards for us to send to Hell." The men laugh at the jest, and the priest steps out of the ranks, and gives a final blessing.

"God, protect all of these brave men ... even the protestants, and unbelievers, for we have need of their strong arms this day. Amen."

"Amen!" The shout comes from a hundred and fifty lips, and about half cross themselves. A single Jew mutters a small imprecation to his own, personal God, whom he cannot name, and draws his sword.

"Riders," Mush calls. "You will stand fast, until I give the order. Then, we ride straight for their centre. If we can cut their line in two, they will break." He sounds confident, but the enemy are trained mercenaries, and his men know they are not likely to flee, like frightened farm boys.

"See that swine in purple?" Richard shouts, so that all can hear him. "That is the head of the snake, my lads. Cut it off, and this day will be ours!"

The ominous wall of gigantic horses is within a hundred and fifty paces, and they start to cross the narrow stream. Richard Cromwell and a party of men have been busy, all morning, digging potholes under the shallow water, and hammering in short, well sharpened, wooden stakes. It is a small hindrance, but might cause a few moments delay.

Colonel Will Draper sees the steady row of massive war horses enter the water, and decides that it is time to make his own opening move. It has taken all his persuasive powers to convince the Governor of Calais to lend his unofficial help, and several days of back breaking toil, but it has been worth it to give them a secret advantage. Will draws his sword, and glances to right and left. His line is unflinching, and ready for battle.

"Now!" he cries into the still air. As if by magic, the outer walls of the two huge haystacks fall away, and reveal Will Draper's deadly surprise. The six twelve pounder canon, that usually adorn the citadel walls in Calais, have been mounted on wheels, and dragged across fifteen miles of rutted roads to this, the carefully chosen field of battle. Tom Wyatt is in charge of the left hand battery, whilst a professional English cannoneer, George

Westernall commands the three huge pieces to the right.

There needs to be no further order to give fire from Will Draper. Each cannon is loaded with the latest horrific weapon to grace the bloody battlefields of Europe. The dreaded chain shot has turned the cannon from a defensive, or siege weapon, into an offensive gun, capable of the greatest destruction. Six flashes are followed by six long spurts of flame, and the unfamiliar rushing noise that betokens the trajectory of the new missiles. Each hollowed out cannon ball splits into two as it flies, and stretches wide the six foot length of heavy chain that joins the half spheres.

The widths of hurtling chains scythe through the air, and slice through everything in their paths. The fearsome heavy horses who have been slowed to a walk by Richard's obstacles are, almost at once, reduced to a pile of screaming, writhing, and dismembered animals, crushing their hapless riders as they fall.

The two volleys are enough to cut down almost every heavily armoured knight. The midday air is rent with the horrible screams of dying horses, and dismembered men. Those not killed by the cannon fire, are plunged into the shallow stream's icy cold waters, where their heavy armour drags them beneath the surface. In the space of minutes, as many drown, as are killed by the murderous chain shot.

The cataclysm is so swift, that Cardinal Baglioni leading the second, more hectic, charge, has no time to slow his advance, or even swerve away from the mayhem. Four hundred mounted men plough into the bloody carnage, and find themselves being unhorsed, or their mounts brought down, as they trip over some unidentifiable carcass, or mutilated body.

"Muskets ... take aim... give fire!" Mush commands, and a ragged volley of musketry is sent into the slowing mêlée of attackers. More of the cardinal's men, but fewer, this time, tumble from their horses, as the heavy lead musket shot hits home. Captain Paulio sees that only by pressing home the attack can they win the day. The professional soldier of fortune screams out his orders, and the well disciplined men who are still mounted, press on. Almost three hundred men burst clear of the scene of carnage, and launch themselves up the slight incline, intent on braking their enemy's thin line of defences.

Tom Wyatt's men have reloaded first, and send another three rounds of chain shot ripping into Cardinal Baglioni's advancing right flank. This is followed by another blast from the right wing, and dozens more men and horses are obliterated. After this second battering, Baglioni's army grind to a halt, and try to draw breath. They have lost a third of their strength, and are yet to close with the Englishmen.

"Pikes.. advance!" Will Draper cries, and the mixed bag of Swiss and English pike-men lower their twelve foot weapons, and begin to march forward. Unarmored cavalry, Will knows, cannot face such an attack, as the horses will swerve away from the sharp points. The remainder of the enemy, see the glistening line of deadly pike heads, and do all that is left for them to do. They split apart, into two unequal groups, and try to gallop around the menacing pike thrusts.

"Charge, lads!" Richard Cromwell yells, as he sees the enemy line break. As one, every mounted man in Will Draper's tiny command gallops into the attack. Will spurs his own mount forward, and rides straight for where the purple clad cardinal is. Angelo Baglioni is stunned into inaction, as he sees his army disintegrate all about him, and does not see the harbinger of his own death, who rides at him with murderous intent.

Richard rides into a knot of the enemy cavalry, and begins slashing about him with a huge war axe, whilst Mush leads his men at any who seem willing to stand their ground. Baglioni's men are professional soldiers, and they do not consider flight, except as a last resort. Run, and you risk being cut down from behind, they think, so they stand fast, and they die well, until the English see they have won, and offer quarter.

"Lay down your arms, and you shall have your lives!" Richard shouts, over the clash of steel on steel. Many of the cardinal's hired soldiers throw down their arms, but as many more, believing they fight for the Holy See in Rome, fight on. Tom Wyatt's cannon are silent now, and he, and his gunners snatch up whatever weapons they favour, and wade into the fray. Though still outnumbering their English enemies, the paid mercenaries have had enough. Those driven by their faith see a priest amongst the enemy, and begin to doubt their cause. It is only when they see Captain Paulio lead the cardinal from the field, that they start to throw down their swords, and beg for quarter.

Will Draper gives chase, as Baglioni gallops away, protected by a few men of his personal bodyguard. The Englishman ducks under a swipe from a mounted man, and runs his sword under his arm. The man screams, and topples from his horse. Will touches his heels to the flanks of his own mount, and gallops towards the fleeing cardinal. A second man charges at him, and Will leans away from the well aimed sword slash. He twists in the saddle, and returns the compliment with a fierce backhanded stroke, that sends his attacker crashing from his mount, with his back sliced open.

Will pulls the horse's head back around, and scours the field of conflict. The cardinal is about a hundred strides distant, and he urges his own mount to flight. Will kicks his horse's flank, and trots after the fleeing man.

"Running away, Baglioni?" Will cries, over the lessening din of battle. "Your army is broken, just as I smashed Malatesta's forces at San Gemini. Surrender to me now, and I will grant you quarter, despite your evil deeds."

"And hang me from a tree later, Draper?" Angelo Baglioni sneers. "I have sworn vendetta against you, and it must be to the death."

"Then climb down from your horse, and let us finish this, here and now."

"You would kill a cardinal?" Baglioni asks. "Do you not fear the retribution of God?"

"Not your god, Baglioni," Will calls back. "What are you, but the bastard son of a pox riddled Paduan bandit? Your brother was a better soldier than you, and, for all his evil doing, he did not run away from me. You are a coward, Cardinal Baglioni."

"Kill him!" Angelo Baglioni orders, and Captain Paulio obeys, without hesitation. He hands the cardinal his own reigns back, and draws his sword. It is a heavy cavalry sabre, designed to slash, and cut, from horseback. Will tightens his grip on his own trusty German-made blade, and nods at the big Italian mercenary.

"You have fought well today, my friend. Surrender, and you will be given honourable quarter," he calls. In answer Paulio swears at him, in Italian, and spurs his horse into a gallop. Will kicks his heels, and his own, smaller mount leaps forward. The Italian leans to the left, and delivers an expert cut with his blade, but Will Draper sways away, and they pass one another, without harm.

Paulio drags his mount around in a tight semi circle, and comes racing back. Will charges, and waits for the next swing. The Italian reverses his tactics, and, leaning to the right, attempts to run the point of his sabre into Will's throat. The Englishman catches the man's point with his own, and lets it run up, and over his right shoulder. They are almost past one another again, when Will Draper delivers a swift backhanded swipe, which rips through the mercenary's leather jerkin, and slashes open a shallow wound in the man's back.

Paulio turns, and feels the searing pain. He knows that he is losing blood, and that he has one last chance of victory. Throwing caution to the wind, he rides straight at Will, and sends his mount crashing into his. Both men tumble to the hard ground, roll apart, and leap up to their feet. The Englishman loses his grip on the fine German sword, and it falls, several feet from where he lands. Paulio sees that he has the advantage now, and lunges at Will. He is a fraction too late with the thrust, and Will Draper is able to step inside his guard, and duck away. He darts to one side, and forward rolls as the Italian cuts at him again. He hit's the ground, and comes up, with his sword in hand, just as Captain Paulio closes in on him, his blade poised for the death blow.

Will manages to bring his own blade up, to block the savage downward cut, and deflects his enemy's blow. He performs a neat half turn, allows the unbalanced man a moment to pass him, then flicks the tip of his sword up at the man's face. He screams in pain, and staggers back, with his left eyebrow split open. The Englishman sees the rage in his opponent's eyes, and knows the moment is here. The big Italian lunges, wildly, and Will stabs at him, with considered calm. The point of the fine German sword catches the man under his chin, and goes up, into the mouth.

Captain Paulio staggers back, and falls to one knee. He drops his sword, at last, and raises a hand, begging quarter. Will brushes past the badly wounded man, and leaps back onto his mount. The renegade cardinal has dug in his heels, and is galloping back towards the safety of Amiens. Will chases, and is within fifty yards of his quarry, when a party of French soldiers ride from the city's gate, and gallop towards them. Will curses, and draws to a halt. The cardinal rides up to the rescuers, and blesses them. Then he turns, and waves at Will Draper.

"I live to carry on my vendetta, Colonel Draper," he calls from safety. "I swear, none of your family will escape, as long as I draw br…"

The boast is cut off, mid sentence, and the cardinal clutches at his chest. A slow, red stain spreads out from his fingers. He looks up, and past Will, before sliding from the saddle. Will turns in his own saddle to look back to where Mush is. The young Jew has followed, and is holding a smoking musket, cradled in his arms.

"Family," Mush calls. "Angelo Baglioni's vendetta was against family, my family. Come, Will, the day is won, and Miriam wishes your safe return."

The riders from the city have no wish to fight. Baglioni was an outsider, with the king as a friend. They have no wish to die for a stranger's cause, and turn back to Amiens.

*

Will Draper and Mush ride back to the scene of the bloody battle, where Richard is organising the systematic plundering of the dead, and the amassing of a small fortune in horses, weapons and purses.

"Mercenaries always carry their wealth with them," he explains, happily, as his friends return. "We will be able to effect a good share out, lads."

"Do not forget the church, my son," Ignatius Loyola informs the big Englishman. "We have much to do, and will need a great deal of gold."

"Ask your Pope Clement," Richard jests. Will Draper shakes his head, surprised, once more, at how jovial men can be in the face of so much death.

"How did we fare, Tom?" he asks.

"We lost eight men," Wyatt replies. "Though Baglioni's casualties were worse. The chain shot alone accounts for over a hundred dead, and our charge doubled that number. What of the cardinal?"

"Dead," Will replies. "We will camp here tonight, and return to Calais on the morrow. Have the enemy bodies covered with the straw, and burned. We cannot spend days burying so many. Then have the men camp further up the hill, to avoid the stench of this fearsome Hell."

"The Battle of Hell," Mush mutters. "An apposite name for such carnage."

The small force do as Will commands, and, after a meal of hot broth, and hard bread, they rap themselves in blankets, and go to sleep on the unforgiving ground. It is the middle of March, and the harsh Calaisis weather has one last surprise for the weary men. In the early hours of the morning, white flakes begin to fall, and by first light they awaken, under a finger's depth of unbroken white snow.

"Will, get up!" John Beckshaw

can hardly contain his excitement, and shakes his master fully awake. "Wake up at once, my friend … for we have the miracle we so badly needed. Look. Hell has frozen over!"

9   Whispers

"The merry little month of May," Thomas Wyatt muses. He is struggling to finish the book he has promised to write for Miriam Draper, and is trying to find couplets that will stimulate his jaded imagination. "Not so damned merry, and not so damned helpful."

"Talking to yourself again, Master Wyatt?" Thomas Cromwell asks, as he saunters past the arbour the poet has occupied in the gardens of Westminster Palace.

"I have lost my muse, Master Tom," the poet replies. "Ever since my return from Calais, my mind has been full of ... other things. The carnage was appalling."

"But necessary," Thomas Cromwell replies. "You helped us all with your expertise, and more than that, you helped save the Draper family from destruction."

"For which I have been handsomely rewarded, sir," Tom Wyatt says. "The king favours me again, thanks to you, I believe."

"It will only last as long as he favours me, young man," Cromwell tells him, truthfully. "Now, I must leave you to find your lost muse. The world has enough soldiers, and not enough fine poets."

"Stay a moment," Tom Wyatt says, softly. "Pray, set your face into a smile, as though I am jesting with you. There is something I think you should know."

"Go on." Cromwell nods, and chuckles, as he is instructed.

"It is only a rumour."

"As is all truth, until it is proven." Tom Cromwell laughs again.

"I spent this last night with Lady Grace Ferriby, one of the queen's women. I hoped her caresses might bring my poetic abilities back."

"Anne will not like you swiving her ladies-in-waiting, Tom," Cromwell replies. "She is a very jealous woman."

"Who is desperate to bear a son."

"What do you know?"

"Only that she was complaining that the king does not visit her enough, and that his skills are … not what they once were."

"And?" Cromwell slaps a hand on his thigh, as if listening to a ribald tale of illicit swiving, or the outcome of a game of chance.

"Then, about a week ago, her mood changed. She became more light hearted, and rather generous."

"Then she is with child?"

"Lady Grace is a silly girl, and does not know when to remain silent." Tom Wyatt is uneasy now, and wishes he had, himself, remained silent. It is only the realisation of what he owes to the man that spurs him on.

"There is more?" Cromwell knows how Wyatt loves to tease a story out. He must be patient, if he is to know all there is to know.

"Anne took a late supper with her brother, George, and her father. Afterwards, the two Boleyn men were in very high spirits, with much back slapping, and fooling. Then, just yesterday morning, the queen felt sick. She locked herself away, with a few of her closest ladies, and was not seen until nightfall."

"Pray finish, Master Wyatt, for my poor old face aches from all this uncalled for smiling."

"Just before Grace came to me," the poet replies, "she was sent to the kitchens, to burn something in one of the fires that always blaze."

"What?"

"Bloodied clouts," Wyatt whispers. "Rags, some of fine linen, all soaked through that did make me think…"

"She has miscarried," Cromwell concludes. "It is not uncommon, within the first few weeks of carrying a child. I wager a bag of gold angels that she has not yet told the king."

"Will you sir?" Wyatt asks. He still loves Anne, and does not wish her any harm.

"Not I," Thomas Cromwell says. "For Anne Boleyn is no fool. She will laugh in my face, and say it was but her normal woman's time. The king will believe her, and I shall look like a conniving mountebank or, at best, an addle-pated old fool."

"Then my news is of no use to you, sir?"

"On the contrary, young Wyatt." Cromwell drops his voice even lower. "It tells me that the woman is having problems in the quickening, and might not be able to hold onto a child. Elizabeth might have been her only chance to furnish England with a legitimate heir."

"Then we say silent?" The poet is relieved, and will be only to happy to stay tight lipped about the affair. It is enough that Cromwell has witnessed his devotion in revealing the secret to him.

"We do." Cromwell thinks for a moment. "Write me a poem about a poor woman, who is driven mad over the loss of her child. I want it to be mournful, and I want it to press home how she fears never to have another child to love."

"A sad subject, sir."

"Which might come in useful, one day," Cromwell says. "Show it to no one, and let me have a copy by the end of the week."

"I am a poet sir, not a shepherd," Wyatt protests. "These things cannot be rounded up, like a straying flock."

"I see. Then make it the next week." Wyatt looks into Cromwell's face, for a sign that he is teasing him, but receives nothing back, save a pointed stare. "Once written, I shall introduce it into the court, where it will be widely read. The message shall be clear to those in the know. It will tell them that Thomas Cromwell knows their secret, and chooses to let them get away with it, for now."

"You connive, sir?"

"I do," Cromwell says, "and with good cause. "Let the queen bring forth a son, and I am finished, along with anyone who might mean her harm… or know ought of her past."

"Then connive away, Master Tom, I will not try to stop you."

*

"How may I be of service to you, my dear, Lady Rochford?" Cromwell asks. He has granted Lady Jane, Countess of Rochford, and wife of George Boleyn, an interview, at her request.

"I need money, sir, and hoped that you, out of your friendship to me in the past, might help."

"Does your husband keep you penniless, Lady Jane?"

"Ever since he found out about myself, and my foolish dalliance with Charles Brandon."

"Then we must see what can be done, my dear," Cromwell says, affecting the air of a kindly old uncle. "Though I do not see George's problem. You once told me he prefers boys to women, did you not?"

"I think I said he preferred anyone other than I, sir," Lady Jane replies, straight faced. She is an adept liar, but sometimes forgets whom has been told what. "I was upset about his rejection of me, and spoke hastily. Such bestial action is punishable by death, is it not?"

"It is, though half the men in court indulge, I hear." Cromwell knows that he and Henry share an aversion to the act, but cannot recall when last it was punished by impalement. "I think the king would only pass sentence, if it touched on his own personal honour."

"George is his brother-in-law, sir," Lady Jane reminded him.

"So he is," Thomas Cromwell says. "That might well upset the king enough to ruin your husband."

"My future is looking grim, Master Cromwell," Lady Jane replies. "George shuns me, and now, Lord Suffolk is tiring of me, and does not send me generous gifts anymore. It is no life being a used woman, and I fear for my future. 'Tis a pity I am not a mother, or even with child"

"I shall speak with both men, my dear," Cromwell says. "Now, tell me, Jane, who does George like, these days?"

"He slept with Charles' mistress a few times, and has bedded some of Queen Anne's ladies, but he does not seem to enjoy it much any more. He spends most evenings playing cards with Queen Anne, and her coven of poisonous cronies."

"What does the queen say of me?"

"Sir?"

"Come, girl," Cromwell snaps, and it makes her flinch.

"She calls you names."

"There, that was not too hard, was it? What names?"

"Master Blacksmith," Lady Rochford says. "When she is most irked by you, she says you are a bastard, and a son of a lowly shilling whore."

"She calls my mother a whore?" Thomas Cromwell smiles with cold contempt at this slur. "Most rich, when coming from that particular quarter. Now, what plans has she for me?"

"She sometimes wishes to see you, and Sir Thomas More, on the same scaffold, and often plots with my husband. She is a wicked woman, sir."

"How long was her last pregnancy?"

"Oh, only a couple of..." Lady Jane almost chokes back the words. "I don't ... I mean, I must not...."

"Speak of such things?" Thomas Cromwell smiles a wicked smile. "How often has the king lain with the queen, these last few weeks?"

"I cannot say," George Boleyn's discarded wife replies, bitterly. "The queen excludes me from many things these days, almost as if she fears me knowing her closest secrets."

"But the king still visits?"

"Of course, he does, now and then," Lady Jane says. "How else would she come to be with child, even if it did not hold?"

"Quite so." Cromwell adds the conversation to the thousand other little snippets he has acquired, and wonders if any of it will ever come to be of any use. He is fully aware that Anne Boleyn might have enough leverage with Henry to have him arrested, at any moment, and he would know nothing of it, until he was incarcerated in the Tower of London. "Now, let me find you a purse of silver, for immediate expenses, my dear girl. Should you need more, and have anything useful to tell me, please, do not hesitate to call on me."

"You are a kind man, sir."

"Thank you for that, Lady Jane," Cromwell replies. "May it always be the case."

*

"Must you attend court today?" Miriam asks. "Little Gwyllam longs to play with you, Will." She is taking a couple of days rest, after having delivered her second child, also a boy.

"I will be home before noon," Will promises. I need only show my face in the Examiner's Chambers, and make sure that John Beckshaw is keeping an eye on things. Since he and Pru took the house in Cheapside, we do not talk as often as I wish."

"He is a competent young man," Miriam replies, as she nurses the new baby. "He loves you well enough, and will always look to your best interests, husband. Will you see Master Thomas at all?"

"I would guess so. He keeps close to Henry these days." Will recalls but three days before, when he called at Austin Friars, and proudly announced the new arrival - Master Thomas Henry Draper. Cromwell had almost cried with pleasure, and promised his namesake a golden future. "Though his thoughts are taken up on more important things. I have asked him to stand as a Godfather to little Thomas Henry."

"He will like that. Give him my love." As soon as Will departs, Miriam will get up from her bed, and return to balancing her accounts. She employs clerks now, but still likes to check everything out for herself. Since her ill starred trip to Calais, she has resolved to stay at home, and make their fortune increase from English shores.

It is June now, and the first shipments of the 1534 vintage Italian, and Portuguese, wines are due, and there are the returns from the Spring shearing to be tallied. Her resourceful rescuer, Stephen Vaughan is now her chief agent in France, and the Low Countries, and handles her business affairs with great skill, and honesty. She loves her ever growing family, but her thirst for commerce grows, with every passing month.

*

"Good day to you, my dear Colonel Draper," the king says. Will has not realised that Henry was sitting in the woven willow arbour, and he bows, to hide his surprise. The king is alone, which Will has never known before. Even in solitude, Henry usually has a gaggle of friends, and hangers on, standing in close attendance.

"You Highness is alone?" he asks, wondering where the personal guard are lurking.

"Yes, I sent them all away," Henry growls. "It is getting so a man cannot enjoy his own company any longer."

"Shall I withdraw, sire?"

"No, of course not. In fact, I want you to sit with me." Henry pats the stone bench, and Will perches on the edge, uncertainly.

"Do you have some special need of me, sire?" he asks, and hopes the answer is 'no', but the king nods his head, ponderously.

"I do, but not of your investigative skills," Henry replies, his voice cracking with emotion. "I need a private word of advice, sir, and can think of no other man to give it."

"Master Cromwell always advises you well, sire." It is the answer that all Austin Friars men are counselled, or recommended, to give. Let Thomas Cromwell carry the weight of office, and keep the king happy.

"I love the fellow well," Henry replies, "but he cannot help me with my dilemma. It is a matter of love, Will. You young fellows know about love, do you not?"

"My wife believes me to be an understanding sort, Your Highness," Will says. "How can I help?"

"How is a man to act, if he finds himself to be in love?" Will is surprised by such an honest question coming from Henry. The man is in his middle years, and has surely seduced his share of women.

"He might declare it from the rooftops, or carefully keep his peace, Your Majesty." Will smiles at Henry's uncertainty. "It is different, in each and every case."

"I can do neither thing," Henry says, in a tight, petulant voice. "For I am not allowed to love. I am married to a woman who… well, never mind. I am married, yet I cannot stay silent."

"It is not unknown for gentlemen to keep a lover, as well as a wife, sire. Even kings have such feelings."

"I knew I could count on you, Will," Henry says. "So, you will arrange it then?"

"Arrange what, sire?"

"For me to meet with the lady."

"I see. Does she have a name?"

"Yes!" Henry nods his head, with vigour.

"Then might you tell it to me, sire, lest I choose the wrong one?" Will says.

"Ha! Of course. It is Lady Seymour."

"Jane Seymour?" Will is taken by surprise again.

"You sound surprised, Colonel Draper," Henry snaps. "Do you think me not man enough for the girl?"

"Your Majesty is man enough for any woman in England," Will

replies. "It is just that Lady Jane Seymour is … not like other women."

"How so?"

"Well, surely, when you speak…"

"We have never spoken."

"Never?"

"No, we just blush at one another, and stand on opposite sides of the room."

"Therein lies the problem, sire," Will Draper says. "I know the Seymour family, and they are an odd bunch. The men are strong protestants, and hold strong views on … certain things. Little Jane, who is under Master Cromwell's wing, is very shy, and virtuous, beyond all measure."

"I have heard that one before, Will." Henry is becoming grumpy.

"We all have, sire," Will Draper says. "They smile, and will not allow a kiss, until they have what they wish. Then, once you bite into it, the fruit is sour."

"Just so," Henry says. "Bitter fruit, where sweetness should flow. Yet my Jane is not like that, you say?"

"She is the absolute personification of virtue, sire. Upon my sacred honour. Master Cromwell sees that the girl is kept so, by sending her small gifts of money, and keeping her in kid gloves. She is more like a daughter to him."

"I had no idea of this." Henry is confused by the information, and his exasperation grows. "Then my love is doomed to die?"

"I did not say that, sire," Will explains, thinking as he goes along. "Master Cromwell would welcome Lady Jane coming under your protection, but the matter is rather delicate. The girl is virtuous, and never speaks, unless she has considered each word. Even if she devotedly returns your love, I do not see how she could ever … respond to it."

"Am I so ugly, and old, Will?"

"No sire… you are married."

"You damn me, sir!"

"Your marriage damns you, My Lord," Will replies. "Though I must say, I am not qualified to advise you on the matter further. Might I withdraw, and speak to a wiser council?"

"Thomas Cromwell?" Henry frowns then. "What if he spurns me, or the girl cannot bring herself to ever love me as I want?"

"What if pigs fly, and cats write poetry?" Will says, and the king smiles, and nods.

"You see how I am, old friend?" Henry says. "I am a ruler who cannot rule his own emotions." Will Draper notes how he has been promoted to the rank of 'old friend', and wonders if it will last beyond his next remark. He could tell Henry the truth, that the girl is quite possibly simple, but docile, and that he will tire of her in a moment, but he cannot shoulder such a responsibility. It is for other, wilier minds, to fathom now.

"Leave it with me, sire," Will Draper promises, "and I shall seek out the best advice I can."

*

"Sweet, suffering Jesus," Tom Cromwell mutters, but a short while later. "Henry really said all of this to you?"

"On my honour, Master Thomas," Will says. "I could hardly stop from laughing. All I could think of was to tell you, and ask for your best advice. The king is in deadly earnest, and seems to genuinely care for the poor Seymour girl."

"He thinks me a friend to young Jane?" Thomas Cromwell has only a vague recollection of some small kindness he has shown a small framed, plain looking girl in the past.

"You bought her some kid gloves, once," Rafe Sadler puts in. "She brought us some minor, but useful, information, and you rewarded her for it. She is a flat-chested, insignificant little thing, and I cannot understand what Henry sees in her. She speaks only when spoken to, keeps her eyes cast down to her little feet, and comes from a terrible family background."

"Ah, yes," Cromwell replies. "Was not the father sleeping with his own son's wife?" Rafe confirms the gossip. In fact, the Privy Councillor has a full working knowledge of the family, its worth to him, and the possible uses he has for them. It amuses him to find out what those about him think they know.

"They have an old manor house, and some excellent woods, and hunting grounds on their land, which is over in Wiltshire," Rafe Sadler explains to Cromwell. "Wulfhall, they call it."

"Then there is the way ahead," Cromwell says. "Queen Anne seeks to ruin us, so we must divert her mind from it. What better way, than inventing a new, prospective lover for la Boleyn to worry about?"

"I do not understand," Will says.

"We encourage Henry's attachment to Jane Seymour, yet keep him far away from the girl," Cromwell says. "The king will mope about, and pay less attention to his queen. She will see she is falling out of favour, yet not know why."

"Henry will not keep his distance long," Rafe says. "The girl is a part of Anne's retinue, and within his grasp."

"The king has his own set of morals, and will not besmirch the reputation of a virgin," Thomas Cromwell tells them. "When he becomes too amorous, I will recommend that her father recalls her to Wulfhall. The prize being snatched away, will make him all the keener on the pursuit."

"To what end?" Will Draper asks. "One way, or another, he will have his own way with the girl. Poor

Jane Seymour cannot go into a nunnery."

"Leave that to me," Thomas Cromwell says. "How are the boys, Will?" He will say no more of his intentions, aware of Will Draper's peculiar style of fluctuating morality.

"Both are doing well, Master Tom. You must come to visit us soon," Will replies.

"I shall, as soon as business permits," Cromwell says, with a sigh. "Gwyllam and Thomas shall want for nothing from me. Nothing!"

Will Draper notes how Cromwell has ended all discussion of the king's new fancy, and understands why. Despite their almost father and son relationship, the Privy Councillor knows that the King's Examiner will only go so far, and baulks at anything too immoral.

Will knows that Thomas Cromwell is already planning some intricate scheme, and that some parts of it are not for his, more honest, ears. His old master sees opportunity in most things, and will use this latest development to further the cause of Austin Friars, even to the detriment of an innocent young woman. Like it, or not, the lives of Jane Seymour, and her family at Wulfhall, are going to change, forever.

*

Cromwell is much taken with the idea of introducing a phantom lover into the royal marriage, but the affairs of state confound his plans for several weeks. It is the end of August before an opportunity presents itself, and he can begin his tinkering. The king is strolling in one of his many gardens, when Cromwell comes upon him, as if by chance.

"Do we have state business, Master Cromwell?" Henry asks, as he sees the Privy Council member approach. The usual hangers on are strolling behind, waiting for the slightest sound, or sign, from the king. Tom Cromwell bows, and shakes his head, as if surprised by the question.

"Not on so pretty a day as this, sire," he says. "It would be most remiss of me, if I were to even cloud your enjoyment, with the dull affairs of the realm. I am here, merely, to deliver a small gift, to a sweet young lady of my acquaintance."

"You sly dog, Thomas," the king replies, and digs him in the ribs. "Would that I could deliver my package to a sweet, and willing young woman." Laughter at the lame jest tinkles from the sycophantic retinue. "Which pretty girl are you wooing?"

"Alas, none, sire. The body is far less willing than the spirit." At this, Norfolk laughs, in sympathy, and the rest snigger, and wink at one another. "I am merely visiting Lady Jane Seymour, with a few squares of pretty silk, to make sleeves with. Her father is an old friend of mine, and I have, foolishly, promised to take her under my decrepit old wing."

"Ah, young Lady Jane," Henry says, his mood perking up. "Is she not the shy little thing waiting on the queen? There, see … she carries Anne's book of prayers for her."

"Indeed she does, sire," Cromwell says. "Might I be excused for a moment, whilst I deliver this parcel?"

"You may not. We shall *both* pay our respects to the ladies, Thomas, for it is time I was introduced to the new girl." Cromwell bows, and the two men approach Queen Anne, and her retinue. He bows to Anne, who sniffs, as if the air is bad, and he beckons to Jane Seymour, who steps forward.

"Hello, Jane," the lawyer says, and takes her right hand in his left. "Your father, and your brothers and sister, send their best wishes, and ask me to see you want for nothing. Are you keeping well, my dearest, sweetest, young girl?"

"I am sir." Jane bobs a slight curtsey, and blushes in the prettiest of ways. "My thanks for your kindness, and consideration, Master Thomas." Cromwell is impressed, and a little flattered, by the simple honesty of the reaction.

"How are the kid gloves I sent?" Thomas Cromwell asks, with fatherly concern. He is the picture of sincerity, and accompanies the enquiry with a warm smile. In a better world, he might have made a fine priest, or a caring doctor. Instead, he shifts for himself, and seeks to further his own ends, shamelessly.

"In reasonably good order, sir," Lady Jane replies, blushing at this unexpected attention from so important a man. "Your servant, Master Sadler, delivered me of six pairs, and they will last me throughout the year." Queen

Anne hears this, and frowns, for Sadler is supposed to be Henry's advisor. She wonders, just as Cromwell hopes, why he is involved in the transaction.

"I am glad to hear it, young lady." Thomas Cromwell puts a fatherly arm about the girl's shoulders, and eases her towards the king. "Now, let me present you to His Majesty. The king treats me as a dear friend, and I hope he can extend that genuine goodwill to you, my dear one. Sire, this is Lady Jane Seymour, of Wulfhall. Her father owns the very best hunting grounds in the whole of Wiltshire."

"Lady Jane," Henry mutters, and bows. Then he holds out his hand, for Jane to kiss the huge ruby ring of state. Instead, whether by ignorance, or design, she kisses the hand itself, and Henry shudders with pleasure. He looks across to his wife, and notes how she frowns in so ugly a manner. "It is a delight having my garden filled with such rare beauty. Your dear ladies do you justice, my dear, and … er …they serve to frame your own particular sort of beauty."

Queen Anne curtseys at the heavy handed compliment, and moves to link the king. She slips an arm through the crook of his, and starts to walk on, leading him away from the rest. Cromwell falls in, a few paces behind. After a moment, he utters a small cry, and excuses himself from Henry's company.

"The gift, sire," he apologises, and scurries back to where Jane is admiring a rose bush. He whispers a hurried explanation to her, and hands over the prettily wrapped parcel. As he does, he glances over to the king. He waits, until he is sure Anne has seen, then nods, and returns to Henry's side.

Queen Anne sees Cromwell's look, and thinks he is the king's messenger, openly passing on a gift from the king, to a pretty lady-in-waiting. She can do nothing but seethe at the perceived insult, and resolves to subject her husband to an icy coldness for the next few days. Of all the girls in court, she sees that Henry insults her, by openly admiring the very plainest one of all.

Thomas Cromwell is quietly pleased with himself. The king is now on speaking terms with Jane, and the queen is convinced that Henry is contemplating the taking of a mistress. Like all vain women, she believes herself to be the centre of everything, and thinks that the world is looking on, and laughing at the insult.

The moment she is alone, she hurls a book against the wall, and curses like a peasant woman. The braver of her ladies try to calm her down, whilst others slip away, and gossip to the court. Henry, they say, has affronted Anne, and looks kindly on plain Jane Seymour.

By nightfall, it will be accepted as a known fact.

*

Anne Boleyn is a woman with a most unforgiving sort of nature, and memorises every small slight she is offered. Cromwell is already a marked man, of course, but she cannot forgive her husband's cruel actions. She resolves to speak coldly to him, at every turn, and make his life as miserable as she dares. Henry's punishment, however, lasts for but a few days, before something else intervenes.

It is on the happy event of Princess Elizabeth's first birthday, in September, that Queen Anne whispers into the king's ear. Thomas Cromwell is standing nearby, wondering what mischief he can get up to next, when he sees the look of joy on the king's face. He feels a coldness twisting like a knife in his heart, and turns to speak with Rafe Sadler.

"Damn it, Rafe, we are undone again," he says. "The queen is with child once more!"

10   Hampton Court Exile

"Are you mad, Will?" Richard Cromwell says. "My uncle cannot run the country from Cornwall!"

"You exaggerate," Will replies, sharply. "Tel him I must speak with him, at once."

"He is busy."

"Must I force my way in, Richard?" Will Draper is on horseback, with John Beckshaw, and they are both heavily armed, as if ready for war. "Fetch him now, if you please … or not." Richard Cromwell is a huge bear of a man, and could handle both men in a fist fight, but the look in Will's eyes threatens him with a pistol ball in the arm. Slowly, he realises that the man means it. He nods, and stands aside.

Thomas Cromwell is coming out of his library, with one of his agents, when he hears the commotion. The sound of horses, and raised voices does not bode well for a quiet day. He goes out into the chill morning air, and demands to know what is afoot.

"Master Thomas," Will shouts. "We must leave London, at once. There is great danger, if we tarry. John's wife,

Prudence, has seen a most terrible thing coming."

"And you believe her?" Cromwell knows about the various prophesies, and, despite being a rational thinker, he cannot explain the girl's strange gift. "I cannot run the realm on the say so of a girl, Will, no matter how pretty she is!"

"Our families are packing, even as we speak," Will tells his old master. "Pru says that to stay in London means certain death. It only remains for us to decide where to go."

Thomas Cromwell considers various courses of action, and decides on the one which will cause the least upset amongst his friends. A wasted day outside the city, until the perceived threat is past will do less harm than rejecting Will Draper's judgement, and thus insulting those who believe in Pru Beckshaw's divine powers. He claps his hands to summon the servants.

"Hampton Court," Cromwell says. "The king is already there, hunting. We shall pay an impromptu visit to His Majesty. Our unexpected early arrival will gladden his heart."

"Or make him think we are all mad," Richard Cromwell mumbles. "I shall start packing. What of Rafe and his family?"

"Notify all who we love," Will says. "I do not know what comes, but it spares no one, according to John's wife."

"Does she ever foretell anything good?" Barnaby Fowler says, as he starts shouting orders to the servants. "Might she not, for once, foresee a surfeit of hot pies that must be eaten?"

"No man fears happy news," Will tells him. "To be forewarned about unhappy tidings is a thing to lovingly cherish... not despise. If Pru says some horror is on the way, I, for one shall run."

*

"I feel like such a fool, Tom," Cromwell mutters to the man standing next to him. They are both dressed as chickens, and are flanked by others in even stranger garbs. Tom Wyatt, the author of the piece, says they represent the abundance of the realm.

"The king will be most pleasantly amused," Archbishop Thomas Cranmer replies through his yellow painted beak. "See the cow, yonder? It is poor Lord Suffolk to the front, and young George Boleyn at the rear end."

"Playing the arse again, I see," Stephen Gardiner, Archbishop of Winchester sneers. He is masked, and dressed in Lincoln Green. He is, for his pains, playing the part of an English meadow. "How come we to be here, like this?"

"Why, summoned by Thomas Cromwell, of course," the Duke of Norfolk says. He is a tree, and has a speaking part in the king's newly written mummery, which he has quite forgotten. "Are we not all here, at either your command, or your request, Master Blacksmith's Boy?"

"Grown men, playing the fool for Henry," the back end of the brown milking cow sneers.

"Ho, sirs!" Tom Wyatt declares. "Does that cow fart treason?"

"Bastard," George Boleyn mutters. He is tired of being the butt of their jests, and thinks that, now Anne is queen, they should be more respectful to him. The return to his court chambers of his wife, whom the king has now tired of chasing, does not make matters any easier either. His only consolation are the evenings spent with his adored sister in her chambers, but since becoming with child again, she invites him less and less.

From the high minstrel's gallery, a dozen court musicians begin to play, and the various costumed courtiers begin to sway from side to side, like flora, or imitate the animals they depict. The rear of the cow tries to turn right, as Charles Brandon, the front end, swings left, and they collide with Norfolk's tree, which explodes with a string of the foulest language, picked up from his time as a land locked admiral.

"You arse faced, stinking dog turd!" Norfolk snarls. "Get out of my damned way."

"You old bastard … ouch!" Tom Howard takes advantage of Boleyn's exposed rear end, and kicks him up the backside, hard.

"Peace," Archbishop Cranmer says.

"Go swive yourself, chicken face," another quite anonymous courtier calls.

"Get off my foot, you pox ridden slut!" Stephen Gardiner snarls at a cowering lady-in-waiting, who is sheathed in the sheerest silk, and represents the westerly wind.

"If I am, then it is from you," the girl replies, sweetly. The archbishop squints, and tries to peer through the narrow slit left for his eyes.

"Judith?" he asks, and gets a fierce slap for his erroneous guess.

"We are but God's creatures," Tom Wyatt intones, "but hark, here is the sun, come to shine on us." Thomas Cromwell can hardly suppress a snigger, as Henry rolls in, wrapped in yellow silk. Being stuck at Hampton Court is beginning to have its advantages, he thinks. The king takes centre stage, and is about to launch into a long soliloquy, when a page bursts into the huge chamber.

"Your Majesty!" the boy cries. "News from London. The sweating sickness has struck, and the city is being ravaged, from end to end!"

'Mistress Pru Beckshaw's prediction?' the king's councillor wonders. Thomas Cromwell is not convinced, but still offers up a silent prayer. His people are scattered about the countryside, his son is in Cambridge, and the majority of the royal court is spared, by the happy chance of a girl's disquieting dreams.

The rotund sun retires to his private chambers, and orders the gates to be closed to any who come from the city. He has a healthy regard for his own life, and does not wish to die like so many of his subjects shall.

*

It takes more than a month for the last strains of the mysterious sweating sickness to leave the city, by which time, almost a third of those who remained behind, are dead. The illness does not discriminate, and strikes down the young, as readily as the old and infirm. In the morning, you shiver, and by dinner, you are either better, or dead. Half of London are infected, and one third die.

"How do I explain your Pru to the king?" Thomas Cromwell says. "If he believes what I tell him, he will want to reward her, and the bishops will want to burn her, for being a witch."

"Pray, say nothing, sir," John Beckshaw begs. "We seek no advancement over this episode. My wife mourns for all those she could not warn, and rejoices that all at Austin Friars who still live."

"By listening to your wife, we have saved the king, and most of the nobility of England," Will says. "Now, we can return to the city, and prepare for Christmas. Austin Friars celebrates the season, like no other house. This year, there will be small children again, and the halls will tinkle with their laughter."

"We can do our Christmas pageant," Richard declares, happily. The good old days, he thinks, are coming back. There shall be presents, feasting, and silly jests. The children will be given wooden toys, and the poor shall be fed like lords. "An Austin Friars Christmas is a joy for all to be a part of."

"Then let us be merry," Cromwell says. "We shall spare no expense. It is as if this sickness has made us all forget the bad things that happen, and we can look forward to a peaceful new year. Peace, and goodwill shall descend onto all men."

"Master," Rafe Sadler is standing in the frame of the door, like a, ginger haired, harbinger of doom. "His

Majesty demands your immediate presence."

*

Thomas Cromwell arrives at the door to the throne room, just as Anne Boleyn is leaving. He bows, and mutters a polite greeting, but she sweeps past him, as if he were invisible. He sees the smug smile on her face, and fears that he is about to hear something which he would rather not wish to know.

"It is not my doing, Tom," Henry says, as soon as Cromwell enters the lavishly furnished chamber. "Would that I could have it any other way."

"What is it, Your Highness?" Cromwell asks. "What troubles Your Majesty so?"

"It is *Her* Majesty."

"The queen is unwell?" For a moment, Thomas Cromwell's hopes are raised, only to be dashed into pieces.

"She is not," Henry admits. "Her mind has turned, once more to the great oath, and those who might refuse to take it."

"None of your subjects have yet refused, sire," Cromwell says, carefully.

"Sir Thomas More has."

"No, sire, he is but studying the complicated legislation, to ensure its complete legality. Only then will he turn to the wording of the oath itself. If it is at fault, he fears perjuring himself over a misplaced comma, or a wrongly phrased codicil. The man loves you, sire, and does not wish you to be misrepresented to your people. If you have men swear to a flawed oath, it will redound on you, all around Europe."

"Yes, yes, I know all that," Henry replies. "I have tried to tell the queen, but she is adamant. The oath must be sworn, by everyone, and within the next few months."

"But sire…"

"Enough now, Thomas. You have fought his corner well, and I applaud your loyalty to the man, but it is your loyalty to me that is now in question."

"By you, My Lord?" Cromwell can feel the ground shifting under his feet.

"By Queen Anne. She sees how you cosset my old Lord Chancellor, and she says you must now prove where you stand."

"How, sire?" Cromwell asks,

with genuine worry in his voice.

"I am putting you in charge of the entire business, from now onwards," Henry tells his leading Privy Councillor. "You must question Sir Thomas More, at once, then frame your charges against him. The queen is adamant, and she will accept nothing less than treason."

"That might be a hard thing to prove, sire." Thomas Cromwell hopes that, even at this late juncture, Henry might relent, and accept a lesser charge than treason.

"I have the greatest faith in you, Thomas," the king says. "Do this one thing for me, and your position at court will be secure again. The queen is in a most delicate state, and must not be upset in any way. Tom More must be charged with treason, tried, and executed, by summer."

"Summer?" Cromwell tries to make it sound an unlikely target to achieve.

"Sooner, if possible," Henry says. "My son is due in late April, or early May, and it will be a gift for his mother."

"As you wish, sire," Thomas Cromwell says, and bows to the king.

There is nothing else to do, or say. He must warn Margaret Roper, so that she and her family can leave the country. As for Sir Thomas, he fears it is far too late. No fancy lawyer's words can save him now.

*

"Will you lead the interrogation personally?" Rafe Sadler asks.

"I will." Thomas Cromwell looks up from his book. "There is to be absolutely no coercion."

"Then he will not swear." Rafe sighs. He likes Sir Thomas, and once had hopes of courting his daughter, Margaret, but cannot see any escape from the inevitable. "He will continue to refuse, but not give any reason. If we charge him, he will refuse to plead, and challenge the legitimacy of the court."

"Quite rightly, for the jury will be packed with all those who most hate him. Norfolk will preside, old Boleyn will sit on the jury, and I must prosecute." Cromwell scratches his chin. "You must warn Will Draper to be ready. I want More's family on a fast boat to France, before Anne thinks to extend her wicked spite to them. Meg will refuse, no doubt."

"I will talk to her," Rafe offers. "Roper is a sensible sort, and will argue our cause."

"What is he, this week?"

"He goes about, swearing that Tyndale is the great truth, and the way ahead," Rafe replies. "He condemns the Bishop of Rome as a dissolute old *rué,* and demands that the king sweeps all the Catholic priests into the sea."

"He is constant, if nothing else," Cromwell says, and they both laugh. "Is the ambassador here yet?"

"*Senõr* Chapuys is waiting outside," Rafe Sadler confirms. The little Savoyard wishes to thank Cromwell for warning him to move out of London, and has brought him a gift of oranges, and a rare book on Irish mythology. "I shall bid him enter. Shall I stay, or do you wish to speak to him in private?"

"You can be about your business, Rafe," Cromwell tells him, "but I have no secrets from you, and you may just as well stay, if you wish." Rafe acknowledges the compliment, calls Chapuys in, and goes off on an errand for Henry.

"Eustace, my dear old friend!" Cromwell embraces the little man, who insists on kissing both of his cheeks, in the way of the French.

"Some oranges for you, Thomas," Chapuys says. "I have also brought you this small gift, as a thank you, for your timely advice. It is written by an Irish monk, and tells of the time when giants ruled in Ireland, and the word of God was unknown. Not unlike present day England, I think."

"Then Henry is our giant," Cromwell jests. "We know God, my friend, but His words are better read in English. Why, even Our Lord Jesus Christ did not speak in Latin, and the testaments were put down in Hebrew."

"Am I here for a lesson in religion, Thomas?" Eustace Chapuys asks.

"You are here to question me about Sir Thomas More," Cromwell replies. "You will ask me what the king intends, and I will obfuscate. You will continue to ask me things, until I make a slip of the tongue, which will lead you to believe that we mean to prosecute him, unto death, if need be."

"Dear God, but this cannot be," Chapuys says. "The man is renowned, throughout the whole of the Holy Roman Empire, and Pope Clement considers him to be a personal friend."

"Damn, I had no intention of letting you draw this information from me, Eustace. I must hope that you do not write to your emperor, the Bishop of Rome, Erasmus, and every learned man in Christendom, to rally them to More's cause. For, if you did that, the king might find himself being called a wicked tyrant."

"Rightly so!" Chapuys is indignant. "Now the truth is out, I must invoke popular outrage, and demand that Henry leaves Sir Thomas alone."

"I fear your actions might not be enough to save poor Tom More," Cromwell says, "but the weight of public opinion might well slow down the legal process. Henry does not wish to lose his honour, for the sake of a shrewish woman's desires."

"Then Anne Boleyn is behind this?" the little Savoyard asks.

"Another slip of the tongue. I did not mean to impugn the queen's good name," Thomas Cromwell tells his friend. "Pray, forget my slip. I would not like the whole of Europe to blame Queen Anne for this shocking prosecution. Nor would I dream of suggesting that Emperor Charles might wish to offer the Mores, and the Ropers, sanctuary from her most vile vindictiveness."

"You are the absolute soul of discretion, Thomas," Chapuys replies. "I shall ascribe everything I know to an anonymous, but reliable, source. Now, let me peel you an orange. They are from Seville, and have a sweetness that is somewhat missing in your sour faced queen!"

*

Miriam takes her place in the carriage, with the baby, Thomas Henry, in her arms, whilst one of her girls looks to the comfort of little Gwyllam. The boy is very sweet natured, and will be easy to entertain on the trip back to Draper's House. Will has sent men on ahead, to open up the big, new house, and get the fires going in every grate.

"You must follow on, very soon," Miriam tells her husband. He kisses her, and the children, and promises to be there by nightfall, in time for supper. She accepts that he and John Beckshaw have business, and contents herself with inviting Pru to take the last seat, and so keep her company. She often thinks of Mush's deceased wife, and wonders if Pru will become as good a friend.

"I only have to arrange transport, my love," he says. "Master Cromwell bids me do it, as an act of friendship."

"Save your efforts, Master Will," Pru says. Her eye lids flutter, and she seems almost asleep. "More shall become less, no matter what the eagle does, and the falcon will fall from the sky, and lie with the black lion."

"What is that you say?" Will is shocked by the girl's words, and looks around, to ensure no one has overheard them being uttered. Pru opens her eyes, and stares at him, blankly.

"Say, sir?"

"Never mind. Do not repeat it," Will Draper tells her. "Now, on your way, my dearest wife, and may God keep you all safe on the road."

"Driver, take the westerly road," Pru says. "For the top road is blocked by a fallen tree." Miriam nods her agreement to the driver, convinced that her new found friend will be right. She comes from a different culture, and can accept the art of prophesy, more easily than the western educated mind.

They are but a few miles into their journey, when a gang of men pass, carrying saws and axes. It seems that a huge tree has come down, and blocks the top road from Hampton Court Palace.

*

"Are you absolutely sure of the words?" Thomas Cromwell asks.

"More shall become less," Will Draper tells his old master. "I take that to be about Sir Thomas, and it does not bode well."

"I think I am meant to be the eagle, but the falcon, and the lion?" Cromwell muses over the strange utterance. Since becoming queen, Anne Boleyn has adopted the image of a falcon as her personal badge, and the Boleyn family crest bears a rampant black lion on it. "Mistress Pru is seldom wrong. It seems that she predicts doom for Tom More, and a fall from grace for the entire Boleyn clan. She must keep this to herself, lest the queen gets to hear of it."

"She forgets, almost as soon as

she speaks the words," Will confirms. "Miriam will keep her safe, and see she does not repeat the treasonable phrases."

"It is how you interpret them," Cromwell says. "If she means to infer the end of More, Anne will love her for it. By the same rule, if Pru is saying Anne and the Boleyns' will fail, the queen will wish to burn her, as a witch."

"We live in very dangerous times, Master Tom," Will Draper says. "When will you have to move against poor Sir Thomas?"

"I cannot put it off too long," Cromwell replies. "Anne will have her spies watching for any delays. I must act, as soon as I am back at Austin Friars."

*

As fate would have it, it is Queen Anne herself who extends Sir Thomas More a stay of execution. As her ladies-in-waiting prepare for the return to Whitehall, Anne starts to shiver. Within the hour, she is delirious, and the physician, Adolphus Theophrasus is sent for by a worried

Duke of Norfolk. The Boleyns, father and son, are already on their way back to London, and Tom Howard assumes responsibility for the immediate health of the queen.

"I dare not visit her," Henry says, pathetically. "Lest I am infected with the sickness."

"Quite so, sire," Thomas Cromwell says. "The king must be kept safe, at all costs. I will speak with the doctor, once he is done, and bring you word of the queen."

"And of the child, Thomas," Henry says. "The queen is almost five months along, and he must live. England cannot afford to lose its future king." Cromwell bows, and almost runs to meet the physician, before he can speak with anyone else.

"Adolphus, old friend," he says, drawing the big man to one side. "How goes it?"

"It is not the sweating sickness."

"Hush, man. I do not wish to know what it is not," Cromwell tells him. "Rather, I would know what it is."

"A passing chill." Theophrasus shrugs. "Nothing more."

"That will not do," Cromwell replies. "Henry is a generous man, but he will not pay much for a mild chill, will he?"

"Then it is more than mild."

"Might we say it is a 'bad chill', Adolphus?"

"We might."

"And might we substitute the word chill for another?"

"A bad fever, which might settle on the queen's lungs?" the doctor guesses.

"How awful," Cromwell says. "Would this involve a lengthy stay in her chambers, under constant supervision ... for the sake of the unborn child?"

"A couple of weeks, at least," Theophrasus advises. "For the child's sake."

"Then the king should stay close by his queen?" Cromwell asks. If the king stays at Hampton Court, he reasons, then he must too.

"Without a doubt." The doctor smiles, and nods, as he perceives what Cromwell is about. "I shall advise that the queen rests herself, and he takes some exercise, if only to take his mind off things. Perhaps he can go out, riding and hunting, for a few weeks?"

"Then that is what I shall tell Henry." Cromwell takes a purse from his belt, and passes it to the physician. "With luck, November will be out, before we can return to London. Then the king will want to be merry right through to Christmas. I see that my business with Sir Thomas might have to wait until the new year."

"I have potions for all ailments," the doctor, a mixture of Greek and Jew, whispers. "I can cure a loved one, or rid you of an enemy."

"Dear Christ, man!" Cromwell understands what the doctor offers, and almost staggers back with horror. He does not mind condemning anyone with the law, but there are some kinds of murder he cannot countenance. "I want Queen Anne confined to her chambers for a few weeks. Then I expect her to be fit enough to return to Whitehall Palace. Do you understand?"

"Of course I understand," Adolphus Theophrasus replies, slapping his friend on the back. "I promise you, Thomas, that the queen will not come to harm at my hands. I shall nurse her back to health, and she will celebrate, by having Sir Thomas More's head cut off, before sending you to the Tower of London."

"Oh, how you cheer me up, Adolphus," Cromwell says. "She will try, but I will prove to be too strong for her. Her father owes me seventy thousand pounds, and dare not move against me. Her brother is a fool, and has no real influence."

"Except with his sister," the physician replies, and grins at some secret inner thought. "Back where I come from, such things are not frowned upon. A brother *should* love his sister."

"Anne knows George is a spent force." Cromwell has a sudden moment of blinding truth. Like Saint Paul, on the road to Damascus, he suddenly sees the way ahead, and curses that he has been so long in understanding how things must be.

"As you say… a spent force," Theophrasus says. "Now, I must attend my patient."

11   Ordeals

"How is your young charge, Thomas?" Henry is being fitted for a new suit of armour, and insists he must be surrounded by his friends. Norfolk and Suffolk are both present, and Tom Wyatt is lounging in an alcove, chatting with Richard Rich. The armourer has watched the king's girth grow, and has had to, carefully, suggest to Cromwell that Henry is too fat to fit the old equipment.

Cromwell is the great facilitator, and has used Tom Wyatt, and Charles Brandon, the Duke of Suffolk to pass on the news. They have achieved this by talking about the new designs coming out of Italy, and wondering if the French king, François will be buying a new outfit. Henry, never one to be outdone by a lesser man, has demanded a new suit of Italian design armour, and the armourer can make it, from scratch, without alluding to the king's burgeoning obesity.

So, Henry parades about in his underwear, for all the members of his court to admire. The forging of the metal is discussed, as is the shape of each piece, and the cleverness of the foreign design. Even the disinterested Archbishops of Canterbury, Winchester, and Westminster, are there, hoping for some small Christmas gift, as a reward for their devotion to the king's great love of jousting.

Stephen Gardiner wants his cathedral in Winchester to have a new roof, and the others have similar hopes. One wants funds to build alms houses for the poor, and wonders at the cost of Henry's armour, which would build six houses, and furnish them. Thomas Cromwell is there to keep them in order, and Rafe Sadler is close by, watching all that goes on. Cromwell realises the king is addressing him, concerning the Seymour girl, whom he has now met on three occasions, and bows.

"If you mean sweet Lady Jane, sire, then she prospers," Cromwell replies. "Her brothers are now at court, and they see she is given respect, and knows her proper place. She never ceases to praise Your Majesty's amazing generosity, despite returning the generous money gift you sent."

"A hundred golden pounds, in a fine jewelled box, Master Cromwell," Henry grumbles. "Was it not enough for the girl?"

"It was a wonderful gift, sire, but most ill conceived." Cromwell can be so honest, because he knows it was not Henry's idea. "It is the sort of thing a callow young man might do."

"George Boleyn said it would work," Henry curses. "I do not know why I listen to the bloody fool."

"Because he is a fool, sire," Cromwell replies. "We all like a good joke, but we should not take advice from the court jester."

"Well said, Thomas." Henry holds out a huge forearm for it to be measured. "I see how it might look, if it were to come out that I send gold to young girls."

"Jane sought only to protect your reputation, sire," Cromwell says. "She knew some would be spiteful, and try to hurt you with gossip."

"The lady's clever wit is surpassed only by her great virtue," Henry concludes. "Still, no harm done, eh?"

"I regret to say that is not the case, sire. It seems the queen has heard, and wishes her to leave the court. Lady Jane's brothers are horrified, and say that such a thing would cast doubt on their dear sister's honour. They are here to make urgent representations to Her Majesty."

"Lady Jane will not leave the court," Henry snaps. "Let me make it plain, that this is *my* court. Not the queen's. I choose who to have, and who to cast off. Lady Jane is a pleasant young thing, and I enjoy the few, brief moments I spend in her company."

"Perhaps that is why the queen always reacts in so vindictive a manner?" Thomas Cromwell says, ingenuously. "Might she see Jane Seymour as a rival for your affections?"

"Damn the woman," Henry replies. "Gardiner, come to me. I would have words, about the queen."

"Sire?" Stephen Gardiner, though now the Archbishop of Winchester, is not a holy man. He was a priest, because the church educated him, and then became a good, though pedantic, lawyer. It is common knowledge that he is distantly related to the king, illegitimately, through his poorer Welsh relatives, and owes his good fortune to the bastardy of his father, rather than his talent. "How may I be of service?"

"What if the queen bears me

another daughter?"

"Then you are doubly blessed, sire."

"God's teeth, Gardiner!" Henry sees that he must speak plainly. "I do not want a second daughter. Can I put the queen aside, if she fails me a second time?"

"That is a question for Archbishop Cranmer, sire," Gardiner tells the king. "I have a legal mind, but his is of a more theological bent."

"Cranmer!" The older prelate scurries up to the king, and bows. He knows Gardiner has dropped him into something, and wonders what is going on. "If I wish to divorce the queen, can it be done? I want a plain answer, mind."

"That is a complex question, sire," Cranmer says.

"Yes, or no, damn it!"

Cranmer looks about him, as if for some moral support, and Thomas Cromwell enters the discussion. The question is too important to be left to priests, and a careless answer could see Anne's power increased, rather than removed.

"As a lawyer, I can best answer you, sire."

"Well?"

"We wrote the law, so that you could *specifically* put aside Katherine of Aragon," Cromwell says. "The marriage was unlawful, and declared null and void, because you cannot marry your brother's wife. To divorce the present queen, you must have a similar reason."

"As I thought," Henry growls. "The woman is rude to me, and tries to isolate me from my friends. She is no fit wife, Thomas."

"Sire, if I speak freely…"

"Do so. I will bear no ill will."

"I might advise you, against the queen, whom is out of favour with you," Cromwell tells the king, "but what if she bears you a son? You would forgive her, for the boy's sake, but the queen would never forgive me."

"I will not let her turn me against you, Thomas."

"Yet you let her have More?"

"You go too far, sir!" Henry snaps. "You all wish to see if it is a boy, and offer me nothing. I care not, and want only my freedom. As for More, he does not take an oath, that you have all sworn to. He is a traitor, Thomas, and you must prove it."

"As you command, sire," Thomas Cromwell says. It is his last attempt, and he can do no more to save his old friend. "As for the matter of a second divorce, it might be possible, under certain circumstances."

"Name them." Henry sees that he might get that which he desires, leaving him free to marry again.

"The law must be seen to be clear. If any man wishes to put aside his wife, there are certain reasons he can cite. She might be related to him, inappropriately, or have committed some act which makes it impossible for the marriage to continue. The list is a long one, and each must be examined, in detail."

"I cannot see how this helps me at all, Thomas."

"The queen might be, quite unwittingly, unfit to be your wife. For whatever the reason. To this end, you must ask your Royal Examiners Office to investigate the possibility of a divorce. Let them see if there is some legality we have overlooked. It must be made clear, that your son remains legitimate, even if you divorce the mother. He cannot be declared bastard, like Princess Mary was."

"Of course not," Henry agrees, because there is no reason to declare a legitimate son to be a bastard. "What else?"

"Secrecy will damage your reputation, sire," Thomas Cromwell tells the king. "The queen must know you wish to divorce her."

"Ah." Henry does not relish the prospect of a screaming confrontation with a pregnant Anne Boleyn, and he is wondering whom he can saddle with such an unforgiving task, when Thomas Cromwell adds an important codicil.

"It must come from you, sire," he says. "The queen will not have it from any other source. You must inform her, before we begin to look at the legalities. That way I, and your other servants, will feel safer in our work."

"It seems I must do everything for myself, as usual," Henry roars. "Then let me get it done with, at once. I shall tell her now."

"Your Majesty, one catches more trout with a line, than a club," Cromwell advises. He cannot believe his good luck, and realises that he might now be rid of Anne Boleyn at little personal cost. "Promise her a couple of fine houses, and a generous allowance."

"I shall promise her the entire world, if only it gets me my freedom!" the king says. He pushes the armourer aside, and clad in his new mail, he stomps off to tell Anne Boleyn that she is no longer loved. He crosses the throne room, barges through the doors to the outer court, and fails to see the low, stone step at his feet. He misses his footing, and falls forward, with an ear splitting crash.

Cromwell is first to reach the king, and he pushes Henry's dead weight over, onto his back. The king's eyes are open, but he is not breathing. The lawyer recalls his soldiering days, and begins to loosen the armour. Behind him, several courtiers stand, in shocked horror. Then one of them cries out that the king is dead, and the outer court is suddenly full of running people. The word spreads, and, by the time Cromwell has slapped Henry's blue tinged face, Anne Boleyn is being told the tidings, by her brother.

"Then Elizabeth, or the child in my belly, shall rule," Anne tells George. "We must act quickly. Find father, and have him gather together some loyal men. That bastard, Tom Cromwell, must be taken, at once. Then we must make sure it is I who becomes Regent of England, not Uncle Norfolk."

"He is with Cromwell now," George says. "I will take some friends, and arrest them both."

"Just Cromwell," Anne says. "Once he is in our power, the rest will follow."

"As you wish, sister," George says. He gathers four friends, and, armed with daggers, they go to take Cromwell. The younger Boleyn has no intention of arresting the man. Instead, he will be stabbed to death, whilst trying to escape. Then he will search out Will Draper, and do the same.

He, and his confederates, burst into the outer court, just as the king is being levered back onto his feet. Thomas Cromwell's slap has shocked Henry back into breathing, and after a minute, he is quite recovered. The lawyer is relieved, then disturbed to see George Boleyn, and his excitable gang of men arrive.

"Guards!" His strident voice stops George Boleyn, and his eager men, in their tracks. "These men are armed!" A half dozen of the palace's guards surround the dagger wielding men, and hem them in with their long shafted halberds.

"George?" Henry does not understand what is amiss.

"Sire!" George Boleyn begins to stutter an explanation. "We thought you were dead... and we were ..."

"Were what, My Lord?" Thomas Cromwell asks. "It is an offence to bring unsheathed weapons into the king's presence."

"I thought..."

"I rather think not," Cromwell replies. He has the man on the defensive, and does not allow time for him to offer a believable explanation. "Take them away, to await the king's pleasure."

"What is it, Thomas?" Henry asks. His breathing is now returning to normal, and he has quite forgotten about his need for a divorce. "What is George up to ... what is going on?"

"Boleyn thought you were dead, sire," Cromwell says.

"The ignorant little bastard," the Duke of Norfolk curses. He sees that, had Henry been dead, the Boleyns would have arrested both he, and Cromwell. Being left to his niece's gentle mercy holds no appeal, and he sides with Cromwell, if only to make sure the king understands what has just happened. "I see what the knave was about, sire. It is written in his treacherous eyes!"

"He thought me dead?" Henry is beginning to realise what has just occurred. "He was coming to arrest you, Cromwell… and you too, My Lord Norfolk, I should guess. But why would he do such a thing?"

"With you dead, there would be a most terrible struggle for power, sire," tom Cromwell explains. "George Boleyn sought to remove me, and the very man who might well become Regent to the rightful heir to your throne"

"Dear God in Heaven!" Henry turns, and lumbers back into his throne room. "Come, Thomas … and bring along Norfolk. We must put something down, in writing. I am the king, and it is God's divine will that I set out the right order of things."

"And the divorce, sire?" Cromwell asks, but sees that the moment is passed, and he must wait for the next time.

"Later," the king replies, as he clanks into his private chambers. "I must first ensure the royal succession."

*

It is late, and Thomas Cromwell is just scratching down the last few words on the parchment. He, Henry, and the Duke of Norfolk, have laboured long, and hard, to enshrine the succession in law. On the morrow, the lawyer will present the new, hastily written, legislation to Parliament, and have it swiftly enacted.

"Then my unborn son will rule England, after my eventual death," Henry says. "Failing that, my little Elizabeth will sit on the throne." Mary is excluded, as the king has declared her to be a bastard, because his marriage to Katherine was not deemed to be valid. It is the best Cromwell can do, and he hopes that the strong Roman Catholic faction does not seek to start a civil war, and try to put the girl on the throne.

"What about George Boleyn?" Cromwell asks. "What do you wish us to do with him, sire?"

"Death." Tom Howard, Duke of Norfolk spits the word out, with the vehemence of a striking snake. "The dirty little turd was coming to murder me, and you too, Cromwell."

"Then it was not treason," Cromwell explains. "He thought only to arrest his sister's enemies. He thought the king was dead."

"That is just like the sort of thing the silly bastard would believe," Norfolk sneers.

"Because of that, he did not realise he was bringing a weapon into the king's presence." Cromwell does not like it, but he must explain the law, even if it helps Boleyn, else the king might come to doubt his word.

"Ah, my blacksmith's boy understands the law, better than any man in England," Henry says, smiling for the first time that night. "Let them stay in the Tower for a few nights, then throw them out. Tell George that it is the very last time I spare him."

"As you wish, sire." Cromwell presents the finished document, and Henry signs it. Norfolk drips hot wax onto the bottom of the page, and the royal seal is applied. The Privy Councillor will obey the king, in his own way. Boleyn will be released, of course, but only after a dose of the most fiendishly refined torture.

He shall have Rafe Sadler visit George, in the Tower, and advise him to write his last will and testament. Will Draper has men within the Tower too, who will drop terrible hints about Boleyn's fate. On the day he is released, he will think he is being taken to the block, rather than being freed. The man will be broken with fear.

"A good nights work, gentlemen," Henry says. "Let us get to our beds, and put this day behind us, for I have seldom had a worst one." There is a knock, and one of the many pages peeps around the door. He sees Thomas Cromwell, who often drops a silver shilling into his hand, and addresses himself directly to him.

"Master Cromwell … someone seeks you out, most urgently. It is the physician, whose name I cannot pronounce."

"Send him in," Henry says. "Is he here to tend my injuries, Thomas? You worry far too much, my friend." A moment later, and Adolphus Theophrasus is standing before them, wringing his hands in dismay.

"Thomas ... Your Majesty ... My Lord Norfolk," he says, with tears in his eyes, "I did all that I could. I am beyond mortal sorrow."

"What is all this about?" Henry demands. He has a vague recollection that he knows this man, but cannot place where he fits into his well ordered world. " You speak of sorrow, sir? Has something gone amiss?"

"Your Majesty, this is Doctor Theophrasus," Thomas Cromwell tells him. "I fear that the queen has miscarried."

Henry Tudor, King of England, falls to his knees, and begins to sob like a child.

*

The miscarriage, Adolphus Theophrasus insists, is none of his doing, and he is as dismayed at the loss of the king's heir as any of Henry's subjects. It seems that the sudden shock of Henry's pronounced death, was too much for her. The doctor was called, at once, but could do nothing to save the unborn child.

"The realisation that she was to be the ruler of the realm made her heart race, and her pulse quicken, to an alarming rate," the doctor advises Cromwell. "I cautioned her to rest, but she would not. It seems she was too busy ordering the arrests, or assassinations, of a long list of people. The news of King Henry's sudden, and miraculous, 're-birth' caused the miscarriage. I am sure of it."

"The king's heir, you say ...then it was a male?" Thomas Cromwell asks. "The lost child could be recognised as such?"

"Without a doubt, Thomas," the physician replies. "The features were well formed, and the male genitalia were there, clear to see. Henry has lost a son ... perhaps his last chance to sire an heir to his throne."

"His last chance?" Cromwell pours out two tumblers of wine, and hands one to the physician. "Tell me everything, Adolphus... omit nothing."

*

"They want me to go to her," the king tells Cromwell. "They say I must be reconciled to my marriage, and show the queen that I bear her no ill will. They say she has been through a terrible ordeal, and I must forgive, and forget."

"Most commendable, sire," Thomas Cromwell says. He drops his voice to a whisper, and stands as close to the king as he dare. "Which 'they' are we talking about? Who, in this realm, dares to tell my king what he must do?"

"The Earl of Wiltshire, of course," Henry replies. "He says the fault lies with those who shouted of my demise. He says the queen was carrying a healthy son, and that she can bear many more."

"Ah, the love of a father for his daughter often blinds them to the real truth, Your Majesty," Cromwell says. "He is distraught, and does not consider what he says properly. It is true, that Queen Anne was carrying a male child, but not a healthy one."

"Dear God, Thomas," Henry sobs. "Are you the only man in England who will tell me the truth?"

"It is my duty, sire," Cromwell replies. He sees that it is time to pile on the agony, and score points, whilst he may. "I had Colonel Draper speak with the court doctors, who all told the same story as Wiltshire … to the exact word.

I spoke with Adolphus Theophrasus, who seems to be a good doctor, who speaks his mind."

"Well?"

"He was there, sire, and he examined the … your son … after it aborted. His medical opinion was that the child was not as far developed as it might be, and unlikely to have gone to full term."

"What reason did he give?"

"I am not a medical man, sire, and I cannot…"

"Do not falter now, Thomas," Henry says. "The truth, and nothing less… I beg of you."

"Very well, Your Majesty. The physician says that the queen's womb was weakened by previous childbirth, and that he believes there to have been previous problems. He states that the queen is no longer young enough to carry a child, successfully."

"Previous miscarriages?" Henry is confused. "Does he not think that the birth of Elizabeth might have…"

"No, sire. He says that the queen has had, at least, one previous miscarriage," Cromwell says. "Upon closer investigation, this proves to be the case. It seems the queen lost a child, mid term, and was not treated properly afterwards, for some reason."

"How can this be?" Henry is beginning to wonder if he ever really knew Anne. "She kept it a secret?"

"One of her ladies let slip that the queen lost a child, very early on, and did not wish you to be told, for fear of you worrying."

"For fear of me questioning her ability, more like," the king growls. "It was kept from me, for her own ends, not mine!"

"I cannot say, Your Highness." Cromwell sighs. "The physician has his doubts, sire. He believes that you may never have another child... at least, not with Queen Anne."

"Once Christmas is done," Henry says, "you are to instruct Colonel Draper that I want a full investigation of the queen's past. I want him to see if any reason exists which might allow for a divorce. He might start with that snivelling bastard, Harry Percy."

"Sire, Lord Percy swore an oath, and you accepted it," Cromwell reminds the king. "If he changes his story, he stands to be charged with perjury. That means he will lose his head, and it will all reflect badly on your own honour."

"Then what?"

"I do not know, sire," Thomas Cromwell replies. "Though there is always something. If it can be proven that the marriage was false, in some way, Archbishop Cranmer will allow a second divorce."

"And who will follow me?" The king is wallowing in self pity, and can think of nothing but himself.

"Why, your own son, sire," Cromwell says. "Once Queen Anne steps aside, you will be free to re-marry. Might I suggest that you select a strong, healthy young Englishwoman. A woman fit to bear the strong sons of a strong king?"

"Have you anyone in mind?"

"Not I, sire. That is for you to decide." Cromwell is starting to bow himself away when he seems to have an afterthought. "Oh, I almost forgot, sire. Ned and Tom Seymour have left court, with their sister. It seems their father is quite unwell, and that he needs to have his unwed daughter close by. Ned Seymour is an old friend of mine, and has asked me to visit his estates, in a few weeks. Wiltshire is unwelcoming at this time of year."

"And?"

"I thought I might leave it, until the hunting season is underway … and then visit Wulfhall, with some close friends," Cromwell says. "We might even build it into a royal progression, if it please Your Highness."

"If it please?" Henry barks with laughter. "Why, nothing would suit me better, old friend. Now, must I still confront the queen?"

"No, sire, that would not be a good idea now," Cromwell replies. "Let her recover, and think you are reconciled to the fate she plans for you. Then, when we have enough evidence, the divorce can be enacted, in as private a manner as is possible. The people will not mourn her absence."

"If I am to play a part, I must let her have that which she most wishes," the king says.

"More?"

"Yes. You must press him, Thomas, and have him swear the oath." Henry holds up a hand, to forestall Cromwell's response. "You will tell him this. Tell him that I love no man better, and wish only that we be reconciled. Tell him that he has but to take the oath, with none but you, and I, present, and I will forgive him completely. Tell him that the moment he swears, I will take him to my heart again, and restore him to his former self. No, even higher."

"A generous offer, My Lord," Cromwell says. "I will go on bended knees to the man, if he so wishes it, and I will beg him to change his mind, and accept your magnanimous terms."

"If he agrees, I will hold him, under house arrest, until I am divorced," Henry concludes. He has thought it, and assumes that it must, therefore, come about. "Then, once Anne is gone, I will have him come to me, and return all that has been taken from him."

"Yes, sire." Cromwell bows, and leaves. He will try, one last time, but thinks that no man on earth is as stubborn as More. Even with such a generous offer, he can see how the man might still refuse, and so choose to bring about his own death.

12   The Last Good Man

The Winter of 1535 proves to be one of the harshest anyone can recall, and the Thames freezes over, from bank to bank, for several weeks. Throughout January, and February, it is all the people of England can do to stay alive. Starvation, and coughing sickness, take their terrible toll, and there is unrest from the Scottish borders, to the Welsh Marches.

"I have written to the Duke of Northumberland again," Will Draper says to Cromwell. "He begs to be excused a trip south just yet, because the Scots are marauding again, in great numbers. They starve, and raid southwards, in the hope of some relief. I say he must come as soon as he can, by order of the king."

"Good, we need him here, if we are to progress against Anne any further," Tom Cromwell says. The formal investigation into Queen Anne has ground to a halt, as those who might know anything have become silent. Anne suspects something, as the king has not visited her bed since Christmas. Her own spies are out, and about, looking for any sign of trouble, and everyone is keeping their heads down.

"We must also press her childhood friends again," Will Draper ventures. "Tom Wyatt must know what sort of a child she was. It might be some childish indiscretion that disqualifies her from the marriage. Though God knows what."

"What do we know about her past correspondence with William Tyndale?" Tom Cromwell asks. "Henry never quite liked the man, and she might easily have overstepped the mark in her writings."

"Anne admires his philosophic outpourings," Will replies, "but she has never done anything indiscreet, other than ask him to reconcile himself to Henry."

"Her sister?" Cromwell asks.

"Living rather quietly in the countryside." Draper mutters. It is not a subject he wishes to have probed too deeply, but his old master is as all seeing as Pru Beckshaw.

"I know Mush visits her, Will." Cromwell likes his young men, and does not wish to press them into anything they do not want to do "Might he not speak with her, and ask a few pertinent questions?"

"She will not speak out about Anne," Will tells his old master. "She runs her farm well, and lives very quietly. I doubt she has even spoken to her sister, let alone the king, these last twelve months."

"Time is running out," Thomas Cromwell complains. "The king asks, almost daily, what progress we make, and then wants to know when he might visit his 'dearest Jane' in Wiltshire. He means to divorce Anne, and replace her with Lady Jane Seymour, before the year is out."

"Then, one way or another, he will have his wish. I wonder at how we have come to create such a king." Will stands, and finishes his wine. Outside, Austin Friars servants are busy serving hot broth, and freshly baked bread to hundreds of starving Londoners. "If he could only look beyond his own needs, and see how his poor people are doing. Henry lives in a fool's paradise."

"Hush, Will." Thomas Cromwell sighs. "He is the king, and we must act within that constraint. Let him try to run his love life, whilst we run his country. Let him think he is despised, and he will turn into a raging despot. We let him have his petty victories, where we must, and he gets to throw aside a queen, or destroy a minister of More's ability. Make him feel unloved, and he will seek out those whom he can blame. The government of this realm would collapse under his oppression, and the people would suffer. So, we give him a few, small sacrifices. It is for the best that way."

"Then he wants More still?"

"Of course." Cromwell sees he must explain the workings of the king's mind to his former agent. "He loves More, because he is honest. This means he wants to save him. However, he knows More does not agree with the first divorce, let alone the second. If More lives, he will urge Henry to return to Katherine. Henry wants Jane Seymour for queen, and sees that More will try to block him. It is, therefore, important that Sir Thomas More is despatched ... if only for his honesty."

"We live in a harsh world, sir," Will replies. Cromwell nods, and looks at the hungry faces. The crowd is dotted with men who are neighbours, but who have now fallen on hard times. The crops fail, the grass is sparse, and even the sheep do not prosper well enough. Men have gold, but there is little to buy with it. Bread is doubled in price, and murder is done over a joint of meat, or a few vegetables. "I hear the French are suffering far worse than we."

"There is plague abroad," Cromwell confirms. "Eustace Chapuys tells me that it started in Vienna, and is already lodging in Paris. Let us pray it stays there."

"Amen to that, Master Tom," says Will. "How is it going with poor Sir Thomas?"

"I have strung it out as far as I can," the lawyer says. "Now, I must interview him. The order is signed to convey him to the Tower, where I must try to keep him alive."

"He should swear the oath." Will knows he voices advice that will never be heeded.

"There are two schools of thought on the subject," Cromwell says. "There is what Tom More thinks, and there is what the rest of the world thinks. He will not change, and he will not give an inch."

"Even a mountain can be worn away," Will Draper says. "What of Bishop Fisher… will he recant?"

"Fisher is as stubborn as a mule. He writes to me from the Tower, begging extra blankets, and better food. Then preaches to me as to the king's vile falseness. I fear he will die also."

"You have much on your shoulders, sir."

"Yes, my head. Which neither Fisher, nor More will be able to say, unless they recant. Once, Rafe and I jested about an unkindness of ravens, and a bastardy of lawyers. Now, I find myself involved with the fall of Katherine, the expulsion of Anne, and the instalment of Jane in her place. What would such a collection be called, Will?"

"Two are in the last stages of decay, and poor Jane has a grim, dark, future awaiting her. Perhaps it is a twilight of queens?"

"How droll," Cromwell replies. "I might tell that to More, when I see him. He is a man condemned, but seems set to outlast most of Henry's women."

"If you see Meg, tell her that I have made arrangements for her and the family to leave," Will tells Cromwell. "Though they might be safer here, rather than France, at the moment."

"We are in the hands of God," Cromwell says. "I hope that He knows where all this will end." Cromwell contemplates a thought that has come, quite unbidden, into his head. If Fisher were to be tried, and executed first, it might either shock the king into staying his hand with Thomas More, or frighten More into finally taking the oath. It is, of course, a wicked idea, but has its merits, in that one important man might be spared.

*

"I thought you had forgotten me, sister," George Boleyn says. "So, what will you have of me?"

"Just your company, brother," Anne says. "Half of my friends have left court, and I am in need of some cheering up."

"I could come to you ... later."

"That cannot be. Henry has not sought out my bed for four months," Anne informs her younger sibling. "There is no chance of me coming with child at this rate, and he seems to be bored with me."

"The king loves you still." George tells her. "He calls you 'his beloved queen' in public."

"Does he?" Anne is stone faced. "Did he ever love anyone, save himself? They say he moons about, writing silly poems about Jane Seymour, and does not go about his kingdom, for fear of catching the plague. Tell me, George, does he still swive that dull witted little wife of yours? Or has he another mistress?"

"My wife claims not to have bedded Henry, and I half believe her. The courtiers all say the same to me, sister. That he moons after Jane Seymour. Suffolk was asking her whereabouts, only this morning."

"She is in the country, and she will stay there," Anne replies, smiling wickedly. "Father sees to that. Henry must be forced back to my bed, so that I might have the chance of another child. If he but once lies with me, I can seek others out, who might prove to be more virile."

"You need no others," George says, stiffly. "I would never fail you, my love."

"You say that… yet you spend your time feeling up the skirts of my own ladies-in-waiting. I think you to be rather… inconstant, little brother."

"You are too cruel, Anne." George paces up and down, and is becoming agitated. "It is true that I flirt with your ladies - who does not? - but I do not bed them. And as for my dearest little wife … she sleeps with everyone, save me and the king."

"Poor Lady Rochford," Queen Anne smirks. "Of all the men in England to choose from, she marries a faithless Boleyn man, and courts an impotent king."

"For God's sake!" George is genuinely frightened at her words. "If Henry cannot behave like a man, there will never be an heir."

"Then Elizabeth will rule," Anne replies. "Henry dare not put me aside, lest the world finds out about his shortcomings. Lady Jane Seymour can sleep with him, for all I care, but only as his mistress."

"He might get her with child."

"Then it will be a bastard," Anne concludes. "No, Henry can never abandon me. He must resolve himself to his fate."

"Until death do you part?"

"Precisely," says Anne. "Once Henry is gone, I can choose whom to be with."

"Do not tease me, sister." George cannot abide the idea of his sister wanting another man, and her re-marriage is quite unthinkable. "I doubt any would put up with your foul little tempers. You would frighten them all away, I fear."

"Harry Norris admires me," Anne tells her brother. "In fact, several about the court would enjoy me, given the chance, and some even dream of being my next husband."

"Then, surely, they must all wish the king to be dead," George Boleyn says. "That is treason. Are they all then so mad?"

"Who knows what goes on in the minds of all these men?" Anne stands, and crosses to the window. She is intent on the scene below, and does not notice a slight shape, moving away from the door. Lady Jane, the wife of George Boleyn, was in search of her wayward husband, and she has heard quite enough.

She tries to commit every word to memory, and puzzles over what some of it means. One day, it will be repeated, and her world will change, forever.

*

"Are you treated well, Sir Thomas?" Cromwell casts an eye about the small cell, and makes a mental note to have the man moved to a larger set of rooms.

"As well as any prisoner." More replies. "What is the weather like, outside, Master Cromwell?"

"Wet, and cold." Cromwell realises that More's window is all of six feet above his head. "The French plague seems content with staying over the Channel, and the food situation is improving."

"Thanks, I believe, to Colonel Draper's wife?" More says.

"Yes. She has a fleet of cogs, and ships, scouring the far reaches of Europe, in search of supplies." Cromwell shrugs. "It is enough to feed London, and with a little left for the rest of England."

"She is a good woman," More says. "Once, she fed only my dear land of Utopia. Now, she succours all of mankind. Ironic, is it not?"

"How so?"

"A Jewess… a despised outcast… feeding the very people who despise her religion." More smiles. "We live in an upside down world, do we not, my friend?"

"Meg, and the rest of your family, are well."

"Abroad?" More asks, more in hope than certainty. His daughter is a wilful woman, and will do exactly as the mood takes her. "Somewhere safe from the queen's spite?"

"No."

"They must leave."

"Your words tell me the answer to my question." Cromwell sits at the small table. "You wish them to be safely away, because you will not take the oath."

"That is so."

"Why not?"

"Because I will not."

"Can you tell me your reasons?"

"Yes, but I will not do that, either," More says. "Suffice it to say, that I cannot see my way clear to go with you on this matter, my dear old friend."

"I will report back, of course, but the council will not accept what you say," Cromwell tells him. "We have strung this out to the limit, Tom, and now, we must pay the piper his price. Either you take the bloody oath, or you refuse. I am instructed to say that we do not need a reason for your refusal. The very act of refusal is to be considered treason."

"Then, at last, I am a dead man," Sir Thomas More says, and shrugs his shoulders. "

"I tried," Cromwell says. "Meet me, part way. Tell me that you are considering things, and could well change your mind, given another week, or two."

"Why stretch things out any longer?" More says. "I will not take the oath, and that is final."

"Then you will surely die," says Cromwell.

"If I must, but I will go to the bosom of my maker with a clear conscience." Sir Thomas holds out a hand, and Thomas Cromwell clasps it, tightly.

"Come with me, Tom," he begs.

"And lose my soul?" More pulls his hand back, as if it is scalded.

"Men who are as good as you have sworn," Thomas Cromwell says.

He knows this is a ridiculous thing to say, for if they swear to save their lives, above their souls, how can they be better? Sir Thomas More is, the Privy Councillor realises, the last good man in England.

"That must be their own concern, Thomas," More replies. "They put their rightful king before Almighty God, so as to validate an invalid marriage."

"Henry wants a divorce." Cromwell's words hang in the damp air, like a spectre at the feast, and More almost laughs in his face.

"From Anne Boleyn?"

"Yes. He tires of her, and wants to re-marry."

"Then Henry is the King of Cloud Cuckoo Land," More tells his friend. It is a popular theme for ribald stories that in the land of Cockayne, or Cuckoo Land, even the most absurd things can happen on an everyday basis. Kings serve paupers, the sad laugh, and the happy ones cry. "He seeks to turn about the well ordered running of a world that does not need, or want, his cockayed ways."

"Then shire horses shall lay hen eggs, cows will fly like ducks, and

Henry have his way," Cromwell says. "He will have you dead, Anne gone, and Jane Seymour as his queen, before Christmas next."

"What… *little* Jane Seymour?" Sir Thomas More finally allows mirth to gain the better of him, and he laughs, raucously. Cromwell sees there is no more to be said, and stands to leave. The cell door swings open, almost too fast, and a grim faced guard lets him out into the corridor.

"See that Sir Thomas's lodgings are improved," he tells the man, "and make sure his food is plentiful, and hot."

"I cannot do that sir."

"What is that?" Cromwell thinks he has misheard. That a common guard might refuse a command from him, is not something he has ever considered to be a possibility.

"Orders, Master Cromwell." The guard actually steps back, so black is the look he receives. "Forgive me, sir. I would not cross you, if it can be avoided, but the orders are directly from the king."

"Given to you?" Cromwell almost knocks the man off his feet with a well aimed thump to his ear. "In writing, you insolent dolt? Can you even read? Who dares to issue orders, using the king's name?"

"Sir Richard Rich, sir," the man gasps out. "He has a sealed document, and says that he is in charge of the prisoner, from this day onwards."

"Rich, you say? See Sir Thomas is kept warm, and well fed, and there is a bag of silver in it for you," Thomas Cromwell snaps. "Ignore me, and Colonel Draper will call to see that you understand better. I shall deal with Richard Rich!"

"He is in the White Tower, sir," the guard offers. He is caught between two powerful forces, and cannot do right for doing wrong. "I seek only to do my duty … yet it is always us common men who must be kicked up the arse, sir."

"I am from the same stock as you, fellow," Thomas Cromwell admits. "Forgive my anger, and do as I bid of you. Master Rich will be along presently, to confirm my wishes." He is almost out of the room when what the man has said sinks home. "Hold, fellow. You say Sir Richard Rich?"

"Yes, sir. Did you not know?"

"That the king has knighted the fool?" Cromwell shakes his head in surprise.

"No, sir … that he has, just yesterday, appointed him to the position of Attorney General."

"Dear Christ, then we do truly live in Cloud Cuckoo Land!"

*

Richard Rich is dining with the Warden of the Tower, and the Master of the Royal Mint who has quarters in the fortress. His position in life seems to become more elevated with each passing day, and well placed people now seek him out as a friend. The king now gives him direct orders, and Queen Anne flirts with him, and begs for him to pass on small items of gossip from the court. Even the Holy Roman Emperor's Savoyard ambassador, Eustace Chapuys, sends him small gifts of money.

Only the day before, Henry has made him into his leading lawyer, and placed him above every other legal mind in England. It is what he has been working towards, and gives him the protection he needs from the likes of

Cromwell, and his cronies. With the full force of the law behind him, he can begin the steady rise to the top of the political dung heap.

He is sipping his second glass of wine, and extolling the great beauty, and regal virtue of Anne Boleyn, when the door is kicked open, and a towering angel of retribution fills the opening. The Warden of the Tower leaps to his feet, and bows to Cromwell. The man is a good friend of Colonel Will Draper, and knows where his true loyalties must ultimately lie.

"Master Cromwell … this is such a pleasant surprise," he gushes. "You must join us in our simple repast. This is our new Master of the Mint, Sir Arthur…."

"I know he is new," Cromwell growls. "I had the last one hanged from an orange tree. Good day, Rich, I see you have forgotten your manners. It is customary to stand, when a better enters the room." Richard Rich stands, and offers a slight bow.

"I think 'equal' might be a better term, sir," Rich sneers. "For I am now knighted, and made the king's new Attorney General." His two companions move a half step further away from him, as if not wishing to be involved with whatever is about to happen.

Thomas Cromwell smiles, and takes Rich's seat at the well laden table. He notes the haunch of venison, and the plentiful supply of hard cheeses, fresh baked bread, and wine. Richard Rich moves down, and goes to sit at the next empty place.

"I see that the wide spread famine is yet to reach His Majesty's Tower of London," Thomas Cromwell mutters. "I do not recollect giving you permission to sit in my presence, Master Rich."

Sir Richard Rich hovers, his backside an inch off the chair, and his face flushes with embarrassment. Despite his recent elevation, Thomas Cromwell is still the leader of the Privy Council, and none take precedence over him, unless it is the king, or a full earl of the realm. So, being a coward at heart, he stands, and waits for permission to sit. Cromwell cuts himself a piece of venison, and tears off a lump of bread, before gesturing for the Warden of the Tower of London, and the Master of the Royal Mint to be seated.

"How goes the new position, Sir Arthur?" Cromwell says, as if to demonstrate his total power. "The king asked me who to appoint, and I thought of you at once."

"Well, Master Cromwell," Sir Arthur replies. "I am grateful for your patronage, and must ever be in your debt."

"Think nothing of it. It gives me pleasure to help an old friend, as easily as I can break an enemy. And how stands the Tower, sir? Has the king any need to worry?"

"The Tower stands fast, sir," the Warden reports. "The ordinance is all in good working order, our 'guests' are all accounted for, and even the ravens are loyal to their king."

"Now, Richard," Cromwell says to the, still standing, young man. "What is this I hear about your breeches?"

"Breeches, sir?" Rich is caught off guard, and does not expect this sort of treatment.

"Why, yes." Thomas Cromwell chews his meat, and one can imagine that it is Sir Richard Rich in his maw, being slowly masticated. "It seems that you are outgrowing them. You seek to give orders, concerning Sir Thomas More?"

"I was…"

"Silence!" The word slices through the room, and pins poor Rich into his place. "The guard tells me you have a warrant of some sort? Show me." Rich fumbles in his purse, and produces a folded document. Cromwell sees that it bears, not the king's seal, but the white falcon of Queen Anne. He holds out a hand, and makes Rich walk over to him with it.

"This is from the Attorney General's Office, yet sealed by the Boleyn woman," Cromwell says, and the two onlookers gasp in surprise. The Privy Councillor is offering a most blatant insult to the queen. "You might as well wipe it on your arse, for all the strength it possesses. My charter is from someone named Henry, and bears his *royal* seal."

"Queen Anne wishes matters hurried along," says a nervous Rich. "And as I am Attorney General, it is my sworn duty." Thomas Cromwell nods, sagaciously at the cowering young lawyer, and waves Rich into a chair.

"Yes, she wants things hurried along … as does the king, Richard.

Though there is a world of difference. The queen seeks her callow revenge, whilst King Henry wishes only to avoid any embarrassing criticism from the finest legal brain in Europe. The king does not wish More dead, at all costs. You understand me, fellow?"

"Queen Anne…"

"Is a dangerous, and wilful woman," Cromwell insists. "Yet she is only a woman. Go against me, Richard, and you will fall with her. I seem to have had this conversation with you before, have I not?"

"I am torn between two camps, Master Cromwell." Richard Rich has even less courage than morality, and wishes he could work his wiles unseen. "You treat me badly, and try to keep me from advancement, whilst the queen promises me things, if only I do as she bids of me."

"I can have you executed for perjury," Cromwell replies. It is a shot in the dark, but the effect on young Rich is most gratifying. His face drains of colour, and his hands begin to shake.

"I do not mean to … do not wish to…."

"Tell me what she asks of you, Richard, and I will try to spare you."

Cromwell's voice is cold, and promises an evil end for the young lawyer, if he makes a wrong move.

"She merely wonders if I might overhear something."

"Said by More?"

"Yes."

"What?"

"She only wondered."

"What words would she have you hear, Richard?" Cromwell stands, and towers over the frightened man.

"That I might ask More to take the oath, and that he refuses me, saying that the king does not have the right to ask. That it is for God, to decide … not a mere man."

"And Sir Thomas, who has spoken to no one, all these months, would suddenly say this to you?"

"Why not?"

"Because you are a liar, a thief, a scoundrel, and a creature of such low esteem, that I might tread in you, rather than on you. If it comes to a trial, and you utter your perjured words, I will see that you are ruined, Sir Richard Rich."

"How can I refuse the queen?"

"The Boleyn name will not save you," Cromwell tells the young lawyer.

"Even were the king himself to order you to lie, I would still take my revenge on you. Let it be my oath. I, Thomas Cromwell do swear to utterly destroy, and confound my enemies, wherever they might seek to hide. Now, my dear Warden, shall we dine?"

"I will say nothing." Richard Rich speaks the words, but knows he is lying to himself. If threatened, he would condemn his own mother, and if paid enough, betray God himself.

"Hush, Richard," Thomas Cromwell tells him. "No more lies. As our new Attorney General you will be expected to lead the prosecution. Once Sir Thomas More is on trial, no power in Heaven, or on Earth, can save him. Your paltry lies will make no difference to the outcome." He raises a glass, and proposes a toast to the company. "Gentlemen, here is to the last good man in England. God save his immortal soul."

"Sir Thomas More," the two dinner companions say, and raise their glasses.

"Better quarters, better food, and a good fire, each evening," Cromwell says to Richard Rich. "Make it so, and I will ignore you, Rich. Fail me, and…" He drains the glass, and throws it into the fireplace, where it shatters into a thousand fragments.

13   Fleas Upon Fleas

"Ah, here comes the Duke of Norfolk, and poor Suffolk is behind him." Cromwell frowns, and tells Rafe Sadler to stay close enough to hear what transpires. "For they do not know how to placate the king, without my advice. He rages, almost daily at them, and swears he is surrounded by traitors."

"He is in a foul mood, because of Bishop Fisher's death, three weeks ago," Rafe says. "He seeks to lay blame."

"He ordered it," Cromwell replies, with a shrug. "The man died for his beliefs, and it has made him a saint, amongst those who still follow the old Roman Catholic ways. What did he expect the world to do … applaud him?"

"Fisher broke down, and recanted. Then he swore the oath, and begged for forgiveness," Rafe reports.

"And they sentenced him to an easier death?" Cromwell has heard the tale, but wonders if Rafe knows something more.

"They did. Cardinal Fisher thought he was to be spared, you see.

When they told him how he had been tricked by Richard Rich, he withdrew his confession, begged forgiveness of God, and denied the king's right to rule the English church."

"And so they killed him anyway," Cromwell says. "Did they not think of the consequences?"

"It seems not. The king's closest advisors all agreed, and told Henry that John Fisher was a traitor, and will be forgotten in a month."

"More fool them," Cromwell replies. "For here we are, already in July, and his fame as a martyr spreads across the civilised world. The Pope will canonise the poor man, before long. Now, hush, and move a little away from me, Rafe."

"Master Cromwell, a word, if you please!" Tom Howard, the Duke of Norfolk calls. He tries to sound affable, and smiles a feral smile ay the Privy Councillor.

"I could give him two," Cromwell sighs. "Though I doubt he would respond to them. Yes, My Lord Norfolk? Are you well? How is the king today?"

"Ranting," Charles Brandon replies, as he catches up with his fellow noble. "He is beset with complaints, and wonders why he is so ill served by those about him. What can we do to reassure His Majesty of our continued devotion, Master Cromwell?"

"Do not be an ass, Brandon," Norfolk snarls. "England is falling to pieces, because its first minister is tied up in legal proceedings, day and night. Henry needs you by his side, Cromwell, as much as I hate to admit it. It was a black day when we brought Cardinal Wolsey down, and a blacker day when Henry made you Sir Thomas's tormentor in chief."

"I cannot fulfil both roles," Cromwell says, though, in truth, he has distanced himself from the affairs of state for a few weeks, because there are some nasty pitfalls to be avoided. The king in France threatens war, because Admiral Travis has done more than just raid his shipping, whilst the emperor demands the immediate release of Sir Thomas More. The Pope is busy excommunicating everyone who even thinks of helping Henry's cause, and the king's own wife spends her time nagging at him. "Either I am a prosecutor of political prisoners, or a

Privy Councillor. It is for the king, in his wisdom, to decide."

"Well, he has," Norfolk informs Cromwell. "He has told me to have Richard Rich put More on trial, at once, and bid you attend him now, as his chief councillor. I will have our new Attorney General press ahead. He must have Sir Thomas tried, and executed, within the week, and you will return England to its former good standing."

"There is no evidence against Sir Thomas, gentlemen" Cromwell says. "I have questioned him, for weeks on end, and he does not utter a single damning phrase. He professes his love for the king, and wants nothing but the best for his country."

"A trivial matter," Suffolk says. "It seems that More has been cursing the king, and saying he is not fit to rule. My own steward heard him, and so did Sir Richard Rich... though he now, strangely enough, says otherwise."

"I shall twist Master Rich by the balls, and have the truth out of him," Norfolk avows. "Then, More must make his peace, for friend or not, I shall have to take his head."

"Then there is nothing else to be done," Cromwell says. "We live in sad times, My Lords, when a king can be swayed by his queen in this way."

"Have a care," Norfolk growls at him. "My niece is queen, and is mother to the heir."

"The female heir, sir," Cromwell replies, softly. "The king would do anything for a son. You are both wise men, and I hope you understand what I mean. Good day." The Privy Councillor is needed by the king, and he leaves the two men gaping after him.

"Sadler, come to me," Norfolk demands. "What does Cromwell mean by that?"

"I cannot say for sure, sir, as I am the king's man."

"Then guess," Suffolk says. "For I know where your love lies, Rafe."

"Very well. The king wants a boy. This queen does not seem to be able to provide one. The king needs a queen who can deliver a male heir."

"Henry would never dare," Norfolk says. "It is one thing to put aside your brother's wife … that was legal … but he cannot divorce Anne. The church would never agree."

"No, My Lord. She must stand aside for the good of the realm," Rafe concludes. "That is what Master Cromwell thinks, and that is what the king will think. Now, if you have no further need of me, I must attend the king, in case he needs my legal expertise."

"Snotty little bastard," Norfolk grumbles.

"Rafe Sadler is a clever man," Suffolk says. "He smells the wind, and knows where to set his sails. Will Anne step aside?"

"Never."

"Even if the king insists?"

"She knows he will not." Norfolk sounds confident, but does not fully understand how the court can be manipulated, and the king subtly influenced. "He is far too honourable."

"Quite," Charles Brandon, Duke of Suffolk says. He is more pragmatic than the older Norfolk, and knows that nothing is immutable when it comes to politics. "I hope your niece realises that which does not step aside, can be put aside."

"She is a wilful young woman, and may not make the right choice."

Norfolk concludes. "I must speak with her father, at once."

"And what of More?"

"Oh, have Rich draw up the charges. Tell him to throw it all in, and make it sound as legal as he can. I will allow Sir Thomas the courtesy of answering the charges, in a closed court, and then have him condemned to death. Shall we say, the day after tomorrow?"

"Not tomorrow then?"

"Good God, no!" Norfolk is scandalised. "I am stag hunting all day, and will not miss it for anything!"

*

"Tell me how it went, Thomas," Henry asks. "I know you will speak the truth. The rest of them, I fear, are not to be trusted."

"As Your Majesty wishes."

"We are alone now, Thomas. Like this, I am but your old friend, Henry," the king says. He resorts to first names when most stressed, and thinks it makes common men more open with him. In fact, it is when Cromwell, and the others, distrusts him the most.

"Well, Henry, they brought Sir Thomas More from the Tower on the first day of this month, and called him to trial. The courtroom was closed to all, but a chosen audience. Sir Richard Rich, your new Attorney General, read out the main charge, which was one of High Treason."

"Treason would have done," Henry mutters. "Why must they always go too far?"

"Rich put the charges, in a hesitant, stumbling way, and then started to read out the evidence. I was forced to stand up, and stop him, for he had made a mistake. I pointed out to the most senior lawyer in the land that Sir Thomas had not yet been asked to plead."

"Christ, but the man is a damned fool," the king curses. He has promoted a man beyond his ability, in order to have a willing stooge, and now he pays the price. "I will be ridiculed, as the king with an incompetent fool as his legal voice. What then, old friend?"

"The Attorney General made some sort of mumbled apology, and asked Sir Thomas to plead. He stated, in a clear, strong voice, that he was not guilty, and added that he had never spoken out against the king, or denied his headship of the Church of England."

"Stout fellow," Henry says. "I cannot believe he ever would, Thomas. What then?"

"Sir Richard Rich looked to the Duke of Norfolk, who nodded, as if giving him permission to speak." Thomas Cromwell pauses for dramatic effect, and sees that the king is hanging on his every word. "Then Rich did testify that Sir Thomas More had, in his presence, denied the King was head of the Church, and that only the Bishop of Rome ... Pope Clement ... could represent God."

"It is what he always thought."

"Perhaps, but I cannot read a man's mind, sire. In all my conversations with him, Thomas More never once spoke a treasonable word against you. I cannot understand why he would then utter such infamies to a man whom he did not trust, and whom he once dismissed, for petty dishonesty." There, Master Rich, that is you paid out, Cromwell thinks.

"Then Richard Rich is not the man I am told he is." Henry seeks to distance himself from a man he now sees is a craven dog.

"Someone has lied to you, Henry," Thomas Cromwell says, softly. "Who would dare do such a thing?"

"Queen Anne proposed him." Then you are paid out, in part, too, madam, Cromwell thinks.

"It was also decided by the jury that Sir Thomas More's silence was 'clear, and irrefutable, evidence' of 'a most corrupt, and perverse nature', whatever that might mean. The man never took a coin that was not earned, and as for him being perverse … I say only that George Boleyn was in court, with a close male friend."

"What?" Henry cannot let this pass. "What do you mean to imply, Thomas?"

"Nothing but that which I have heard rumoured about court, Henry," Cromwell says. "You asked me to have Colonel Draper investigate the Boleyn family, in regard to the likelihood of a second divorce, and he reports back, on a weekly basis. It seems that the father uses the treasury like his own personal bank, and that George has unusual tastes in the privacy of the bed chamber. He lacks proof yet, but knows that the young man is, in some way, corrupted."

"Dear God, I am beset by evil, Thomas." Henry is in danger of slipping into one of his maudlin broods, which results in nothing being decided. Cromwell realises that he must work fast.

"For evil to triumph, it only needs good men to look away," he says, sharply. "Perhaps, Henry, because of your own innate goodness, you have looked away too often? Forgive my criticism of you, dearest friend, but you are almost too honest to be a king."

"But king I am!" Henry is enthused by Cromwell's clever rhetoric, and lurches to his feet. "So, they have managed to kill my dear friend then?"

"Sir Thomas went to the block, this morning, sire. His final words were to beg your forgiveness, because he could not abandon his God. I took the liberty of commuting the sentence, to simple beheading. Richard Rich, after speaking with both the Boleyns, wanted him drawn, part hanged, and disembowelled first, but I knew you would be revolted by such an act of blatant barbarity."

"You did well, my friend." The

king frowns. In a few short sentences, Thomas Cromwell has pointed out why his court is so blighted. "Urge Colonel Draper on to complete his report. I want my divorce, and once I have it, I want George Boleyn, if he is found to be guilty, to be tried as a sodomite."

"And the father?"

"If he is stealing, then he must be punished."

"Rich?"

"If I remove him now, I will be the laughing stock of the realm," Henry reasons. "Leave him in place, but have Master Sadler fulfil his usual duties. See that Rich receives nothing more than his usual salary, and let him find his own living accommodation. He is no longer welcome in my court, and I do not wish to see his face again."

"As you wish, sire." Cromwell has most of what he wants, and feels uncomfortable using the king's given name. "We must now brace ourselves for the backlash which Thomas More's death will bring. Those who tried him should have known the ill will it would cause, both here, and abroad. It was bad enough when they killed poor Fisher."

"The French call me 'Bloody Hal'," Henry moans. "As if it were all my doing."

"Yes, Lord Norfolk was remiss in rushing into things with Fisher," Cromwell says, with a sigh. "He is far too headstrong to be a good advisor to the king. Why, was he not one of those who so badly treated Cardinal Wolsey?"

"Yes, it was he, Harry Percy, and Anne … dripping their poison into my ear." Henry has something else to feel indignant about. "Did I never tell you how, on the day he died, I was ready to forgive him, and restore him to power?"

"He knew it, sire."

"How can I be sure?"

"I was his man, Your Majesty," Cromwell reminds the king.

"Of course. I remember now. He sent you to me, did he not?" Henry is twisting history, but it salves his conscience, and makes him feel better.

"That is so, sire. He sent me to court, saying that I was to wait on you, until you sent word to release him. It was in your mind to forgive him, when certain people conspired to ruin him, instead. I recall how Percy begged to be sent to fetch the cardinal, and how he overstepped his authority, and arrested him, in a most cruel way. It was the sudden shock of it all which broke his heart. Even at the end, I am told he kept faith with you, and swore his undying love."

"He said so?"

"Colonel Draper was present," Cromwell says, creating his own little twist. Draper had been there, but not at the bedside, when Cardinal Wolsey breathed his last. "He brought word to me, and I told you, sire. You were almost inconsolable. Then you bade me stay on, and help you in the council."

"A happy day, Thomas," Henry says. "When you leave here, today, I wish you to make up a list. Put upon it all those who have failed me, twisted my words, or betrayed my love, and we will attend to them, in good time."

"As you command, sire." Thomas Cromwell needs to make no such list up. He has a book at Austin Friars, and it is full of names. The black, leather bound volume was started in his days with Wolsey, and contains the names of everyone who conspired in his downfall. One by one, each name shall be stricken through.

Austin Friars is a gloomy place that evening. Sir Thomas More was known, and liked by all within its walls, and even the servants mourn his passing. As if by mutual consent, everyone in the big house gathers at the kitchen table at supper time, and conducts a short, intimate service, which concludes with a heart felt prayer, and a good meal.

"He gave me a penny, once," Young Adam, the stable keeper, says, as they sit around the kitchen. "That's to keep you honest, fellow, he told me. A penny, I ask you!"

Thomas Cromwell is standing in the door, and he smiles at the story. As a youth, he too had received a coin, but a silver shilling, with the same injunction from the man, who was then studying to be a man of the law. He has used a similar device since on most of his people. Here, it says, stay honest, and prosper by it.

It works with most, but Thomas Cromwell recalls how Digby Waller preferred evil, and how Richard Rich's inner weakness will let him down. Still, he thinks, for every bad one, there is at least a dozen good ones. Colonel Will Draper is a case in question. Since coming to him, as a near penniless soldier of fortune, he has exceeded all expectations, and remained loyal to the Austin Friars cause.

His nephew, Richard, is making his way as a merchant, and often acts as a front man when the more 'died in the wool' old merchants will not deal with Miriam Draper, because she is a woman. He is proud to remember how he saw the girl's worth, and helped her build her business up to what it now is. Her ships roam the world, and her dealings with the Spanish and French, help his agents go where they could not, previously.

"Where is your trusted right hand, Will?" he asks.

"On the king's business, Master Thomas," Will replies, vaguely. "He and his wife are looking into certain matters, appertaining to the queen's affairs."

"Pray, keep me informed, Will," Cromwell tells him, and the King's Examiner simply nods. He serves two masters now, and must be careful what he tells to each. If pressed, he will always come down on the side of Cromwell, but he must not be seen to be too partisan.

"How is the king?"

"He talks of making up lists, and of vengeance."

"Is that good, or bad for us?" Will asks.

"Good, one hopes. You might even be able to give George Boleyn a kick up the arse, to pay him back for burning down your house."

Will holds his peace. Word has come to him that some great secret has been uncovered, that involves Boleyn, but he does not wish to act too soon. John Beckshaw and his wife are on the scent, and will report back, when they have found something out. Inside, he is no different from Cromwell, and wants to wreck those who have crossed him.

"Did you attend the execution, Master Tom?" Mush Draper asks. He was fond of the garrulous old Sir Thomas, and could not watch him die.

"I had to," Cromwell says. "It was good that, at least, one friend was with him, at the end."

"Amen," Barnaby Fowler intones, and one or two even cross themselves. Cromwell smiles at the unconscious action, and wonders if Rome can ever be truly eradicated from his England.

"I wager that arsehole Richard

Rich was there, in his new finery," Will says.

"He was." Cromwell grimaces at the thought of the man rising so high, and so quickly. "He was as a flea on my back, and I am a flea upon Norfolk who is a flea upon the king. We all fight for our place in the sun."

"I wonder who Henry lands on?" one of the servant lads muses, and the entire room erupts into laughter at the coarse innuendo. Poor Henry, they think... all dressed up, and no-one to hop upon!

*

"Thank you, for sparing me a moment of your time, Master Cromwell." Margaret Roper is dry eyed, and as dignified as any queen. She curtseys to the Privy Councillor, and places a sealed document on the desk before him. Cromwell does not look at it, and gestures for her to take a seat.

"You are always welcome at Austin Friars," he tells her. "Though you should not travel unaccompanied. There are those who would do ill to any who loved your father."

"I will not sit," Margaret replies. "The letter is for you, and was written by my father, just before they took him to the Tower. As for me, I come begging a favour."

"You want the body?" Cromwell guesses. It is beyond his power, as traitors are usually dismembered, after death, and their remains scattered to the corners of the realm.

"No, I know that cannot be," she tells him, "but his head is to be stuck on a spike, for the rabble to laugh at. Can you spare him that indignity, sir?"

"I shall send word to the Warden of the Tower, within the hour," Cromwell says. "Have your husband call on him, tomorrow, and he will hand over your father's head. The fellow will expect a reward for this, so take this purse, and give it to him."

"You are kinder than you need to be."

"I loved your father, Meg, and I used to bounce you on my knee once." Cromwell stands, to signify the end of the business. "If I could have saved him, I would. All I can promise now, is to deliver retribution, where it is deserved. Master Fowler!" Barnaby Fowler, who is only in the next office, comes bustling in.

"Master?"

"Find a couple of reliable young fellows, and have them escort Mistress Roper back to Utopia."

"I shall be honoured to take the lady home, sir." He bows, and beckons Meg out into the corridor. Cromwell closes the door behind her, with a finality that makes her sigh. "You must forgive Master Cromwell's shortness, Mistress Meg. He does not know how to handle grief very well, but his heart is bigger than most men's, and it is in the right place."

"He is a busy man," she mutters. Meg Roper understands that she is now, despite her gender, the head of the More family, and worries at what the future holds for them all. "I doubt he has time for my trivial worries."

"That is not so," Barnaby replies, leading her out into the sunlight. "The master has already instructed me to arrange a small pension for your step-mother, and bids me find plenty of work for your husband in the law courts. Roper is a sensible fellow, and has taken the oath.

My master loved your father well, mistress. He did all he could to avoid so terrible an end, and he does not wish to see you penniless."

"He said nothing of this," Meg says. The information lifts some of the weight from her shoulders, and gives her hope for the days ahead. "I should return, and thank him."

"No, mistress, you should return to Utopia, and pass as quiet a life as you can." Thomas Cromwell's man frowns, and decides to be frank with her. "Until Queen Anne's fangs are drawn, you will not be safe. Her bile is enough to poison everyone of your family. I wish you would all consider going to France. Colonel Draper can have you all on a boat, within a couple of hours."

"My father could not run away, Master Fowler," Meg replies, softly, "so, how can I?"

*

Thomas Cromwell spends a long time studying the letter, and wonders if there is some hidden meaning in the words. In the end, he decides that it is exactly what it purports to be … a last goodbye, from a dear friend. It starts with Dear Tom, and goes on to thank him for his friendship, and devotion to his family. Then it commends his wife, and family to him, and begs Cromwell to help them, where he can. It concludes with an assertion that he will soon be walking with God, and advises Thomas Cromwell to follow in the same, well trodden, footsteps.

"Too late for me, old friend," Cromwell mutters, as he folds the paper, and slips it into a drawer. "Perhaps it is even too late for England."

"Master?" Mush is, as he often does, these days, loitering close by. "Did you call?"

"Did I then speak out aloud?" Tom Cromwell's brow creases in consternation. "I must be careful, for some thoughts do not bear voicing, lest the wrong ears perceive, and understand them."

"There are no dangerous ears in Austin Friars, sir," Mush replies. "I saw Meg Roper leaving. Will she not leave England?"

"No. I fear her only safety lies in even more death."

"You mean Anne?" Mush dislikes the queen, as he has seen how she treats her own sister, and distrusts her more than anyone.

"Do you still bed her sister?" Cromwell regrets the words, even as they leave his mouth. "I do not seek to judge you, Mush. Forgive me, but… "

"You want to know where she stands," Mush says, completing his master's thought. "She is frightened of Anne, and is afraid what will happen, should she fall from grace."

"The king would not harm her."

"No?" Mush smiles, and shakes his head, disbelievingly. "She knows something … about her sister. I do not know what, but it frightens her that she has the knowledge."

"Can you coax it from her?"

"Perhaps." Mush considers how casually they talk of betraying a lover, and feels a pang of sorrow that he has become so hard. "She wants to come back to court. If I can promise her a place, and all that goes with it, she might speak."

"Then promise it to her, Mush," Cromwell says. "If we do not find a way to remove the queen, we will all soon follow Sir Thomas More to the block."

"Leave it with me," Mush says. "Might I promise her marriage?"

"To you?" Cromwell shakes his head. "That can never be, my dear boy. Henry would see it as a plot against him. Imagine it, lad. Lady Mary Boleyn, allied with the house of Cromwell is a step too far, I fear. No, we shall find her a decent gentleman, and an estate in the north."

"Then we must part?" Mush is surprised that he is not more upset at the prospect. In truth, he still loves the wife he lost, and can only ever look upon Mary as a loving friend.

"Can you?" Cromwell asks. Mush feels a lump in his throat, and has to clear it with a short cough.

"Yes," he replies, softly. "Though it shows me to be a lesser man, I can."

"Then go to her. Make her offers, and find out what you can," Thomas Cromwell says. "It was always going to end this way, Mush. Mary Boleyn must go on without you. She will fare better than you think, and anonymity will be her friend. Let history fasten onto her sister, and spare Mary from too close an inspection."

"Then I am to break with her, and promise an estate in Cheshire, and a solid gentleman farmer to marry," Mush confirms. "For what is in her head?"

"Yes."

"You will keep your word, about her reward?"

"Mush, when have I ever betrayed you?" Cromwell says. "Your woman shall go north, and spend her days in happy anonymity. Must I take yet another bloody oath?"

"Be damned to swearing, Master Tom," Mush tells him. "A man must promise with his heart... and not with clever lawyers words. Shake my hand, and it is done."

"Good man," Cromwell says, and he hopes that he will always be able to earn this young man's trust, and devotion.

14 A Forest of Traitors

Will Draper yawns, and sits up in bed. On the floor below, he can hear Miriam, and her maids, preparing the house, and the two children for the day ahead. He smiles at the thought of the caring husband, father, and gentleman, he has become, and calls for his own manservant.

Young Adam appears, as if by magic, carrying a bowl of warm, rose petal scented water, and a freshly stropped, single edged razor. It is the youth's duty to shave his master's chin, with practiced ease, then help him dress for the day in his newest hunting finery. He has an invitation to join the king, whilst he jaunts about the woodlands surrounding Hampton Court Palace.

"Did you manage to have my sword edged?" Will asks, as the blade scrapes over his chin. The boy's hand remains as steady as a rock. He wipes some excess lather from the blade, onto a towel draped over the back of the chair.

"I took it to Big Caleb… the blacksmith, over in Cheap Street, sir," Adam replies. "It costs tuppence, but he does make a very good job of it, master."

"And the pistols?" Will asks.

"All cleaned, sir," Adam tells his master. He is expected to carry out many tasks, and has to be in constant attendance, but does it willingly. He knows that, if he pleases the colonel, he will be considered for a position in the King's Examiners Office, once he reaches his later teens. "I also warned the stables to have Moll readied, sir. She will enjoy a good gallop. I assume you are still riding down to Hampton Court Palace today?"

"Damnation to it, boy, but I wish I could avoid this invitation," Will replies. "The king does love his stag hunting though, and likes to surround himself with those he considers to be close friends. That means George Boleyn will be there, and I shall have to keep a hold on my temper."

"I hear that Master Cromwell is preparing a surprise for His Majesty," Adam says, scraping away the last of his master's stubborn stubble.

"You hear too much," Will says, and smiles to lessen the reproof. His young servant is a close friend of the Austin Friars people, and picks up much useful gossip. "Speak up, lad. What is Master Cromwell up to then?"

"A visit to the country."

"With Henry?"

"Yes. He has written to the Seymour family, at Wulfhall, and warned them to expect a royal visit."

"Ah, I wondered when he would make his move," Will Draper muses. "Fresh country air, good hunting, and Mistress Jane at the dinner table. Master Tom knows what a poor picker the king is, and seeks to be the royal matchmaker this time."

"Methinks wicked Queen Anne will not like that," Adam says, with a wry grin. "I doubt Queen Katherine will be much pleased either."

"Yes, the king has a veritable queue of consorts," Will jests.

"Not for long, perhaps?" Adam tells his master. "My friends at Austin Friars tell me that Master Chapuys is a frequent visitor these days."

"Eustace Chapuys?" Will wonders why the little Savoyard ambassador is becoming so politically active of late. "Does he still hope to put Katherine back on the unsteady throne?"

"He begs Master Cromwell to

let him visit the queen," Adam explains.

"Anne?"

"No...Katherine ... The Dowager Princess of Wales."

"Why?"

"She is stricken down with some ague, and is dangerously ill, I hear."

"Again?" Will Draper shakes his head at the latest news. "It sounds like another ruse. Keep your eyes and ears open, lad. I want to know if Master Cromwell is foolish enough to allow this visit."

"He will refuse," Adam says. "It is all he can do. Is there anything else I can do for you, sir?"

*

"How goes your investigation, Draper?" The words cut across the gathering of titled men, and court hangers on, like the slash of a keen knife. Will Draper is busy, checking Moll's girth strap is tight enough. She is a cunning old girl, and knows enough to breath in at the right moment. Will waits, until the Welsh Cob exhales, and pulls it as tight as he can. Then he turns, as if just noticing George Boleyn is even included in the king's boisterous hunting party.

"Which one, Boleyn?" he replies. "The king bids me look into any matter that he deems worthy. Why, just the other day, His Majesty bade me look into the privy, where he feared there was something foul. I looked, and saw you coming out, and the problem was solved at once."

"Ho!" Henry is already mounted on his huge hunter, and towers over his subjects like some ominous cloud. "Well riposted, sir. You see the thrust of the jest, George? Methinks Colonel Will knows a bad stink when he sniffs it. Now, stop your mewling noise, and mount up." Henry notices Boleyn's horse, and nods in appreciation. "A very fine steed, George. New, is he?"

"My steward bought him at the last Nottingham fair, sire." George smiles, smugly, basking in the king's attention.

"Oh, I thought I hanged him," Henry replies, and tries to recall the details. "Did he not try to burn down Colonel Draper's house?"

"My new steward, sire," Boleyn answers. "Haskins was a bad lot, and paid for it with his life. Your Majesty brought his crimes to my attention, and I am grateful for…"

"Stringing up your personal steward?" Will says, sharply. "I wager the king knows well enough what his servants get up to."

"Well said, Will," the king says. "Though I do not see how we can bet on it … lest I number them all off, and that will take all week."

"Might I suggest another, more interesting wager, sire?" Will asks. He knows Henry's love of a bet well, and is sure it will pique his interest.

"First to bay the hart?" Henry guesses. "Or who will be first to take a tumble?"

"Your Majesty is renowned for his many tumbles," Will replies, with a sly wink at the king. "Few here could even try to match him with the ladies."

"Ha!" Henry's laugh is loud, and demanding of attention. Everyone in earshot must respond by either laughing, or applauding at everything that amuses him. "Let us not try to enumerate our tumbles, sir, lest we make the company blush!"

"Then let me issue a challenge," Will says. "How much did your fellow pay for your stallion, George?"

"Enough." George Boleyn does not like the sound of this sudden challenge. He knows that, in any fight, Will Draper would drub him. "Why should it concern you?"

"My guess is thirty pounds," Will says. "Any more, and you have been robbed. I challenge you to a race, George. Your handsome beast, against my little Welsh cob. I wager thirty pounds that Moll can win the day." Boleyn is relieved that his fighting skills are not to be tested, and pleased at the challenge. His own horse is three hands higher than Moll, and almost twice the size. He has hunted the beast across his Kent estate, and knows he can cover five miles at a strong gallop.

"Done." George is still smiling when Will takes his hunting bow from Moll's saddle, and crosses to Henry.

"Sire, your arm is still the strongest in this gathering," Will says, as he offers up the bow. "Send an arrow into yon woodlands, and we shall use it as a marker."

"A race… oh, what a wonderful idea!" Henry bends the bow, with practiced ease. He is over six feet tall, and still possesses a powerful pair of shoulders. The arrow arches high, and strikes home in the upper branches of a huge oak tree. "There is your mark, gentlemen. First to round the oak, and arrive back here, wins the wager. Agreed?"

Will nods, and takes the bow back. He returns to Moll, and is just mounting her, when George Boleyn kicks his heels into his horse's flanks. The huge beast spurts forward, and is twenty paces clear, before Will can urge Moll into pursuit.

"Cheating bastard!" the Duke of Norfolk cries to Henry, who can only roar with laughter. Charles Brandon, and the rest can only join in. Norfolk growls, and calls his support for Will Draper, against his disreputable nephew. "God be with you, sir, and damn that worthless arse to Hell!"

George Boleyn is a good rider, and lighter than Will Draper, by several pounds. He has a clear advantage, and gloats at the prospect of finally giving the upstart Draper his comeuppance. His horse is striding out well, and Boleyn risks a look over his shoulder, to find that Draper is within five or six paces of him. He digs in his heels, and bends low over the horses neck, urging it on.

Will Draper has chosen his race course well. The big stallion has stamina, and is used to many long miles running, whilst his own Welsh cob is small, and bred for speed. In open battle, the little mare can cover a quarter mile in thirty or forty heart beats. Better still, she is trained to respond to her master's knees, which leaves the rider free to carry weapons in each hand.

Boleyn reaches the huge oak, still four paces clear, but fails to account for the sharp turn. He pulls the horse around, as hard as he dares, but still has to describe a large arc. Will leans to his right, and Moll turns in the space of two strides, and is around the big tree. Will lets her have her head, and she surges forward, as if she had no weight on her back.

Will Draper is almost alongside Boleyn now, and he prays he has judged it right. He knows Moll's turn of speed has its price, and that she will tire quickly now. The little cob seems to sense the importance of the gallop, and pushes on, until she is a half length clear. George Boleyn is horrified that his arch enemy is besting him again, and pulls his horses head hard over, making his mount swerve into the flank of Draper's mount.

If timed better, the manoeuvre would have knocked Moll onto her haunches, but the collision is badly executed, and Boleyn's mount stumbles. The big horse goes down, in a flail of arms, legs, and screams. Moll's final burst of speed sends her back to the roaring crowd around Henry, where she slows, and begins to blow hard. Will leaps from her back, and gives her an affectionate slap on the neck.

"By God, sire," Will calls to the king. "It seems poor George Boleyn has beaten you to the first tumble of the day after all!"

"And one I willingly grant to him, Will," Henry roars. "For it is one he truly deserves!"

*

In the end, it is only George Boleyn's tender feelings that are hurt. Both horse and rider manage to recover, and hobble in, a very poor second. As is the way, amongst the court, George must follow the official line, and laugh, along with the king, at how he has been soundly humiliated, once more.

"A well earned thirty pounds, Will," the king says, as they sit down to dinner, that evening. "I trust Boleyn has paid up?"

"It is of no matter, sire." Will bows, and moves into the seat allocated to him by the king's Master of the Halls. It is not amongst the highest places, but is well situated to hear what is being said. "I knew my Moll can out run any horse, over a quarter distance. It was not a fair challenge."

"Blasted little turd," Norfolk growls, as he sits to the king's right hand side. Suffolk will take the left, and the men only hunting party will sit, each according to their perceived station. "What sort of a gentleman cheats like that?"

"Enough now," Henry replies. "Boleyn is not the worst of men. Did you note how those fellows felling trees looked at us, as we passed?"

"Empty bellies make for poor subjects, sire," Brandon says. "Once the harvests start to come in, they will cheer us again."

I'll wager that there were many in the forest today, who would wish me harm," Henry mutters.

"Then we shall cut down every tree," Will says. "When there is nowhere for them to hide, we shall see what we shall see."

"The king is well loved," Suffolk puts in. He is close to the king, and dislikes such fears being pandered to. "His people love him, and his nobles serve him well."

"I do not think there is anyone, of any real consequence, here today who means him harm," Will says. The king glances about the room, and frowns. Will Draper's words have struck home, and he notes that the Earl of Wiltshire is absent.

"Boleyn, where is your father?" The words tumble out, angrily, and the chamber falls silent.

"He has business, sire … on his estates."

"In Kent?" Henry asks.

"No, sire. He is in Wiltshire," George replies. There is something amiss, and he does not understand what it can be. He has taken his usual humiliation in good stead, and cannot see what his father's day to day business has to do with anyone. "He is trying to raise money, to pay the tithe you require of him."

"Tithe?"

"You assessed the Earldom, sire," Thomas Cromwell informs the king. He has just arrived at Hampton Court Palace, and is still in his riding cloak. "I dare say that is what the boy means. I am pleased to see how diligently he attends to his debts. One can only hope he is as prompt with settling his debt to me."

"Thomas, my dear old friend," Henry calls, and waves him forward. "The Master of the Halls is remiss, placing you so low down my table. Charles, shift yourself over, and let dear old Cromwell sit with me. There, that is better. Now, tell me, truthfully, old friend, does Boleyn owe everybody?"

"I know not, sire," Cromwell says, easing himself in between Suffolk and the king. "I know he owes you, and I, about one hundred and twenty thousand. As for the rest, I fear he uses his relationship to the crown as surety."

"More fool them," Henry says, and winks at his favoured Privy Councillor. "For the relationship is but through marriage. Which reminds me, we must talk ... later, after these wine sodden souls are all abed."

"As you wish, Your Majesty." Thomas Cromwell catches Will Draper's eye, and gives him a nod of polite recognition, as if they seldom met. "Colonel Draper... how are you?"

"Well sir."

"Excellent. I was just about to spring a surprise on the king, and I am pleased that you are here, for it saves me writing to you."

"A surprise, Thomas?" Henry is suddenly alert. "It takes something quite magnificent to surprise a king. What have you hidden up your sleeve for me?"

"A royal progression, sire."

"Oh, a progression," Henry says. He is greatly disappointed, and wonders why Cromwell thinks it such a wonderful thing. Royal progressions are seldom more than a few decent meals, and hundreds of subjects wishing to complain to the king, in person.

"To Wiltshire, sire." Cromwell smiles, as the king's face lights up in pleasure. "I thought we might visit the Seymour family, in Wulfhall, where you will be most welcome."

"The queen will not like it." Henry begins to see pitfalls, where none exist. Cromwell has thought of everything.

"The queen is not invited," he says, softly. "A messenger will arrive, shortly, hinting that there is some sort of unrest in the county. You will gather a few friends, and loyal servants, and gallop off, to quell the disturbance."

"Is there unrest?"

"There is always unrest, sire," Will Draper says. "The common folk enjoy a good grumble, when things are hard. Though it is a strange coincidence that the Earl of Wiltshire is visiting there, at this very moment."

"The damnable fellow," the king says, lowering his voice from a boom, to a more normal tone. "He is as difficult to deal with as his daughter."

"Then a few days hunting at Wulfhall will help lighten Your Highness's mood," Thomas Cromwell says. "For he is not invited either."

"Clever fellow," Henry says.

"I trust I am invited, Cromwell," Norfolk says. He is straining to listen in, and does not wish to be outside the chosen few.

"Of course, My Lord,"

Cromwell says. "You must come, if only to keep you from whispering to your niece."

"Blast the woman," Norfolk says. "I say we leave them all behind, and round up a few of the local girls instead. Just like the old days, Hal. Hunting by day, and tumbling willing village girls by night."

"Our swan song," Henry mutters. Not that he will ever admit it, but the years are catching up with him, and he suffers from the usual curses of ageing. "Damn it, why not? I shall want Charles with us, of course, Thomas, and send for that cheeky young rogue, Tom Wyatt. He will liven things up with his cleverness, I dare say. Who else shall we have, Norfolk?" The old duke, who has been carefully primed for the moment, glances at Cromwell for reassurance, and receives a slight nod back.

"Harry Percy is back from trouncing the Scots," he offers, and waits for the harsh refusal. Instead, Cromwell jumps in with a few well chosen words. The Duke of Northumberland has been well punished these three years past, and must be a changed man, he says to the king. Henry frowns, and tries to recollect why he dislikes the fellow so much.

"Might he not now feel your generosity?" Cromwell concludes.

"Besides," Will Draper says, "he is a mighty roistering sort, and can bawd with the very best of us."

"Then it is done," Henry says, slapping a hand on Cromwell's back. "See to it, my friend. I trust the ban on ladies does not extend to the Seymour family itself?"

"I do believe Lady Jane will be at home, sire," Cromwell murmurs. "Will that be a burden to you? I thought Your Majesty liked the dear girl."

"Ah, but does the lady return those feelings, Master Thomas?"

"Her brothers assure me that she talks of nothing else, save the kind words her king once spoke to her."

"Did she truly refer to me as 'my king', Thomas?"

"It seems the lady is smitten, sire," Cromwell says. "She is a shy girl, and not fond of those young men of her own age. They must seem fickle, and puny, when compared to you."

"Just so." Henry ponders for a moment. "Let us speak of these things anon … when little ears are not listening."

"The trip is for men, sire," Will says. "Not boys. George Boleyn can sit at home, and practice his needlework, with the ladies."

"Ha!" Henry sees a jest where none is intended. "Let us hope his needle is up to the job!" Those around him chuckle, but the remark reminds the king that he has, himself, bedded Boleyn's wife, and that he also found it impossible to thread that particular eye.

"More wine, sire?" Rafe Sadler leans over the king's shoulder, and fills his goblet to the rim. "Would Your Majesty care to be entertained?"

"What is there?"

"Some local girls, who wish to demonstrate their singing prowess to you, and Donald Kee, a travelling jester, who has been touring the northern counties, of late"

"Have him come in," Henry says. "Send the singers away, but give them a few coins for their trouble. I have no appetite for caterwauling virgins tonight." Rafe Sadler nods, and moves away from the long table. He beckons over a tall, thin man, dressed in bright apparel, and gestures for him to perform.

"Why, bless my merry old prodder," the man declares, as he dances in front of the king. "Does not this fellow look like someone I know?"

Henry takes a moment to catch on, then throws himself into the jest. He stands up, places his fists on his hips, then juts out his big chest.

"They call me Hal," Henry calls to loud laughter, and some clapping.

"Then they call me Don," the jester replies, quickly. "For my father was an ass, sire. It is no fun being a Don Kee!"

"Ho!" Henry is as easily amused as he is roused to anger. "The fellow is a donkey, you see, Cromwell? Come tell me another, my little ass."

"Little arse, Hal?" The jester scratches his head. "Then it is all the better to avoid a kick. Has the king ever been to Yorkshire?"

"It is a troublesome place," Rafe Sadler calls out. "Why, they never pay their taxes on time."

"The men all court the prettiest sheep, and they say that no sister is safe from her brothers!"

"Dear Christ, Sadler… but the man is a marvel," Henry cries. "Pretty sheep indeed!"

The jesting goes on, but Thomas Cromwell has lost interest in the crude fooling. At the back of the hall, he sees a peculiar look come over George Boleyn's face. The young man seems not to have a taste for the jests. Perhaps one has struck close to home, Cromwell thinks. Then he recalls the rumours about Boleyn's sexual preferences, and wonders what is hidden within the devious little swine's black heart.

"Hee haw!" Donald Kee is doing a passable imitation of an ass, and is trying to mount a passing servant, much to the king's merriment. Cromwell is distracted for a moment, and when he looks back, George Boleyn has slipped away.

"Off to visit his new mistress," Will Draper says in Cromwell's ear. "It seems he has some secret love, and takes great pains to keep her hidden away."

"Why would he do that?" Cromwell asks. "Boleyn does not love his wife, and tups where he wishes."

"Perhaps he fears the king will

steal her away," Will guesses.

"Poor George," Cromwell concludes. "He can swive a flock of sheep, if he likes, as long as he keeps away from Jane Seymour."

"I cannot see the Seymour brothers letting Henry have his way for nothing," Will says. "They are a mercenary lot, and will want a few thousand acres in return."

"Would that the price were so low," Cromwell replies, with a gentle smile. "You know, little Jane still remembers when I sent her some gloves. She is a sentimental girl, and I do not want her hurt. I must see that the Seymour price is met... in full."

"You mean marriage?"

"What else?" Cromwell sighs. "It is almost time to start the negotiations. I must explain to Queen Anne that she has to step aside. Unless I have powerful arguments, she will sweep me aside, and poison Henry against me."

"My investigation into the queen progresses, sir," Will Draper says. "Though it is nothing but vague whisperings at the moment, I think there is something to find."

"What about lovers?"

"Since she married?" Will shakes his head. "Even she would not dare. Before … now that is a different matter. It is a pity we cannot have Harry Percy change his tale once more."

"The duke swore an oath, on the Holy Bible, in front of the king, and two bishops," Cromwell says. "Even Christ could not break that one down. I have arranged for Percy to be at Wulfhall, when the king visits, but I doubt it will help much."

"Then I must continue my investigation," Will Draper replies. "The father and brother are sure to be swindling the king, somehow. That might be enough to move Anne. The threat of her nearest relatives being charged could be just what we need."

"Anne is a hard woman," Cromwell says. "I want to convince her to step aside, for her own sake. Henry is set on Jane, and I do not know how far he will go to get what he wants."

"God help us if he ever realises his true power," Will says.

"You mean God help Anne, I think." Cromwell claps, because the king is clapping. The jester is being pelted with food, and silver coins, and he is scrabbling around the floor, gathering all he can. Good paydays are few and far between. "Our fool is a wise man. Perhaps we should gather in whilst we can … and wait for the storm."

"If the queen thinks she is going to lose, she will raise more than a storm," Will says. "She has powerful friends in the West Country, thanks to her liberal dispensation of titles. She could have a dozen barons rise up in rebellion. An army of twelve or fifteen thousand men, ready to march on London."

"Then we must whisper in other ears, and have enough troops ready to counteract such a move," Cromwell replies. "I think we can rely on Brandon, whose Suffolk yeomanry number five thousand. They are a sturdy band, and will stand behind the king. I think the Master of Ordinance will remain loyal."

"Miriam sends him gifts, often, so that he will keep his warships in the channel. It ensures pirates stay clear of her shipping."

"Then he is a friend?"

"I drink with him, and our families dine together, now and then.

He is as loyal as any to Henry, and can command fifty artillery pieces, at a day's notice."

"Then London is safe," Cromwell says. "Anne Boleyn will not think to start a civil war, because she considers herself to be too clever to lose. She may not be able to bring forth a healthy boy heir, but my spies tell me that she has ways of pleasuring the king that few others know. Let her get him alone, often enough, and she will turn him against every one of her enemies."

"Then we must outthink her, sir," Will replies. "The woman has nothing but malice in her heart, and would ruin half of England, to keep her crown."

"Then find me something to use," Cromwell tells the King's Examiner. "Give me enough, and I will scare her into abdicating her position. Let me be able to threaten death and destruction on her precious clan, and she might relent."

"And if she does not?"

"Step aside?" Cromwell sighs at the prospect. "Then I must give her such a push, that she topples from the top of the hill to the its very base. If I do this, she will be utterly ruined. Her titles… all of them… will go, and every man's hand would be against her. She might even have to go back to France, with her tail between her legs. May God curse the day her damned father ever brought her back to England!"

"Perhaps there are secrets across the English Channel?" Will Draper guesses. "Though I cannot think how to get at them."

"No, look to her earlier years," Cromwell concludes. "There must be something that she wants to keep quiet."

15   The Interview

It is the first day of November. Almost four months since the execution of Sir Thomas More, and the tide of recriminations, and external threats seems to have turned, at last. The French have sent their formal regrets over the perfidious death of a great philosopher, the Pope has reinforced his excommunication of the king, and Eustace Chapuys has placed his master's strong objections on record, with England's new Lord Chancellor, Sir Thomas Audley.

The little Savoyard is actively working against Queen Anne, whom he refers to as 'that French whore', at every opportunity, and he no longer cares to be secretive about what he writes, despite his letters being covertly read. On one occasion, he even opens with the salutation 'My dear Cromwell', just to show his distaste for his old friend's methods.

"I could not save him from death, Eustace," Thomas Cromwell complains, when next they meet, over dinner at Miriam Draper's house. "I did all I could for the man, and I loved him most dearly. How can you think otherwise?"

"You have the king's ear." Chapuys thought he was to dine with the family, and is not expecting a Cromwellian presence. It vexes him to argue under Miriam's roof, for he loves her and her family dearly.

"I have but one of them," Cromwell replies, tartly. "The other still belongs to the Boleyn family, and they never tire of filling it with poisonous lies."

"That whore … forgive me, Miriam … will destroy your country," the ambassador snaps. "She seeks nothing but power for herself, and her disreputable family. The Boleyn name is even stolen, to make them sound grander."

"True enough," Miriam says, as she pours wine into their glasses. "They were once the Bullen family, and earned their money by cutting thatch, and game keeping. I, of course, was forced to change my name too, thanks to the anti Jewish laws in this country."

"Then you had to change it again," Will Draper puts in. "When you were foolish enough to marry me, my dear."

"I can repent that at leisure, my sweet," Miriam replies, cheekily. "Besides, I have the best of the deal. I have a fine house, a good business, and all our children shall be Jews. The blood descends through the female side with my people."

"An excellent system, my girl," Cromwell says, happy for the change of subject. "For it is a wise man who knows his own father." The table erupts into laughter, but Eustace Chapuys is not to be put off.

"With Sir Thomas dead, there is no one to stop the queen," he says. "More heads will roll before the year is out."

"Not mine, Eustace," Cromwell replies. "The king tires of her, as you often predicted, and longs for a son. It has come to the stage where he does not even visit the queen anymore. Instead, he dallies with bed warmers and chamber maids, or spends himself on various ladies-in-waiting."

"You mean Lady Rochford?" Chapuys says this to show that he is not without his own spies. He does not yet realise that they are Cromwell men, who feed him whatever information their real master wishes.

"Amongst others," Cromwell says. The king has been swiving a cousin of Anne Boleyn for some weeks now, but he wishes to keep her name secret, for the moment. "Quite apart from that, the king wants a male heir, and that means a wife who can bear him one. That woman is plainly not Anne Boleyn."

"He cannot think to put his wife away again?" Miriam says. She shares in the conversation of the men comfortably, and often provides food for thought. "The new church would not allow it. The bishops would all look like fools … or pawns of the king. Even the people, who mostly dislike the queen, would frown on a frivolous divorce."

"Truly spoken," Tom Cromwell says. "So, we must find another, less painful way. We must allow the queen to exit with grace, and a pocket full of gold."

"Then you must speak with her, my friend," Eustace Chapuys says. It is hard to stay angry with Cromwell, who always seems to have some clever move in reserve. "I do not envy you that task. The French Whore would just as soon cut off your head and place it on a spike, as listen to reason."

"She will listen," Thomas Cromwell says. "She must."

*

"Master Thomas Cromwell is here, Your Highness." Lady Jane Rochford leaves a slight pause between her announcement, and the queen's title. She means to remind Anne of her own grievances, and sting her into treating her better. "He has been waiting for almost an hour."

"Do not dare to reproach me, sister … or I will have you sent back to Kent, where my dear brother can ignore you to his heart's content. It does Cromwell good to wait for me, for it reminds him that he is the servant, and not the master here. Now, I am ready, so have him enter."

George Boleyn's wife's face reddens, and she goes to fetch Cromwell from the outer chamber. The Privy Councillor is chatting with Mark Smeaton, the new musician, who has just arrived from Antwerp. The young man is thin, and pale looking, and seems surprised at Cromwell's open friendliness.

"You must know the De Groosen family," Thomas Cromwell says. "They are related to … ah, here is Lady Rochford, come to fetch me. I must go, but we will speak again, Master Smeaton. Here, take this … to keep you honest." He falls in, behind Jane Boleyn, and follows her into the queen's outer chambers. Mark Smeaton looks down at the silver coins in his hand, and smiles. Then he wonders at such generosity, and the thought reminds him of his many sins, and makes him wonder if they are common knowledge.

"Cromwell, at last," Queen Anne says. "I thought you would never come."

"You expected me, Your Highness?" Of course you did, he thinks. You know that the moment is here. From this day on, things will never be the same again.

"Yes. The king is unhappy, so he sends his dog."

"The king does not know I am here, madam," Cromwell says. "I am here, in the hope of avoiding a very great tragedy."

"The answer is 'no', Master Cromwell." Anne turns her back on him, and puts her hands on her hips, in imitation of her husband's favourite stance.

"Might I not put the question first?" Thomas Cromwell spreads his hands in supplication. "That is the usual form."

"Speak." Anne spins about, and glares at the Privy Councillor.

"The king wishes to have a son." There, that is the nub of it, he thinks.

"Then he must come to my bed more often, sir."

"He cannot. He feels that this estrangement cannot be reversed, and wants you to step aside." This here is the solution, if you but see, Cromwell adds, silently.

"Step aside?" Anne Boleyn laughs. "I am the queen, not some cheap mistress to be bought off with a promise."

"The king would be most generous. He asks only that you make the first move. You must ask to be released from your marriage vows, for the sake of the realm. You must state that you cannot provide a male heir, and wish to step aside. Medical evidence will be found to support your claim. Henry would be blameless, and could then seek an honourable divorce."

"And what of me?" The queen is surprised at the cleverness of it. She must beg Henry to release her, and he does, with much wringing of hands. Poor Henry, foiled by the failure of his wife's womb, and what a brave lady, to sacrifice her position for the good of England.

"All your lands and titles, except 'queen' would be yours to keep," Cromwell explains. "Your brother, and your father will be retained at court, if they wish, and all current investigations into their dubious financial affairs would cease."

"I see. Quit, and you will leave my family alone." Anne smiles, and crosses to sit in one of the window bays. "Let me make a counter offer, Master Cromwell. Resign all of your posts, and retire to Austin Friars. Do this, within the next week, and I will stay my hand. Refuse, and I will have you dragged from your office. Your wealth will be confiscated, and your people condemned as thieves, and traitors. The king is like a willow, Master Cromwell. Tomorrow, he will bend the other way, and I will be back in his favour."

"I fear not, madam." Thomas Cromwell does not know why he is wasting his time with her. "The king wishes to re-marry, and provide England with a male heir."

"What, from the little, narrow hipped, Seymour cow?" Anne is almost shaking with anger now, and wants to smash Cromwell's façade of polite firmness down. "He will soon find out what a lame duck she is, and come crawling back to me. I am the mother of the rightful heir to the throne. Elizabeth is the foundation of a new dynasty. The new church … any church … would refuse him a divorce. They know that to back a second divorce would show them to be straw men, under the king's thumb. The people are not yet ready for that, sir."

"If you consent…"

"Enough!" Queen Anne waves a fist at him. "He will get a divorce, but only if I consent. Canterbury and Winchester will not agree to his demands. Both bishops know such a divorce would ruin England's honour."

"But you might consent?" Cromwell sees a chink of light, but also fears a trap. "Under what circumstances?"

"That he comes to me, and begs the favour," Anne says.

Cromwell sighs. Is this all you have, madam, he thinks. Force the king into a private meeting, and hope to sway him by appealing to his sense of honour … or guilt?

"The king cannot be seen to be in favour of a divorce, My Lady," Cromwell reasserts. "He must be able to say that the idea was yours alone, and that you wish it, for the sake of the monarchy. Do this, and your family will rank alongside Norfolk and Suffolk in the realm. You will be the Dowager Queen, mother to the second in line to the throne. Elizabeth will grow up, legitimate, in line for the throne, and rich."

"And if Henry does not sire a male child?"

"Your daughter would be queen." Cromwell sees the glimmer of temptation in her eyes, but it flickers out.

"No, I cannot take the risk." Anne throws herself into a chair, and puts her fist under her chin. It is something she does when not getting her own way. She is now at her most dangerous. "If the Seymour cow brings out a boy, Elizabeth is relegated a place. Let her bring out a second male child, and my daughter will be nothing, but a minor princess, to be bartered abroad."

"I assure you…"

"And I assure you, Cromwell. Remove yourself from this business, or I will reach the king, and sway him to my side again. Then I will ask him how a common little man like you comes to rise so high. Henry fears clever men, Master Cromwell. Remember how I brought down Cardinal Wolsey… and Sir Thomas More? Are you so much better than they?"

"It is for the king to choose, madam," Cromwell says. "He is not renowned for his patience. After all, he is a king, and kings always get what they wish for. He will have Lady Jane as his wife, whether you abdicate, or not."

"He will not put me aside."

"He might, if the evidence against you is enough," Cromwell says. It is his final move, and he hopes the woman sees sense. He has laid out every course that might lead to a happy ending, and must finish with a threat. "Should the king find out that you have betrayed his trust in some way, he will have you put in a nunnery."

"There is nothing to find, sir!"

"You must take the word of one who knows about these matters, Your Majesty," Cromwell says, coldly. "There is always something to find. Always!"

*

"Play something for me," the queen demands. "Something to liven the spirits." The new musician, who is in court under the wing of George Boleyn, plays. He is not that accomplished, and his playing is little better than a competent amateur.

George Boleyn is quite aware of the young man's short comings, but still recommends him to his sister, as a pleasant fellow, who will be a willing, and loyal servant. Anne adopts him, at once, and refers to him as her sweet little puppy dog. Her brother, who knows Smeaton is an effeminate homosexual is happy.

He seeks to surround the queen with bland, uninteresting men, whom she could never come to love more than she loves him, and is rather successful at the task. Mark Smeaton is an effeminate catamite, and no threat, whilst others, like Henry Norris, are so dull that Anne scarcely knows they are there.

Smeaton and Norris, he muses, will keep his beloved sister out of temptation's way. They are like some great Caliph's eunuchs, protecting her from harm. One day, George thinks, Henry will be dead, and Anne will be free to follow her own heart. Once the young, and easily manageable, Elizabeth is on the throne they need not be so discreet.

Were he not such a coward, George Boleyn would gladly hurry Henry on his way, with poison, or some contrived accident, but he lacks the courage, and must bide his time.

"One day," he thinks. "One day!"

*

"Is it settled, Master Cromwell?" Henry can tell from his councillor's diffidence that it is not good news.

"Not quite, sire," Cromwell replies. He bows, and asks if he might move closer. The throne room is crowded with ears, eager to pick up any gossip they can. Henry nods, and he steps to within a few inches of the king. "The queen, as I expected, makes a counter offer, which is almost too derisory for me to recount."

"Tell me, sir," Henry says, his voice cold, and hard. "What does she dare reply that makes my most favoured man hesitate?"

It is time for Cromwell to begin the fight in earnest. The queen, in reply to his offers, has threatened his own life, and that of all at Austin Friars. He must do all he can to ensure their safety.

"The queen says that … you must beg her for a divorce," the Privy Councillor says. "And that she might then consider it."

"Must?" Henry almost explodes. "She demands that I seek her out? Would she have me genuflect at her feet too?"

"Sire, I fear she did not understand what she…"

"You defend her, fellow?" The king is shaking with rage.

"Not I, sire," Cromwell replies, quickly. "It is just that she seemed to be a little… out of sorts. It was as if she was under a spell which makes her contrary. She confounded everything I said. She refused an easy abdication, with the retention of most of her titles, and all of her land. It was as if she knows something I do not. Has she some power over you, sire?"

"I am the king," Henry blusters. "I bend to no one, Cromwell. No one."

"Then she knows something, or expects something to happen," Cromwell muses. "Has anything odd occurred of late, sire?"

"Like what?" Henry says. He is the king, and as such, never notices anything, unless it is for his own personal benefit, or pleasure. "You must speak plainly, sir."

"Are there any fresh faces about court, for instance?" Cromwell asks. "Or have you made any … new friends?"

"Damn it, Cromwell, a man must have his relief," Henry says. "How did you know?"

"Someone mentions something to someone else, and that person speaks to another, who knows a man, who knows Cromwell's man," Cromwell explains. "It is just that your new 'friend' is a cousin of the queen. She is a close friend of the queen, who suddenly finds Your Majesty attractive."

"Dear God ... the whore!" Henry is stunned to discover that it is not his charm and sexual prowess which keeps his new mistress happy. "You mean she is a spy?"

"Sire, I cannot say," Cromwell replies, honestly. "It might be that she desires to be your mistress for many reasons, but we must wonder if she is placed by you, so that some evil plot can be unfolded."

"You think she means to murder me?"

"I do not, sire," Cromwell says, sticking to the truth. "Though such a thing has been attempted before. I simply urge caution. Do not allow the girl to know your thoughts. Take your pleasure with her, then discard her. Find someone who does not like the queen. That should not be too hard."

"Ho!" Henry sees the fooling against the queen, and admires Cromwell for making so bold a jest. "She will have no friends, if she continues her stubborn ways. I have a mind to speak to her, in a stern way, and put her mind on the right track."

"No, sire, that would be unwise. Forgive my abrupt, yet honest, way of speaking, but it would be a mistake."

"What then?" Henry puts his hands on his hips, and strikes a pose he thinks makes him look like a great statesman. "God knows, I trust you, Thomas, and you may speak as you wish to me. I love you, and will always listen to your words of wisdom."

"Sire…"

"Call me Henry," the king says, softening his tone. "Dearest Tom, speak your mind."

"Very well, Henry," Cromwell replies. "Ignore her. Pretend you have no knowledge of her foolish demand. Make sure you are never in her company, alone. Either refuse to see her, or send for a trusted advisor. Master Sadler is a trustworthy fellow, and the Earl of Suffolk is a true friend. Let them note what she says, and listen to them. Rafe Sadler is sound, and will see if she is laying any traps for you. Above all, do not ask her for a divorce. The impetus must come from the Boleyn camp."

"Then the church are with her?" Henry is bemused. He has ridded himself of the Catholic Church of Rome, only to saddle himself with a new church, which will not support him.

"Not at all, Henry," Cromwell tells the king. "They tolerate her, because she is queen. They must support her, if you seek a divorce, without reasonable grounds. They are happy to support you, if she asks for a divorce."

"Then she must ask," Henry says. "That is down to you, Tom. Make her ask. I will keep my part of the deal, and refuse to see her, from this day forth. I will also get rid of the viper in my bed. Charles Brandon always says it is better to tup the servants, and slip them a shilling or two."

"Yes sire," Cromwell says. He is not comfortable using the king's given name, and reverts as soon as he feels able to the customary form of address. "That is a method much used by the Duke of Norfolk. They do say that over half of his tenants can lay claim to his noble blood."

"Well said, Thomas," Henry says with a smile. His good humour is slowly returning, and he is reassured that Cromwell will obtain that which he most wants. "Uncle Norfolk is a veritable satyr."

"And uncle to the queen, sire." Cromwell watches as the king digests the observation, and a look of mistrust creeps across his features. "I have taken the liberty of alerting Lord Suffolk to the possibility of conflict. I believe Colonel Draper has ordinance at the Tower of London, and awaits the word. Should anyone feel inclined to dispute the throne, we are ready to crush them."

"Dear Christ, Cromwell, am I beset on all sides?" Henry is beginning to see what a quagmire he is about to cross, and all for the sake of a woman. Civil war, the church, a spy in his bed, and a recalcitrant wife, all combine to ensure he will not sleep that night.

"Not at all, Your Majesty," Cromwell says, with a beatific smile. "You are surrounded by loyal friends, and good advisors. The army and its cannon are under the watchful eye of Colonel Draper, and I am ever mindful of your safety."

"Then I am a lucky man to have you, Tom," the king says. "I wish you would let me elevate you. A knighthood perhaps, or a baronetcy ... to start with."

"No sire. Why give the opposition ammunition? They already say that I am a lowly commoner, who has risen above himself. They think it is by roguery, rather than by hard work, and loyal devotion to my king. Leave me be, until all our aims are fulfilled, and then consider if I am worthy of reward."

"As you wish," Henry says. "Though know this, sir ... you are my man. I trust no one before you ... not even Charles, or old Uncle Norfolk. I will not hear any evil against you, and I will support you in every way I can. I so swear."

"I have the king's oath," Cromwell says, as he bows his way out of the room. "No man could wish for more."

*

"Is it done then?" Rafe Sadler asks, once Cromwell comes into the outer chamber.

"As best I can," Cromwell tells him. "Henry has promised not to speak to the queen, from now onwards. I have poisoned Norfolk's well, just in case, and put the thought of civil war into the king's mind. He thinks that the poor Mary Sheldon girl he swives is a Boleyn spy, and he has sworn an oath to support me."

"In public?" Rafe Sadler is stunned at this, as he constantly warns the king about making rash promises, let alone swear dangerous oaths.

"At least six courtiers heard," Cromwell says, with a wide grin on his face. "I will give my nephew their names, so that he can have them make depositions to that effect. I doubt they will refuse Richard, for he has a certain, forceful way with people."

"Now what?" Rafe Sadler is the king's advisor, but is bonded to Cromwell, and Austin Friars, by deeper ties. "How do we make the queen surrender to us?"

"Fear," Cromwell says. "It is the last, most powerful, arrow in my quiver. "They say the queen is fearless, but everyone has a weakness. Uncover that secret fear, and she will abdicate."

"Has Will Draper found anything out yet?"

"It is as if she were a nun," Cromwell confesses. "But there is something, I know it. I saw it in her eyes. I will find it out, and use it to make her lay down her crown."

*

"You did not come home last night, sir," Lady Jane Rochford says to the back of her husband. He seldom bothers to acknowledge her, and has grown worse since her affairs with the Duke of Suffolk, and the nonsense with the king.

"I have no home, madam," George Boleyn answers. "I am here for a change of clothes, and will be gone, before one of your lovers comes a-calling. Who is it this week, Henry, Charles Brandon, or some other? What about Tom Wyatt? They say he will stick it in anything with a…"

"Sir!" Jane Boleyn, Countess of Rochford strikes his back with her clenched fist. "You go too far. I found myself deserted by a husband who does not want me. I was seduced by Suffolk, who sought only to spite you, and was then handed on to the king. Who can refuse the king, sir? I did not see you challenging either man over me. You allowed them to use me."

"You could have refused Brandon." George replies. He does not love his wife, but he does not want her used to embarrass him at court. "The man is a Cromwell dog, and is friendly with that bastard, Draper. You have been a fool, madam, and I am done with you. I will not support you any more, and I do not wish to speak with you again."

"These are court chambers, husband," Lady Jane replies, tartly. "I will live here, and continue to wait on your sister, the queen. If you refuse to support me, I will seek redress from other quarters."

"Do as you wish. I have no taste for a whore, madam!"

Jane Rochford steps back, as if slapped. Her husband's words have finally poisoned her mind against him, and though it might take her months to find the courage, mixed with foolishness, to act, she will have her revenge. There is a half formed knowledge in her that knows she holds the power of life and death in her hands, and she need only wait for the right time to speak, and the right person to tell.

"You think you can treat me this

way?" she cries. "Wait until Henry tires of your sister, sir. Oh, I know he has visited her a few times, since More's death, but I doubt it is enough to save the marriage!"

"Have a care," George Boleyn says, coldly. "The king does his duty by Anne, and the Boleyn line will prosper, despite your curses. Now, get out of my sight!""

*

"His Majesty is much taken up with affairs of state," Charles Brandon says, in an off hand manner. "He cannot spare the time to see you, Anne."

"Can he not, my Lord Suffolk?" Anne Boleyn smiles, and makes as if to side step Henry's closest friend. He forgets himself, and reaches out a restraining arm. "You seek to manhandle me, sir?"

"My pardon, lady, but the king does not wish to speak with you. You should, perhaps, listen to the good advice given to you by Master Cromwell."

"What, abdicate my rightful position?" Anne Boleyn smiles again. "I fear the king would be most upset, should I do something so irresponsible. Why, it would cause great unrest amongst his people."

"You think too much of yourself, madam." Charles Brandon has never cared for the Boleyns, and has always resented Anne for coming between he and the king. Now Cromwell is on the case, he is sure the queen's days are numbered, and he can throw caution to the wind. "Get yourself back to Hever Castle, and put on mourning black, for your marriage to the king is dead."

"Pray, do not upset me, Lord Suffolk," Anne replies. "For it is bad for my unborn child." Brandon almost chokes. For a moment, he thinks she is lying, but he sees the look of triumph in her eyes, and is overcome with a wave of nausea. "That is what I come to tell the king. Will he be so quick to cast me off, once he knows I carry the future of England in my belly?"

"How?" Brandon cannot understand it. Henry has sworn that he has not lain with the queen for months, and has no love for her.

"After More died, the king was confused, and upset. I came to him several times... and consoled him. He has his weaknesses, you see. After the last time… well, these things happen, Charles, and I find I am with his child."

"His Majesty will be most pleased." It is all Brandon can say.

"His Majesty will be eager to make things up with me," Anne says. "The Seymour's must go back to Wulfhall, Mary Sheldon must stop warming Henry's bed, and Master Cromwell must look to his own self. The man has done me a grave injustice, and must pay the expected penalty."

Rafe Sadler is loitering close by, and hears what has come about. He calls over one of the court messengers, and whispers into his ear. The boy nods, and sets off running to Austin Friars. The seemingly impossible has happened, and Thomas Cromwell's fate is once more in the balance.

~End~

Many thanks for reading this book. Other titles in author Anne Stevens 'Tudor Crimes' series are:

Winter King
Midnight Queen
The Stolen Prince
The Condottiero
The King's Angels
The King's Examiner
The Alchemist Royal

We value what you, our readers think. Here are a few of the most recent comments on Amazon, about our epic series:

5 out of 5 stars. **Definitely recommended**
By Big Bando on 16 Jan. 2016.   Verified Purchase.
What can I say, except another great read. Can't put these down, once I start reading them!

5 out of 5 stars **Angelic!**
By **AB**, writing about 'The King's Angels, on 8th November 2015.
This series is going from strength to strength, and I await the next slice of Cromwell and his Austin Friars mob, eagerly. I cannot wait for my next Tudor fix!

5 out of 5 stars   **Great book**
By summer63 on 9th January, 2016.   Kindle EditionVerified Purchase
Great characters, brought to life by good writing.

Would recommend (Winter King)

5 out of 5 stars   **Enjoyed every bit of it!**
ByAmazon Customer on 24 June 2015   Verified Purchase.

Brilliant, I enjoyed every bit of it!   (Winter King)

5 out of 5 stars
By C. J. Parsons on 28th October 2015.   Kindle Edition   Verified Purchase

'A gripping read, well written.'

5.0 out of 5 stars

By **swan2** on 10th August 2015.

Format: Kindle EditionVerified Purchase.

Quite short, so read in a couple of days. I love the shardlake series, and it reminded me a bit of them. A good read for the holidays.
ps
I worked out the killer quite early on!

5 out of 5 stars   **More please!**
By B B ...... 2016.   Kindle:Verified Purchase

This was the first one in the series that I read, and I was not disappointed. Have since read all the others. More please!

Printed in Poland
by Amazon Fulfillment
Poland Sp. z o.o., Wrocław